Our Endless Numbered Days

Our Endless Numbered Days

CLAIRE FULLER

FIG TREE
an imprint of
PENGUIN BOOKS

FIG TREE

Published by the Penguin Group
Penguin Books Ltd, 80 Strand, London WC2R ORL, England
Penguin Group (USA) Inc., 375 Hudson Street, New York, New York 10014, USA
Penguin Group (Canada), 90 Eglinton Avenue East, Suite 700, Toronto, Ontario, Canada M4P 2Y3
(a division of Pearson Penguin Canada Inc.)
Penguin Ireland, 25 St Stephen's Green, Dublin 2, Ireland (a division of Penguin Books Ltd)
Penguin Group (Australia), 707 Collins Street, Melbourne,
Victoria 3008, Australia (a division of Pearson Australia Group Pty Ltd)
Penguin Books India Pvt Ltd, 11 Community Centre,
Panchsheel Park, New Delhi – 110 017, India
Penguin Group (NZ), 67 Apollo Drive, Rosedale, Auckland 0632, New Zealand
(a division of Pearson New Zealand Ltd)
Penguin Books (South Africa) (Pty) Ltd, Block D, Rosebank Office Park,
181 Jan Smuts Avenue, Parktown North, Gauteng 2193, South Africa

Penguin Books Ltd, Registered Offices: 80 Strand, London WC2R ORL, England

www.penguin.com

First published 2015
001

Copyright © Claire Fuller, 2015

The moral right of the author has been asserted

The title was inspired by the album *Our Endless Numbered Days*
by Iron & Wine, released through Sub Pop in 2004

Set in 12/14.75 pt Dante
Typeset by Palimpsest Book Production Ltd, Falkirk, Stirlingshire
Printed in Great Britain by Clays Ltd, St Ives plc

A CIP catalogue record for this book is available from the British Library

HARDBACK ISBN: 978-0-241-00393-0
TRADE PAPERBACK ISBN: 978-0-241-18533-9

www.greenpenguin.co.uk

For Tim, India and Henry

I.

Highgate, London, November 1985

This morning I found a black and white photograph of my father at the back of the bureau drawer. He didn't look like a liar. My mother, Ute, had removed the other pictures of him from the albums she kept on the bottom shelf of the bookcase, and shuffled around all the remaining family and baby snapshots to fill in the gaps. The framed picture of their wedding, which used to sit on the mantelpiece, had gone too.

On the back of the photograph, Ute had written 'James und seine Busenfreunde mit Oliver, 1976' in her steady handwriting. It was the last picture that had been taken of my father. He looked shockingly young and healthy, his face as smooth and white as a river pebble. He would have been twenty-six, nine years older than I am today.

As I peered closer, I saw that the picture included not only my father and his friends, but also Ute and a blurred smudge which must have been me. We were in the sitting room, where I was standing. Now, the grand piano is at the other end, beside the steel-framed doors which lead to the glass-house and through to the garden. In the photograph, the piano stood in front of the three large windows overlooking the drive. They were open, their curtains frozen mid-billow in a summer breeze. Seeing my father in our old life made me dizzy, as though the parquet were tipping under my bare feet, and I had to sit down.

After a few moments I went to the piano, and for the first time since I had come home I touched it, running my fingers without resistance across the polished surface. It was much smaller than I remembered, and showed patches of a lighter shade where the sun had bleached it over many years. And I thought that maybe it was the most beautiful thing I had ever seen. Knowing that the sun had shone, and the piano must have been played, and people had lived and breathed whilst I had been gone, helped steady me.

I looked at the picture in my hand. At the piano my father leaned forward, his left arm stretched out languidly whilst his right hand tinkered with the keys. I was surprised to see him sitting there. I have no recollection of him ever sitting at the piano or playing it, although of course it was my father who taught me to play. No, the piano was always Ute's instrument.

'The writer, he holds his pen and the words flow; I touch the keyboard and out my music comes,' she says with her hard German vowels.

On that day, at that tiny moment in time, my father sat uncharacteristically relaxed and handsome in his long-haired, thin-faced way, whilst Ute, wearing an ankle-length skirt and a white blouse with leg-of-mutton sleeves, was striding out of shot, as if she could smell the dinner burning. She held my hand and her face was turned away from the camera, but something in the way she carried herself made her look displeased, irritated to be caught with the rest of us. Ute was always well built – big-boned and muscular –

though in the last nine years she's become fat, her face wider than in my memory, and her fingers so puffed, her wedding ring is locked in position. On the telephone, she tells her friends that her weight gain has been due to the agony she lived with for so many years; that she ate her way through it. But late at night, when I can't sleep, and creep downstairs in the dark, I have seen her eating in the kitchen, her face illuminated by the fridge's interior light. Looking at the photograph, I realized it was the only one I'd ever seen with the three of us in it together.

Today, two months after I'd come back home, Ute had been confident enough to leave me alone for half an hour before breakfast whilst she took Oskar to a Cub Scout meeting. And so, with one ear listening for the sound of the front door opening and Ute returning, I rummaged through the other drawers in the bureau. Already it was easy to cast aside pens, notepaper, unwritten luggage labels, catalogues for labour-saving household devices, and key rings of European buildings – the Eiffel Tower jostling against Buckingham Palace. In the bottom drawer, I found the magnifying glass. I kneeled on the rug, a different one from that in the photograph – when was it changed? – and held the glass over my father, but was disappointed to discover that enlarging him didn't show me anything new. His fingers were uncrossed; the corner of his mouth was not turned up; there was no secret tattoo I had missed.

One by one, from left to right, I focused on the five men in front of him. Three of them were squashed together on the leather sofa, whilst another sat back on the sofa's arm, his hands behind his head. These men wore scruffy beards and their hair long; none of them smiled. They looked so similar they could have been brothers, but I knew they were not. Confident, relaxed, mature; like born-again Christians, they said to the camera, 'We have seen the future and disaster is coming; but we are the saved.' They were members of the North London Retreaters. Every month they met at our house, arguing and discussing strategies for surviving the end of the world.

The fifth man, Oliver Hannington, I recognized instantly although I hadn't seen him either for many years. The camera had caught him sprawling across an armchair, his legs in flared trousers, dangling over one side. Smoke curled through his yellow hair from a cigarette he held in the hand that propped up his head. Like my father, this man was clean-shaven, but he smiled in a way that suggested he thought everything was ridiculous; as though he wanted posterity to know he wasn't really interested in the group's plans for self-sufficiency and stockpiling. He could have been a spy who had infiltrated them, or an undercover journalist producing news stories which would one day expose them all, or a writer, going home after meetings and working all the mad characters into a comic novel. Even now, his strong-jawed self-confidence seemed exotic and foreign; American.

But then I realized there must have been someone else in the room – the photographer. I stood where the person holding the camera must have stood, and with a corner of the photograph between my lips, I positioned my hands and fingers to form a square frame. The angle was all wrong; he or she must have been much taller than me. I put the magnifying glass back in the drawer, then surprised myself by sitting on the piano stool. I raised the key lid, transfixed by the neat white row of keys, like polished teeth, and put my right hand over them – so smooth and cool – where my father's had been. I leaned to the left, stretched my arm out across the top and something moved inside me, a nervous fluttering, low down in my stomach. I stared at the photograph, still in my hand. The face of my father stared back, even then so innocent he *must* have been guilty. I went again to the bureau, took the scissors from the pen pot and snipped around my father's face so he became a light grey mole on the tip of my finger. Careful not to drop him and lose him under the furniture, to be vacuumed up by Ute's cleaner, and with my eyes fixed on his head, I reached up under my dress with the scissors and chopped through the silky fabric in the middle of my bra. The two cups which had irritated and scratched fell apart and my body was freed, like it always had been. I tucked my father under my right breast so that the warm skin held him in place. I knew if he stayed there, everything would be all right and I would be allowed to remember.

2.

The summer the photograph was taken, my father recast our cellar as a fallout shelter. I don't know if he discussed his plans with Oliver Hannington that June, but the two of them lay around the sunny garden, talking and smoking and laughing.

In the middle of the night, Ute's music, melancholic and lilting, drifted through the rooms of our house. I would roll over in bed under my single sheet, sticky with the heat, and imagine her at the piano in the dark with her eyes shut, her body swaying, charmed by her own notes. Sometimes I heard them long after she had closed the key lid and gone back to bed. My father didn't sleep well either, but I think it was his lists that kept him awake. I imagined him reaching for the pad of paper and the small pencil stub he kept under his pillow. Without switching on the light, he wrote, '1. General list (3 people)' and underlined it:

Matches, candles
Radio, batteries
Paper and pencils
Generator, dynamo, torch
Water bottles
Toothpaste
Kettle, pots
Pans, rope and string

Cotton, needles
Steel and flint
Sand
Loo paper, Disinfectant
Toothpaste
Bucket with a lid

The lists read like poetry, even though the handwriting was a boyish version of my father's later frantic scribblings. Often the words strayed over each other where he had written them in the dark, or they were packed together as though tussling for space in his night-time head. Other lists sloped off the page where he had fallen asleep mid-thought. The lists were all for the fallout shelter: essential items to keep his family alive under the ground for days or maybe even weeks.

At some point during his time in the garden with Oliver Hannington, my father decided to fit out the cellar for four people. He started to include his friend in the calculations for the quantity of knives and forks, tin cups, bedding, soap, food, even the number of toilet rolls. I sat on the stairs, listening to him and Ute in the kitchen as he worked on his plans.

'If you must make this mess it should be for just the three of us,' she complained. There was the noise of papers being gathered. 'I am uncomfortable that Oliver should be included. He is not one of the family.'

'One more person doesn't make any difference. Anyway, bunk beds don't come in threes,' said my father. I could hear him drawing whilst he spoke.

'I don't want him down there. I don't want him in the house,' Ute said. The scratch of pencil on paper stopped. 'He is witching this family – it gives me the creepers.'

'Bewitching and creeps,' said my father, laughing.

'Creeps! OK, creeps!' Ute didn't like to be corrected. 'I would prefer that this man is not in my house.'

'That's what it always comes down to, doesn't it? Your house.' My father's voice was raised now.

'My money has paid for it.' From my position on the stairs I heard a chair scrape against the floor.

'Ah yes, let us pray to the Bischoff family money that funds the famous pianist. And, dear Lord, let us not forget how hard she works,' said my father. I could imagine him bowing, his palms pressed together.

'At least I am a professional. What do you do, James? Lie across the garden all day with your dangerous American friend.'

'There's nothing dangerous about Oliver.'

'There is something not right with him, but you will not see it. He is only here to make trouble.' Ute stomped from the kitchen and went into the sitting room. I shuffled my bottom up a step, wary of discovery.

'What use will playing the piano be when the world ends?' my father called after her.

'What use will twenty tins of Spam be, tell me that?' Ute yelled back. There was a wooden clunk as she lifted the key lid, and she played one low minor chord with both hands. The notes died away and she shouted, 'Peggy, she will not ever be eating the Spam,' and even though there was no one to see me, I hid my mouth behind my hand as I smiled. Then she played Prokofiev's Sonata Number 7 – fast and furious. I imagined her fingers sliding on the ivory like talons.

'It wasn't raining when Noah built the ark,' my father bellowed.

Later, when I crept back to bed, the arguments and the piano playing ended, but I heard other sounds, ones that sounded almost like pain, although, even aged eight, I knew they meant something else.

There was a list that mentioned Spam. It was on the one titled '5. Food etc'. Under the heading my father wrote, '15 calories per body pound, ½ gallon of water per day, ½ tube of toothpaste per month', then:

14 gallons water
10 tubes toothpaste
20 tins condensed chicken soup
35 tins baked beans
20 tins Spam
Dried eggs
Flour
Yeast
Salt
Sugar
Coffee
Crackers
Jam
Lentils
Dried beans
Rice

The items meander, as if my father were playing the 'I went to the shops and bought . . .' game by himself – Spam reminded him of ham, which made him think of eggs, which took him to pancakes and on to flour.

In our cellar he laid a new concrete floor, reinforced the

walls with steel and installed batteries that could be recharged by pedalling a static bicycle for two hours a day. He fitted two cooking rings, running off bottled gas, and built alcoves for the bunk beds – all made up with mattresses, pillows, sheets and blankets. A white melamine-topped table was placed in the centre of the room, with four matching chairs. The walls were lined with shelves, which my father stacked with food and jerrycans of water, cooking utensils, games and books.

Ute refused to help. When I came home from school, she would say she had spent her day practising the piano, whilst 'your father has been playing in the cellar'. She complained her fingers were stiff with neglect and her wrists ached, and that bending down to look after me had affected her posture at the keyboard. I didn't question why she was playing more often than she used to. When my father emerged from underneath the kitchen, his face red and his bare back shiny, he looked as though he might faint. He glugged water at the kitchen sink, put his whole head under the tap, then shook his hair like a dog, trying to make me and Ute laugh. But she only rolled her eyes and returned to her piano.

When my father invited members of the North London Retreaters to our house for meetings, I was allowed to open the front door and show the half-dozen hairy and earnest men into Ute's sitting room. I liked it when our house was full of people and conversation, and until I was sent up to bed, I lingered, trying to follow their discussions of the statistical chances, causes and outcomes of a thing they called 'bloody Armageddon'. If it wasn't 'the Russkies' dropping a nuclear bomb and obliterating London with just a few minutes' warning, it would be the water supply polluted by pesticides, or the world economy collapsing and the streets being overrun with hungry marauders. Although Oliver joked that the British were so far behind the Americans that when disaster came we would still be in our pyjamas whilst they would have been up for hours protecting their homes and families, my father was proud that his group was one of the first – perhaps *the* first – to meet in England to discuss survivalism. But Ute was petulant about not being able to practise the piano with them lounging around, drinking and chain-smoking late into the night. My father loved to argue and he knew his subject well. When the alcohol had flowed for a few hours, and all agenda items had been covered, the meetings would dissolve from well-ordered discussion to argument and my father's voice would rise above the others.

The noise would make me throw off my bed sheet and sneak downstairs in my bare feet to peep around the sitting-room door, where the odours of warm bodies, whisky and cigarettes drifted towards me. In my memory, my father is leaning forward and thumping his knee, or stubbing out his cigarette so burning tobacco flies out of the ashtray and melts crusty holes in the rug or scorches the wooden floor. Then he is standing with his hands clenched and his arms held tight to his sides as if he is battling with the impulse to let his fists fly at the first man who stands up to disagree with him.

They wouldn't wait for one another to finish speaking; it wasn't a debate. Like the words in my father's lists, the men shouted over each other, interrupting and heckling.

'I tell you, it'll be a natural disaster: tidal wave, flood, earthquake. What good will your shelter be then, James, when you and your family are buried alive?'

Standing in the hall, I flinched at the thought, my fists balled, and I held in a whimper.

'Flood? We could bloody do with a flood now.'

'Look at those poor buggers in that earthquake in Italy. Thousands dead.' The man's words were slurred and he had his head in his hands. I thought perhaps his mother was Italian.

'It'll be the government that lets us down. Don't expect Callaghan to be knocking on your door with a glass of water when the standpipes have run dry.'

'He'll be too busy worrying about inflation to notice the Russians have blasted us to hell.'

'My cousin has a friend at the BBC who says they're producing public information films on how to make an inner refuge in houses. It's just a matter of time before the bomb drops.'

A man with a greying beard said, 'Frigging idiots; they'll have nothing to eat and if they do the army will confiscate it. What's the frigging point?' A bit of spittle caught in the hairs on his chin and I had to look away.

'I'm not going to be in London when the bomb falls. You can stay, James, locked in your dungeon, but I'll be gone – the Borders, Scotland, somewhere isolated, secure.'

'And what will you eat?' said my father. 'How will you survive? How are you going to get there with all the other fools heading out of the cities as well? It'll be gridlocked, and if you get to the countryside, everyone including your mother and her cat will have gone too. Call yourself a Retreater? It'll be the cities where law and order are restored soonest. Not your commune in North Wales.' From behind the door frame, I swelled with pride as my father spoke.

'All those emergency supplies in your cellar are meant to be just that,' said another man. 'What are you going to do when they run out? You don't even have an air rifle.'

'Hell, give me a decent knife and an axe and we'll be fine,' said my father.

The Englishmen carried on arguing until an American voice cut through them all: 'You know what the trouble is with you, James? You're so damn British. And the rest of you – you're all living in the dark ages, hiding in your cellars, driving off to the country like you're going on a fucking Sunday picnic. You still call yourself Retreaters; the world's already moving on without you. You haven't even figured out that you're survivalists. And, James, forget the cellar. What you need is a bug-out location.'

The way he spoke was authoritative, with an assumption of attention. The rest of the men, my father included, fell silent. Oliver Hannington lolled in the armchair with his back to me, whilst all the others stared out of the window or at the floor. It reminded me of my classroom, when Mr Harding said something none of us understood. He would stand for minutes, waiting for someone to put their hand up and ask what he meant, until the silence grew so thick and uncomfortable that we looked anywhere except at each other or him. It was a strategy designed to see who would crack first, and nine times out of ten it would be Becky who would say something silly, so the class could laugh in relief and embarrassment, and Mr Harding would smile.

Unexpectedly, Ute strode through from the kitchen, walking in that way she did when she knew she had an audience, all hips and waist. Her hair was tied in a messy knot at the back of her neck and she was wearing her favourite kaftan, the one that flowed around her muscular legs. Every man there, including my father and Oliver Hannington, understood that she could have gone the long way round, via the hall. No one ever described Ute as beautiful – they used words like striking, arresting, singular. But because she was a woman to be reckoned with, the men composed themselves. Those standing sat down, and those on the sofa stopped slouching; even Oliver Hannington turned his head. They paid attention to their cigarettes, cupping the lit ends and looking around for ashtrays. Ute sighed: a quick intake of breath, an expansion of her ribcage and a slow exhalation. She berated the men as she walked past them to kneel in front of me. For the first time, my father and his friends turned and saw me.

'Now you have woken my little Peggy, with all your talks of disaster,' Ute said, stroking my hair.

Even then I knew she did it because people were watching. She took my hand to lead me upstairs. I pulled back, straining to hear who would break the silence.

'There is nothing bad going to happen, Liebchen,' Ute crooned.

'And a bug-out location is?' It was my father who surrendered first.

There was a pause, and Oliver Hannington knew we were all hanging on his answer.

'Your very own little cabin in the forest,' he said, and laughed, although I didn't think it was funny.

'And how are we going to find one of those?' one of the men on the sofa asked.

14

Then Oliver Hannington turned to me, tapped the side of his nose and winked. In the glow of his attention I let Ute tug me by the hand up to bed.

When the work on the fallout shelter was coming to an end, my father put me into training. It started as a game to him – a way to show off to his friend. My father bought a silver whistle, which he hung around his neck on a length of string, and he bought me a canvas rucksack with leather straps and buckles. Its side pockets were embroidered with blue petals and green leaves.

His signal was three short blasts on the whistle, which were sounded from the bottom of the stairs. Ute would have nothing to do with this either; she stayed in bed with the sheet over her head or played the piano, propping the top board fully open so the sound reverberated throughout the house. The whistles, which could happen at any point before bedtime, were my signal to pack the rucksack. I ran about the house, gathering the things from a list my father had made me memorize. I flung the rucksack on my back and sped down the stairs in time to an angry 'Revolutionary Étude' by Chopin. My father would be looking straight ahead, the whistle still in his mouth and his hands clasped behind his back, whilst I raced around the newel post, the rucksack bouncing. I rushed down the cellar stairs two at a time and jumped the last three. In the fallout shelter, I knew I had about four minutes to unpack before my father blew the whistle again. I yanked out the chair at the head of the table, facing away from the stairs. And from the rucksack I pulled out a pile of clothes – underwear, denim dungarees, trousers, cheesecloth shirts, jumper, shorts, nightie – and, making sure they didn't unfold, placed them on the table. My hand went back in the rucksack to snatch the next item, like a lucky dip at the funfair. Out came my comb, placed horizontally just above the nightie; to the left, an extending spyglass; my toothbrush and toothpaste, side by side on top of my clothes; and next, my doll, Phyllis, with her painted-on eyes and her sailor suit, beside them. In a final rush, I produced my blue woollen balaclava and squeezed my head inside it. Despite the heat, matching mittens were meant to go on next, and when everything was perfectly aligned on the table and the rucksack was empty, I was supposed to be sitting quietly with my hands on my legs, looking straight ahead towards the gas stove. Then the whistle would go again and a nervous excitement would run through me, as my father came down the stairs for the review. Sometimes he straightened the comb or moved Phyllis over to the other side of the clothes.

'Very good, very good,' he would say, as though it were an army inspection. 'At ease,' and he would give me a wink and I knew I had passed.

On the final occasion that my father and I performed our drill, Ute and Oliver Hannington had been invited to be our audience. She, of course, refused. She thought it was point-less and childish. Oliver Hannington was there, though, leaning against the wall behind my father when he blew the first three whistles. Ute was in the sitting room, playing Chopin's 'Funeral March'. At first, everything went well. I gathered all the items and went down both sets of stairs in double-quick time, but I made an error in the laying out, or maybe my father, in his excitement, blew the second whistle too soon. I ran out of time and the mittens were not on my hands when the two men came down the cellar stairs. With my pulse racing, I stuffed the mittens under my legs. They itched the skin where my shorts ended. I had let my father down. I wasn't fast enough. The mittens became wet beneath my thighs. The warm liquid ran off the chair and pooled on the white linoleum beneath me. My father shouted. Oliver Hannington, standing behind me, laughed, and I cried.

Ute rushed down to the cellar, swept me up into her arms and let me bury my face in her shoulder as she carried me away from 'those absolute awful men'. But like the closing credits of a film, my memory of that scene ends as I am rescued.

I cannot remember Oliver Hannington leaning in his indifferent manner against the cellar shelves with a smirk on his lips after I wet myself, although I'm sure that he did. I have imagined but I didn't see him take the cigarette from his mouth and blow the smoke upwards, where it would have crept along the low ceiling. And I didn't notice how red my father's face became after I let him down in front of his friend.

3

At the end of June, Ute went back to work. I'm not sure if she had simply had enough of being at home with us, or she craved a more attentive audience; it wasn't because she needed the money. 'The world wants me,' she liked to say. Perhaps she was right. Ute had been a concert pianist – not one of those second-rate piano players who is part of a third-rate orchestra – Ute Bischoff, at eighteen, had been the youngest-ever winner of the International Chopin Piano Competition.

On rainy afternoons I liked to sit on the dining-room floor and take out her records from the sideboard. It never occurred to me to listen to them, instead I played my *Railway Children* album over and over until I could recite it by heart; and whilst Phyllis worried about the boy in the red jersey, I examined the cardboard sleeves of Ute's music in minute detail: Ute sitting at the piano, Ute taking a bow on stage, Ute in an evening gown and with a smile I didn't recognize.

In 1962 she had played under the baton of Leonard Bernstein in the opening concert at Philharmonic Hall in New York.

'Leonard was ein Liebchen,' she said. 'He first kissed me, and *then* he kissed Jackie Kennedy.'

Ute was lauded and feted; she was handsome and young. When she was twenty-five and on a tour of England, she met my father. He was her stand-in page-turner, and eight years her junior.

For the three of us, their meeting became one of those stories that every family has – often repeated and regularly embellished. My father shouldn't have been at her concert at all. He was a ticket-taker, covering someone else's shift when Ute's regular page-turner tripped over a purchase line back-stage and smashed his nose into the counterweight. My father, never squeamish, was wiping the blood from the floorboards with a rag when the stage manager tugged on his sleeve and asked in desperation if he could read music.

'I admitted I could,' said my father.

'But that was the big problem,' said Ute. 'My page-turners must always be watching me, not reading the music. Look for the nodding of my head, I say.'

'I couldn't. I was in awe of you.'

'The silly boy, he must turn too early, and then he turned two pages,' Ute said, smiling. 'It was absolute disaster.'

'I wrote you a note to apologize.'

'And then you invited him to your dressing room,' I joined in.

'And then I invite him to my dressing room,' Ute repeated.

'And she gave me a lesson in page-turning,' my father said, and he and Ute laughed.

'Such a handsome, clever boy,' she said, cupping his face with her hand. 'How could I not fall in love with him?'

But that was when I was five or six. When I was eight, asking for the story got me a quick 'Oh, you don't want to hear that boring thing again' from Ute.

For the public and critics, her relationship with James Hillcoat was a scandal. Ute was at the height of her career and she gave it all up for the love of a seventeen-year-old boy. They married the next year, as soon as it was legal.

The day the fallout shelter was completed, Oliver Hannington left, and when I came home from school, Ute had gone too, on a concert tour of Germany which I knew nothing about. I found my father lying on the sofa, his blank eyes staring at the ceiling. I ate cereal for tea and stayed up until the television screen swam in front of me.

The next morning my father came into my bedroom before I got up and said I didn't have to go to school.

'School, schmool.' His laugh was too loud, and I knew he was pretending to be happy for my sake. We both wanted Ute to be at home, huffing at a sink full of washing-up, making the beds with loud sighs or even deliberately thumping on the piano, but neither of us would say it to the other. 'What's the point of sitting in a classroom when the sun's shining and there are plenty of things to teach you at home?' he said. Without him saying so, I understood that he didn't want to be alone. We put up a triangular two-man tent at the end of the garden, just where the parched lawn gave way to bushes and ivy-covered trees. At night we had to wriggle inside it feet first; by morning the guy ropes had loosened and the top ridge had sagged, until it was only inches above our bodies.

Our house – a large, white, ocean-going ship of a building – stood alone on the crest of a gentle slope. The garden, which rolled downhill, had been designed and planted long before our family had moved in, but neither of my parents took care of it and what had once probably been separate and well-kept spaces now blended one into the other. A swing seat stood close to the house on a brick terrace, which was disintegrating whilst the moss and creeping thyme thrived. At the edges, the brick crumbled into the encroaching lawn so that it was no longer possible to see where one ended and the other began. In the sunshine of that summer, the grass all but disappeared from the centre of the lawn, rubbed away by our feet, growing lank and yellow only around the sides. My father made plans on paper for a vegetable patch – scale diagrams of the distance between rows of carrots and runner beans and the angle of the sun at particular times of the day. He said he had grown radishes when he was a child, spicy roots the size of his thumb, and wanted to teach me to do the same, but he only got as far as marking out the area he had in mind and was too easily distracted even to put a spade in the ground.

At the bottom of the garden, clumps of dock and dandelion had taken root, their downy heads spreading seeds in the smallest breath of wind. A wild blackberry lorded it over all the other plants, sending thorny advance guards arching into the air, each with hundreds of buds packed into tight whorls. And all the while, under the straggling flower-bolted beds, the treacherous plant was sending secret messengers, which reappeared as far up as the terrace in small flowerless tufts. The end of the garden was a wild and exciting place for an eight-year-old, because beyond the raggle-taggle border was the cemetery. The scented overgrowth gave way to towering trees, enveloped in twisting ivy all the way up into the canopy. My father and I waded through the nettles, our arms held above our heads to avoid the stings. The daylight under the trees was lazy and the air always cool.

We trod narrow paths into the dilapidated cemetery that led the way to the sweetest elderflower bush, a patch of ground elder which had found sunlight, and the best tree for climbing. I could stand on its lowest branch, and my father would give me a leg up into the tree's crotch, where its branches, each the size of his waist, curved up, then outwards. With our legs dangling either side, we shuffled along one of these, me first with my father close behind, until we could look down through the waxy leaves, to the graves below. My father said it was called a Magnificent Tree.

The cemetery was closed to the public – lack of council funds had locked its gates the year before. We were alone with the foxes and the owls; no visitors or mourners came, so we invented them. We pointed out a tourist in a Hawaiian shirt with his loud wife.

'Oh gee,' said my father in an American falsetto, 'look at that angel, isn't she just the cutest thing!'

Once, we swung our legs above an imaginary burial.

'Shh, the widow's coming,' whispered my father. 'She's blowing her nose on a lace handkerchief. How tragic, to have lost her husband so young.'

'But just behind her are the evil twins,' I joined in, 'wearing identical black dresses.'

'And there's the despicable nephew – the one with egg in his moustache. All he wants is his uncle's money.' My father rubbed his hands together.

'The widow's throwing a flower on to the coffin.'

'A forget-me-not,' my father added. 'The uncle is creeping up behind her; watch out! She's going to fall into the grave!' He grabbed me around the waist and pretended to tip me off the branch. I squealed, my voice ringing amongst the stone mausoleums and tombs surrounding us.

*

When I should have been in school, the garden became our home, and the cemetery our garden. Occasionally I thought about my best friend, Becky, and what she might be doing in class, but not often. We sometimes went into the house to 'gather provisions', and on a Wednesday evening to watch *Survivors* on the telly. We didn't bother to wash or change our clothes. The only rule we followed was to brush our teeth every morning and evening using water we brought to the camp in a bucket.

'Four billion people on the planet and under three billion own a toothbrush,' my father would say, shaking his head. The sunshine didn't stop, so we spent our days foraging and hunting. My back and shoulders burned, blistered, peeled and went brown whilst I learned what was safe to eat from the trees and plants of north London.

My father taught me how to trap and cook squirrels and rabbits, which mushrooms were poisonous and where to collect the edible ones like chicken-of-the-woods, chanterelles and penny buns, and how to make ramson soup. We pulled up the stalks of nettles and dried them in the sun, then, sitting on the edge of a grave, I watched him strip away the plant's exterior and twist what had been foliage a few minutes before into a fine braid. I copied him because he said the best way to learn was to do things myself, but even with my small fingers, the cord I produced was clumsy and malformed. Still, we made hangman's nooses of them and tied them to a branch that we propped up against a tree.

'The squirrel is a lazy creature,' said my father. 'What is the squirrel?'

'A lazy creature,' I said.

'He always takes the path of least resistance,' he said. 'What does the squirrel do?'

'He takes the path of least resistance.'

'And what does that mean?' He waited for my answer, which didn't come. 'It means he'll happily run up this branch and get his stupid head stuck in a noose,' my father said. 'In fact he'll happily run up this branch over his dead friends and still get his head stuck in a noose.'

When we returned to our traps the next day, two slight corpses dangled from the tree by their necks, swaying to and fro from the weight of their own bodies. I dared myself not to look away. My father untied them and put the nooses in his pocket 'for next time'. That evening he tried to show me how to skin them, but when his knife came down on the first neck, I said that I didn't think we had enough kindling and perhaps I should go and collect more. When he had finished, he skewered the skinned animals on a stick he had whittled to a point, and we cooked them over the fire and ate them with ramsons and boiled burdock roots. I picked at mine – the squirrel looked too similar to the animal it had once been, and tasted like chicken which had been out of the fridge for a day too long.

We didn't give a thought to what we were doing to the garden. We only considered our next meal – how to find it, how to kill it and how to cook it. And although I would have preferred Sugar Puffs with gold-top milk in front of the telly, I joined in the adventure without question.

My father dug stones out of the rockery with a trowel and built a fire pit in the middle of the scuffed earth, a little way from our tent. We tied ropes across our shoulders and dragged half a fallen tree trunk around the gravestones and back to the garden so we had something to sit on. Chairs from the house would have been cheating. We dug a pit in a dusty flower bed and made a shallow grave for the bones and skins of the animals we ate. My father showed me how to make char-cloth using a shirt that he had me fetch from his wardrobe in the house. According to my father's rules, this wasn't cheating. I brought it down still on its metal hanger and he sliced the cotton into pieces with his knife. He said if we'd been near a river the hanger would have made perfect fishing hooks and we could be having smoked trout for our dinner. Every evening I lit a fire with his flint and steel, which he always kept with him – flashing the sparks on to the char-cloth, then transferring it to the dry tinder we had gathered.

'Never waste a match when you can light a fire with flint and steel,' he said.

After we had eaten and I had brushed my teeth, we sat on the log and my father told me stories about catching animals and living wild.

'Long ago, in a land called Hampshire,' he said, 'there was a family who lived together in die Hütte. They survived off the land and no one ever told them what to do.'

'What's a Hütte?' I asked.

'A magical, secret place in the forest,' my father said with a catch in his voice. 'Our very own little cabin, with wooden walls, and wooden floors, and wooden shutters at the windows.' His voice was deep and smooth; it lulled me. 'Outside, we can pick sweet berries all year round; chanterelles spread like yellow rugs under the trees; and in the bottom of a valley a Fluss overflows with silvery fish, so when we're hungry and need supper, we can just dip our hands in and pull three out.

'One for each of us,' he said as I leaned against him. 'You, me and Mutti.'

'Does she like fish?'

'I think so. You can ask her soon.'

'When she gets home from Germany.' I was almost asleep.

'In two weeks and three days exactly.' He sounded happy.

'That's not long, is it?'

'No, not long until we have Mutti back.'

'What else about the Hütte, Papa?' I didn't want the conversation to end.

'Inside there's a stove to keep us warm on long winter nights and a piano for Mutti to play.'

'Can we go there, Papa?' I yawned.

'Perhaps,' he said as I closed my eyes.

He carried me into the tent and tucked me inside, my body brown from sun and dirt, but my teeth clean. 'How do we get there?'

'I'm not sure, Peggy. I'll work it out,' he said.

4.

The next morning, Oliver Hannington was sitting on the swing seat next to the house when we walked back from the cemetery carrying a brace of squirrels and a basket of ground elder. The sun was high behind him, his face in deep shadow. He was rocking back and forth, trying to blow his cigarette smoke out through a hole I had torn in the canopy weeks ago, when I had been fighting pirates from the swing seat's deck. When Oliver succeeded, puffs of grey cloud signalled a warning like a native Indian campfire.

'Hi,' said Oliver, still looking upwards. On his lap was a black and white newsletter, and although it was upside down I could make out a drawing of a man wearing a vest and holding a large hammer. At the top of the page were the words 'The Survivor'. Oliver gave up blowing and looked at us. 'Jesus,' he said, making the word twice as long as it was at Christmas. I was suddenly conscious of my dirty clothes and unwashed hair and, looking at my father, noticed he had sprouted a beard whilst we had been living in the garden.

'We've just been messing about in the woods for a bit. Peggy wanted to see what it would be like to sleep outside,' said my father. 'In fact I was just starting to think that it must be about time for a bath.' He handed me the squirrels, which were bound together by their tails, and sat down beside Oliver, who shuffled a little further along the seat.

'Jesus,' said Oliver again. 'You really do need a bath. And

what have you there, little girl?' Oliver smiled with white straight teeth and beckoned me forward so he could peer into the basket hanging over my arm. 'Nice, spinach grown by dead people.' He laughed.

I couldn't have explained why, but even then I knew Oliver Hannington was dangerous.

'Take the squirrels down to the camp, Peggy, and go inside and wash,' said my father. It was the first time in the previous fortnight he had given me an order. I carried the animals back to the smoking fire, dumped them on the ground, then moped up the garden to the seat, where my father and Oliver were swinging and laughing. My father took a cigarette from the open packet which Oliver held out to him, and lit it using a match. An angry, choking feeling stuck inside my throat.

'Papa, you shouldn't smoke,' I said, standing in front of them.

'Papa,' said Oliver in a squeaky English accent, 'you shouldn't smoke.' He laughed and exhaled through his nostrils like a dragon.

'Go and wash,' my father repeated with a frown.

In the bathroom, I pushed the plug into the bath and I said aloud, 'Let's have some hot water, Mrs Viney.'

Without an answering reply or a tired laugh from Ute, my voice sounded small and pathetic. I sat on the edge of the bath while it filled, then cried as I slid down into the water. When I was submerged the only noise was the hum of the blood in my head. I didn't understand why my father had become more like a parent when we had walked up the garden, but I knew that he had, and understood it had something to do with Oliver. When I resurfaced, I thought about my father's friend falling backwards off the seat and banging his head on a rock, the blood soaking away into the earth, or cooking him squirrel stew and telling him it was chicken. He would gobble it up and one of the tiny bones would stick in his gullet and make him choke. For the first time since she had left, I wanted Ute. I wanted her sitting on the edge of the bath and complaining that I was taking too long. I wanted to be able to beg her to imitate the mother from *The Railway Children*, until she relented and said, 'You must never, never, never ask strangers to give you things. Now, always remember that – won't you?' and I wanted to be able to laugh because the words sounded so funny in her German accent. On my own, I washed and pulled out the bath plug, leaving a soapy tidemark which I didn't clean. I dressed in my bedroom and leaned out of the window, over the glasshouse.

I could see my father's knees and calves, hairy and brown, his shoes flat on the dusty ground. Oliver's legs in jeans, at the other end of the seat, were splayed wide, in the way that some men sit. As I watched, my father opened his legs too.

'I've finished,' I shouted down in a voice that was so full of resentment, I was sure my father must notice.

Oliver stood up and stretched. 'I could do with a shower. It's so damn hot in this country. Why do the English still only have baths?' He pulled at the front of his shirt, and I caught a glimpse of blond hair against brown chest.

'Well, I'm going first,' said my father. He pushed past Oliver and charged across the patio towards the house. Oliver gave a whoop of delight, lobbed his cigarette into the flower bed and raced after my father. I saw them running through the glasshouse, and heard them bursting into the sitting room and chasing each other up the stairs, laughing and swearing. I stood in my bedroom doorway as they stumbled and careered past, Oliver tackling my father, leaping over him into the bathroom and locking the door. My father came into my room, panting and smiling. He sat on the edge of my bed.

'It'll be nice to sleep on a proper mattress with sheets, won't it, Peggy?' he said.

I shrugged.

'Come on, it'll be fun having Oliver around. You'll see.' He nudged me, gave me a tickle, then picked up a pillow and biffed me around the head with it, so that I fell backwards, laughing. I snatched another pillow and went to whack him with it, but he was already standing, already leaving the room. I heard him bang on the bathroom door.

'Don't be long,' he called to Oliver, and went into his bedroom.

I lay back on my bed and put the pillow over my head so that the house was quiet, as if no one were there; as if all human life had disappeared in an instant. I imagined the blackberry's tendrils continuing their reconnoitre of the upper terraces of the garden and reaching the house, crawling on their bellies – army-style – under the doors. The ivy which grew up the exterior wall would ease itself inside and spread like a green rash across the ceilings. And the bay tree, standing in the front garden, would stretch long, tenacious root-fingers into the sitting room, lifting and buckling the parquet. I wished I could fall asleep, cradled in the middle of the vegetation, and not wake for a hundred years.

It was airless under the pillow, so after a while I flung it off and ran downstairs and outside. Oliver had left his news-letter on the swing seat. I picked it up and went down to the bottom of the garden where the fire still smouldered. I held a corner of the paper against an ember, blowing on it until the fire caught, then laid the pages flat so the flames licked across them until they had transformed into black flakes. I looked at the squirrels. They were where I had left them, beside the fire. They could have been two miniature men, sunning themselves side by side – lying on their backs with their white tummies showing. I gave them a shove with my toe and thought about how dinner wasn't going to be ready for hours.

Our camp was abandoned when Oliver arrived. We moved back into the house without any discussion. We made toast with white sliced bread that my father bought, along with Oliver's cigarettes, from the corner shop, or heated tins of steak pie and peas we chose from the shelves in the fallout shelter. Each day, the sun leached more colour from the tent that we had left to sag in the garden, and the ground around it dried and cracked into tiny ravines.

On the third afternoon of Oliver's visit, the doorbell rang. I was spooning mouthfuls of Sugar Puffs at the kitchen table and watching two flies circle in the thick heat. Every time their paths crossed, they buzzed at each other in irritation. I had to unstick my legs to raise myself off my chair, and so Oliver, with only an orange towel around his waist, got to the front door before me. I hung back at the end of the hall, waiting to see who the visitor was.

'Hi,' said Oliver in a way that roused my curiosity and made me want to see beyond his body to the doorstep.

'Oh,' said the person. 'Hello.' The voice, a girl's, hesitated. 'Is Peggy in?'

'Come in,' said Oliver, then turned back into the house and yelled, 'Peggy!'

I saw Becky standing on the doorstep at the same time as Oliver saw me loitering near the kitchen.

'You've got a visitor,' he called to me. 'Come in, come in,' he said to Becky.

He held the door open and she walked past him, wide-eyed and smiling but looking at anything except the unknown semi-naked man in my house. Oliver followed her into the kitchen and went to the sink.

'Either of you kids want some water?'

He filled a glass for himself and we stood and watched his Adam's apple bobbing whilst he drank. He filled the glass again and held it out to us, but Becky, breaking from the spell we were under, grabbed my hand and pulled me back down the hall and up to my bedroom.

'Who was that?' she said, flinging herself on to my bed.

'Just my dad's friend, Oliver Hannington.' I stuck my head out of the window to try to breathe cooler air. 'He's staying with us for a bit.'

'He looks just like Hutch.'

'Who's Hutch?'

'You know,' said Becky, 'the blond one from *Starsky and Hutch*.' She had pushed off her shoes and was propping up her bottom and cycling her legs, her school skirt falling around her waist, revealing regulation blue knickers. Just looking at her exercising made me feel hot.

'Anyway, where have you been? You've got loads of catching up to do.'

'What do you mean? I've been here.'

'Mr Harding keeps asking me where you are. We've been doing right angles. I said I didn't know, maybe you've been poorly. Have you been poorly?'

'Not really,' I said.

From the garden we heard Oliver shouting something about ice. Becky crawled across the bed, pulling herself along by her arms on to the carpet and letting her legs flop behind her. The two of us crouched at the window and watched Oliver lying full out on the swing seat, reading a book. He had bent the cover back so he could hold it in one hand, and he had swapped the towel for a pair of shorts.

'Well, you'd better come tomorrow,' said Becky. 'It's the last day of school.'

In the garden, my father appeared with two glasses filled with an orange drink. He handed one to Oliver and they chinked them together.

'I'm going to bring in Buckaroo,' Becky said.

In the morning, I dressed in my grey skirt, white shirt and blazer, made a packed lunch and went back to school. Everyone was already at their desks when I arrived. Mr Harding peered at me over the top of his glasses but made no comment as I sat in my chair.

'What game did you bring?' whispered Becky.

'KerPlunk,' I said, and she nodded her approval.

Mr Harding must have written a note in the register, because when we were setting up our games Mrs Cass, the school secretary, came and said the headmaster wanted a word with me. I had been expecting it and, anyway, I was embarrassed to discover that most of the straws were missing from the game I had brought in.

'So, Peggy Hillcoat, where have you been?' Mrs Cass asked as she marched me down the corridor. It smelled of sweat and plimsoll rubber. She didn't wait for an answer. 'I've telephoned your house at least four times in the past two weeks, trying to get hold of you or your mother. I even came round once and it's not exactly on my way home.'

We turned the corner, where the smell wasn't as strong and the floor changed from linoleum to thin green carpet, indicating that we were approaching authority.

'You can't take holiday willy-nilly, you know. You're in a lot of hot water, young lady.'

She told me to sit on one of the comfortable chairs outside the headmaster's office. The fabric showed the tears and stains of years of pupil and teacher distress. Through the frosted-glass door, I caught a glimpse of the headmaster sipping at his teacup, making me wait until called for.

'I understand from Mr Harding that you've been absent for two weeks, without your mother informing the school,' said the headmaster after he called me in.

'She died,' I said, without a plan.

'Your mother?' said the headmaster. His eyebrows rose and plunged madly, and he managed to look both desperate and surprised. He pressed a button on his desk, which buzzed in the office across the hall.

'She was killed in a car accident in Germany,' I told them both when Mrs Cass had responded to the headmaster's summons.

'Oh, my goodness,' Mrs Cass said, her hand going to her

mouth. 'Not Ute. Oh no, not Ute.' She looked around and behind her as if she wanted to sit down, but became distracted and instead said, 'You poor, poor child.' She clasped me to her, pressing me into her soft bosom, then took me back to the chair and brought me thick, sweet tea in a cup with a saucer, as if it were me who had just learned of the car crash and not her.

Through the door, the headmaster said, 'Surely we would have heard. Isn't she that famous piano player?'

Mrs Cass's answer was too quiet to hear but it involved a lot of gasps, head shaking and hand clasping.

When I had finished the tea, she guided me back to my classroom, her hand on my shoulder, both caressing and propelling me forward. She took Mr Harding aside and had a whispered exchange with him; his expression moved from boredom to shock to a crinkled face of sympathy when he glanced at me, waiting at the front of the class.

On the first row, Becky mouthed, 'What did you say?' and I tried to mouth back, 'I told them she died in a car crash,' but the words 'car crash' were too difficult to communicate without saying them out loud. Rose Chapman nudged and leaned towards Becky, who, in a hiss, translated my words into, 'Tabitha died in a rush!' The Chinese whisper spread from group to group, where children gathered around marbles, counters and dice. Mr Harding told me I was excused; I packed up KerPlunk and left.

At home over the next week, I saw little of my father and Oliver. Once, they went down to the high street and brought back fish and chips, laying theirs out on plates and eating with knives and forks at the dining-room table. Oliver got out the cutlery with the ivory handles and selected Ute's crystal Spiegelau goblets from the sideboard for the red wine they had bought at the off-licence.

'Prost! Toast! Die Bundespost!' shouted my father, and both men laughed in a slurred way whilst the crystal chinked. I carried my dinner, still wrapped in newspaper, into the sitting room and ate it in front of the telly. I went up to bed soon after. I lay still with my eyes shut, but sleep didn't come and I worried I had forgotten how to do it. I hummed the theme music to *The Railway Children* and imagined that Ute was downstairs, conquering the piano, whilst at the kitchen table my father was flicking through the newspaper. Everything and everyone were where they were supposed to be. But I was still awake when my father and Oliver stumbled upstairs, calling goodnight to each other.

If the two men weren't laughing, they were arguing. With all the windows in the house open to try to let in a breeze, I heard their shouting no matter which room they were in. They sounded like a Retreater meeting for two – the real ones had been suspended for the summer; apparently even survivalists took holidays. I tried to ignore them, but would find myself straining to make out each word. My father shouted the loudest, lost control first; Oliver's voice remained a steady, measured drawl that sliced through the other's fury. The arguments seemed to be the same ones, going around and around again: the best bug-out location, city versus the country, equipment, guns, knives. The noise would reach a crescendo, then a door would be slammed, the flare of a match as a cigarette was lit in the dark garden, and the next day all would be forgotten.

One evening I heard a noise from the hall, and it took me

a moment to realize it was the phone. When I picked it up, Ute was on the other end.

'Liebchen, it is Mutti.' She sounded a long way off. 'I am sorry I haven't called earlier. It has been difficult.' I thought she must mean that there weren't many telephones in Germany.

'Papa and I have been living in the garden.'

'In the garden? That sounds nice. So you are OK, and are you happy now that school must be finished for the holidays?'

I was worried she would ask about the lessons I hadn't been to, but instead she said, 'Has the weather been warm in London too?' She sounded sad, as if she would rather be at home, but then perhaps trying to make me laugh, she continued, 'Last night, a fat lady fainted from the heat, when I was on the second bar of the Tchaikovsky. I had to start again from the beginning; it was absolute shambles.'

'I'm very brown,' I said, rubbing dust off my legs and realizing I hadn't had a bath since the day Oliver had arrived.

'How lovely it must be to have time in the sunshine. I am inside every day, in the car or in the hotel and then in the car again to get to the performance.'

'Do you want to speak to Papa now?' I asked.

'No, not yet. I want to find out more about what my little Peggy has been doing.'

'I've been cooking.'

'That sounds very helpful. I hope you've tidied the kitchen afterwards.'

I didn't answer her; I didn't know what to say.

After a few seconds, in a voice I had to strain to hear, she asked, 'Perhaps you could get Papa now?'

I placed the receiver on the padded seat beside the phone and saw that my hands had made dirty marks on the yellow plastic. I licked my fingers and rubbed at the smudges.

When I told my father who it was on the phone, he jumped up from the swing seat, where he had been lying in the sun, and ran into the house. I went down to the bottom of the garden, where I had been baking burdock roots in the hot ashes of a fire I had made by myself. Without understanding why, I thrashed at the embers with a stick, scattering them like glow-worms into the evening. A few landed on the tent, burning black-rimmed holes through the canvas and the liner. When the fire was a grey blotch on the threadbare lawn, I walked through the house and up to my room.

An argument between my father and Oliver was building in the kitchen. It moved to the sitting room and on into the glasshouse; I put my head out of the open window. Below me were two shadows, lit by the lamplight that spilled from the sitting-room door. When I put my fingers in my ears to block out the sound, the black shapes became silent dancers, their movements choreographed, each action planned and rehearsed. I pressed my fingers in and out again in quick succession, which made the argument come to me in bursts of noise, disjointed and staccato.

'You f'
'ker. What'
'itch. How cou'
'you're pathet'
'an anima'
'ucking ani'

And then Oliver laughing, like a machine gun, jerky and uncontrolled. A dark object – an ashtray or a plant pot –

broke off from one of the man-shadows and flew past the other into the glass roof. There was a pause, as if the glass sheet were holding its breath, then it trembled, rippling outwards and splitting apart with a tremendous noise. In a reflex action, I ducked even whilst the glass rained down on the men below. The father-shadow crouched, his hands over the top of his head. Oliver yelled, 'Whowwaa!' as his shadow backed towards the sitting-room door and disappeared inside. My father's shape stayed bent, so that, from my position above him, he stopped being a man with arms and legs and a head and became a crow with a beak and wings. He made a noise like a crow too. I watched him, my hands on the windowsill and my eyes just above them, whilst the sound of Oliver moved through the house – to the kitchen and upstairs to the guest bedroom. I heard drawers being opened and closed, the long rasp of a suitcase zip. Then Oliver burst into my bedroom and I saw myself as he must have seen me, crouching by the window in the dark.

'Seen enough, have you, little girl?' he spat. 'Get a kick out of spying on adults, do you? Well, don't worry, I've seen enough too. Of you and your dear papa.' He laughed bitterly. 'And let's not forget the remarkable Ute. It seems I've given them both a present they won't forget in a hurry.' He left and went downstairs.

For a second I was frozen, then, thinking he was going back to the shattered glasshouse, I spun around and looked out of the window again. But the front door slammed, shaking the house, and below me, my father's crow-body jerked as though it had been caught in one of our traps, and then it slumped. I crept back to bed and lay with my eyes bulging into the darkness and my ears straining to hear the next sound, which never came.

In the morning, I was woken by three short blasts of the whistle. My father stood at the bottom of the stairs, legs apart, head up. The backs of his hands had plasters stuck on them in several places, and there was another over the bridge of his nose.

'Pack your rucksack, Peggy,' he said, using his military voice. 'We're going on holiday.'

'Where are we going?' I asked, worrying what Ute would say about the broken roof and the glass all over the floor when she returned.

'We're going to die Hütte,' said my father.

5.

At breakfast, I agreed to sit at the kitchen table to eat, instead of in my bedroom or on the floor of the glasshouse, where I could escape the stuffy warmth of the other rooms. Ute and I negotiated, and she said if I sat down with her and took time with spooning my porridge she would stop asking questions. I told her I would, because my father's face was tucked away in a secret place. I knew she would continue to ask questions. She couldn't stop herself.

The kitchen table had shrunk since I had been away, but everything else had multiplied and I found the kitchen was the most unsettling room of all. The quantity of things, the overwhelming choice of what to look at, pressed me to my chair and made me shut my eyes. The row of pots with always available tea, coffee and sugar; larger containers marked 'self-raising' and 'plain'; a blender gathering greasy dust; a roll of soft paper on a wooden stick; tall glass jars showing off a food called spaghetti, still in a bag; a shiny toaster that I avoided eye contact with; hooks with assorted mugs; a white fridge made multicoloured by magnets. I couldn't understand why a family of three needed seven saucepans when there were only four rings on the cooker; why the utensil pot held nine wooden spoons if there were only seven pans; and how we could ever eat the amount of food available in the cupboards and the fridge.

Oskar was at Saturday morning Cub Scouts, helping to tidy the grounds of an old people's home. I knew Ute had chosen this particular morning, with Oskar away, to ask me to sit at the table, because she thought that sitting down to eat with my eight-year-old brother might be one step too far. Oskar, Oskar, Oskar: I had to keep repeating his name, to remind myself that he existed; that a boy had been born and had grown for eight years and eight months without me knowing. He was almost as tall as me, but so young. I was still shocked, every time I looked at him, to think I was exactly his age when my father and I left this house. Whilst Ute was ladling porridge, made with water – the way I liked it – I wondered whether the Scouts had taught Oskar how to light a fire without matches, or how to catch squirrels by their necks, or use an axe with one smooth, swift motion. Perhaps they were things he and I could discuss another day.

At the table, Ute tried to engage me in conversation.

'Do you remember that summer?' she asked, her mouth still full of z's and v's, even after all these years. Straight away she began with a question, even though she had promised.

I shrugged an answer.

'I have been thinking of your father, the summer you went away,' she said. 'Went away' was the phrase she always used – innocuous, with no blame attached. 'I think perhaps I was too old for him. Too steady. He wants to have fun with his friend Oliver.'

'Wanted,' I corrected under my breath, but she didn't hear; she was staring through and beyond me.

'They were like boys. They were swinging the garden seat too high. I was afraid it would be damaged, and also the grass with their shoes. That seat belonged to your grandmother; Omi had it delivered all the way from Germany, you know. And then, when they were so hot, they took off their shirts and ran around the garden, playing at tomfoolery with the hose, even though the Water Board said it was not allowed. I watched them from your bedroom window, then I went down to ask them to be careful with the seat.' She paused, recollecting. 'Oliver, he teased me and said, "Jawohl." Maybe that's when it started. Yes, maybe then.'

I didn't ask Ute for these confidences, but still they spilled from her, as if, in the telling, she was assuaging some kind of guilt. In my mind's eye I saw my father, so unaware that one push with his heels against the earth, in time with Oliver Hannington, or a single yelp of delight when a splash of water hit his freckled back, would create a hairline crack in his family's footings. Ute said my father didn't give a damn; that it was all about quick pleasures for him. But the evidence of the fallout shelter still below the kitchen, and the lists I had found down there, told me a different story.

Ute's eyes refocused on me and the way I was eating. She asked whether I was enjoying the porridge, and I became aware that I was shovelling it into my mouth and swallowing, although it burned my tongue. I slowed down and nodded, chastised. I scraped the bowl clean and she gave me a second helping. I had filled out since I returned – my breasts swelling into my new bras, the elastic on my pants leaving a red groove around my hips and stomach, the shadows under my cheekbones fading to pink.

'What did you like to eat when you were away?' Ute asked in her bright and cheery voice.

I wondered if she imagined a daily menu where I had been able to check on the freshness of the fish, if I didn't fancy the nut roast. I considered answering, 'Reuben and I ate raw wolf, ripped apart with our bare hands, and after we had eaten it we used the blood to paint stripes across our noses,' just to see the look on her face. But it was too much effort.

'We ate a lot of squirrel,' I said, keeping my voice level. 'And Kaninchen.'

'Oh, Peggy,' she said in a concerned tone, and reached out a hand to me, but I was quick and pulled mine back. She tucked her hands under the table and pursed her lips.

'When you were away –' she started to say.

'When I was taken,' I cut in.

'When you were taken,' she repeated. 'When I understood you had really gone, I went down in the cellar. You remember the cellar, how it was like?'

I nodded.

'All those shelves with food, tins and tins of food. I went down in the cellar and it was just how your father had left it, natürlich. Packets with rice, dried peas, beans – all with dust everywhere.' Ute sounded as if she was repeating a story she knew well, one she had told many times, to many people. 'I tried to imagine what you were eating, whether it was healthy, and I worry you are hungry, wherever you are. I take a tin of baked beans, another of peaches and one of sardines from the shelves and I put them on the table in the cellar. The table is still down there, you can see it, but I threw the food away years ago. An absolute waste. I took a tin can

44

opener and a fork from the drawer under the cooker, and a metal plate. And I line them up on the table, Peggy, just how you liked to line up all those things from your rucksack, remember? I line the tins neatly beside the fork and the plate, and I look at them. It made me cry, thinking about where you could be, and maybe my little daughter still arranging the things from her rucksack.' Ute's voice broke, and I looked up from my empty bowl. Her face was stricken; tears had welled in her eyes and it occurred to me that they were genuine.

'I was crying,' Ute continued, 'but still I sat there, because I thought you could be sitting somewhere too, with your doll and your nightie lined up. And I open the beans and the peaches and also the Sardinen with the little Schlüssel, the little key. I was pregnant, natürlich . . .' She paused, to calculate. 'Expecting Oskar since two months, I think, and feeling very sick. With the fork, I eat the beans and peaches and Sardinen. I eat them at once, and all the time crying, crying. I make myself swallow, because maybe you don't have the food you like. I eat until I am sick.'

I couldn't work out what response she wanted. Should we cry together and hug, or was she expecting me to volunteer a story of my own? So I just sat, looking down at my bowl again, with my licked-clean spoon placed to the side. It, too, reminded me of the tidy piles of my belongings, taken from my rucksack. The idea that I was still putting things in lines made me smile, but I hid it from Ute, behind my hand. Minutes passed, with both of us silent and not even the scrape of cutlery on porcelain to make the kitchen seem lived in. Eventually I said, 'Oliver Hannington ate some of the food from the cellar.'

Ute jumped backwards in her seat, the legs of her kitchen chair grating against the floor. It wasn't a response I had anticipated, and for the first time since I got home we really looked at each other – my eyes seeing into hers, and hers looking back into mine; both of us trying to work the other out, as if we were new to each other, which we were. And then the moment was gone. A mask had come down over her face, the same mask that Dr Bernadette uses – calm, beneficent, like one of the stone angels in the cemetery.

'Really?' Ute asked. 'Is that true? Oliver Hannington?' Her overreaction made me curious, as though there was something I had missed, something that was right under my nose.

'He told us we should eat the food and replace it, so it didn't go out of date,' I said.

'You are sure? He came to stay, with James? When?' she asked, jumpy.

There was an itch under my right breast as she said my father's name, and I rolled my shoulder to get rid of it.

'Just before. Just before . . .' I trailed off. It hadn't occurred to me that she didn't know this. Every session, the first thing Dr Bernadette said to me was, 'Whatever you say in this room will stay in this room.' The same line, every time. After each session I would come out to the waiting room dry-eyed, and I could see Ute was disappointed. I would sit on an upholstered chair whilst she went in to see Dr Bernadette. I would wait for twenty minutes, and each time Ute came out she would be dabbing at her eyes with one of the pink tissues that the doctor kept handy on her coffee table. I had assumed that everything I said to Dr Bernadette was repeated to Ute.

'There was an argument,' I said. 'Oliver argued with, with . . .' I couldn't work out what name to use. 'My father.'

'Oliver,' she repeated. 'What did they argue about?'

'I couldn't hear,' I said. 'The glasshouse roof got smashed. And then we left.' Ute looked stunned. I wondered if by some miracle the glass had been repaired before she had got home, or whether my memory of it was wrong.

'I didn't know how the glass got to be broken,' she said. 'I wondered if maybe a boy, a neighbour, had thrown a stone. The policemen – the detectives – did not believe in me. I am sure they listened to the telephone, I could hear "click, click" when I picked up.' Ute's words tumbled out, one over the other. 'After a few months, when you are still not found, they came to the house and they are digging up the end of the garden, where they say there is fresh earth. Fresh earth! I do not have time to dig the garden in my situation. They find, how do you say it? Gebeine, animal bones and fur. I say, I don't know how they get there, under the ground. They beated through the cemetery with sticks and with dogs. I yell at them in German. "Ich bin schwanger!" I shout. They tell me that you say to your headmaster that I am dead. I do not understand why you would say that. I cry for a long time, and it is Mrs Cass – you remember Mrs Cass from school?'

I nodded.

'It is Mrs Cass who comes to see me to make sure I am all right, who looks after me. I am worried about the baby inside and what will the neighbours say. It is absolute stupid. My little girl is gone with my husband, but it is months, years, before they believe it is not up to me.'

She was exhausted and angry. And I saw how it might

47

have been for her, crying and worried and alone, suspected of murder, with Oskar growing inside her. But I sat with my hands in my lap and said nothing.

6.

The holiday my father had promised wasn't a holiday. There were no beaches or sandcastles, no ice creams, no donkey rides; my father said we would rest when we got to die Hütte. The bushes at the sides of the path we walked along were nearly grown together, as if to say, this path is not for humans. My father was having none of it. He beat them with a stick he had picked up when we left the road. Walking behind him, I heard the thwack of stout wood whipping the bushes into shape. They didn't stand a chance. Puffs of summer dust rose with each beating. I kept my face turned down, trying to match the rhythm of his footsteps whilst a ray of sunshine burnished the bony nodule at the top of my back. Earlier, when I had been in front, I had lifted my face upwards and seen layers of green upon green, and peaked hills the shape of poured sugar. Beyond them, double their height, was a menacing spine of dirty brown rock with ragged gashes of white. But now, walking just behind my father, I saw only the dust that had settled on the hairs of his bare legs, like the flour that Ute sifted over her Apfelkuchen pastry. Above the legs was the bottom of the shorts, and above that was the rucksack, as wide and as tall as my father's back. Our tent was tied to the bottom of it with twine. Billycans clinked in time with water bottles, which swung against the rabbit wires. *Thump, chinkle, jangle, ding; thump, chinkle, jangle, ding.* In my head I sang:

'There are suitors at my door, oh alaya bakia,
Six or eight or maybe more, oh alaya bakia,
And my father wants me wed, oh alaya bakia,
Or at least that's what he said, oh alaya bakia.'

The shade the trees cast was ancient and scented. The smell rushed me back to Christmas in London, and I wondered if this forest was where our tree came from. Last Christmas Eve I had been allowed to clip on the candle holders, strike the matches and light each candle. Ute had let me open one Christmas present from under the tree because she said that when she was a girl that's when she had opened all of hers. I chose one of the presents that came in the box from Germany, and unwrapped a tube that folded up into itself. A spyglass, Ute said, which had belonged to my dead German grandfather. She tutted and said that Omi must be clearing out her drawers and giving away all sorts of rubbish. I stood on the arm of the sofa and looked through it at Ute's enormous head as she played the piano and sang 'O Tannenbaum' until her voice went croaky. She said we had to stop because the branches on the Christmas tree were sagging and it might go up with a whoosh at any moment. As we blew out the candles I saw her eyes had filled with tears. They didn't fall but collected between her lashes until her eyes sucked them back in.

The memory made me suddenly, desperately homesick; a physical sickness, as if I had eaten something bad. More than anything, I wanted to be in my bedroom, lying on my bed, picking at the piece of wallpaper that was coming loose behind the headboard. I wanted to hear the piano in the sitting room below me. I wanted to be at the kitchen table, swinging my legs, eating toast and strawberry jam. I wanted

Ute to push my long fringe out of my eyes and tut. And then I remembered that Ute wasn't even at home but was playing someone else's stupid piano in Germany.

I forgot Christmas and shivered at the idea that no human being had ever walked this way before. My father had said this was a path made by deer, and so I walked like a deer – lifting my knees and tiptoeing without snapping even a twig with my cloven feet. But a deer wouldn't have had to carry a rucksack overstuffed with the anorak my father had bought for me, even though it was far too hot for coats. I slowed and my father, who carried on walking at the same pace, became a figure I could hold between the thumb and forefinger of my right hand. Every now and again he turned to look at me and his mouth puffed into the shape of a sigh, so that even from a distance I could see that his eyes were screwed into a hurry-up frown. Then he would turn back and carry on walking. I wondered what would happen if I stepped off the path into the trees. Imagine how his face would change when he looked around and I was no longer behind him? He would drop his rucksack and run back in panic, shouting, 'Peggy, Peggy!' I liked that thought, but when I glanced sideways into the forest the trees were denser than those in the cemetery at the end of our garden. From the path, the daylight was just two or three trees deep; after that there were no chinks of light, just trunk after trunk, fading into black. 'We could get lost for ever in there,' Phyllis whispered from my rucksack.

Up ahead, beyond my father, was bright sunlight, and forgetting the forest and the deer and Christmas, I ran to catch up. He was standing at the very edge of the trees. Rolled out before us was a meadow of bright grass, falling away to a deep valley. So deep, we couldn't see the bottom. After that, the land rose up again to more dark pines and meadows. The monster hills that had been there before had disappeared. I took a step forward into the light, soaking up the sunshine. I stretched out my arms and imagined rolling over and over down the hill and back up the other side. I would roll for ever. I was a cold-blooded lizard and the sun gave me energy. I went to run, but my father caught me by the shoulder.

'No!'

He pulled me back into the shadows.

'Look.' My father, still squeezing my shoulder, pointed to the left, along the edge of the forest. It was as if we actually had become deer and were standing at the very limit of our territory, deciding whether a taste of fresh grass in the open was worth the risk. At the side of the meadow were six haystacks, tall and pointed, like shaggy wigwams. They were green with age, as though they had been there for years, left behind from a harvest long ago.

'If there are haystacks, there are people,' hissed my father. I didn't understand why this was a problem. We had met lots of people on our trek through Europe: the French lady who gave me boiled sweets on the ferry across the Channel, the man behind the desk in the car-hire office who tweaked my cheek, overalled men in petrol stations, grubby boys who collected our money at campsites, and foreign girls who sold us loaves of bread. My father had avoided conversations with people who spoke English, hurrying me away from the girl with long hair who said she was from Cornwall and let me have a bite of her lolly when I was waiting outside a supermarket for my father, in an unnamed French town.

'My name's Bella,' she said. 'That means beautiful. What's yours?'

I was struggling to swallow the cold lump of ice so that I could tell her I was called Peggy, when my father came back and dragged me away. I would have liked to talk to her, to say the way she smiled reminded me of Becky.

I looked up and down the meadow. 'What people? Where?' I asked my father. The view stretched for miles, down into the valley and back up the other side, but all was green – there weren't any buildings, not even a barn.

'Farmers, peasants . . .' My father paused. 'People. We'll have to go around the edge of the forest. Further to walk, but safer.'

'Safer from what, Papa?'

'People.'

My father readjusted his rucksack and set off along the treeline, keeping the meadow just out of reach to our left. And I followed on behind.

I wanted to ask how long it would be until we got to die Hütte, if Ute would be joining us, and whether there would be chickens there as well as fish and berries. We had left our hired car on the outskirts of a town days ago and caught a train that carried us across fields and forests and through long black tunnels. My overwhelming impression had been of green and blue – grass, sky, trees, rivers. I had laid my forehead against the window and let my eyes go out of focus. It was hot on the train and stuffy. Every time I moved, the smell of dust rose from my seat, like the air blown from the vacuum cleaner when Ute was in the mood for housework. The journey was uneventful, apart from a brief stop in a town of tall chimneys blowing smoke, and factories advertising cigarettes on their walls. An official-looking man shouted into our carriage in a language that sounded like German, and everyone rummaged in bags and pockets. My father handed over our passports and tickets. The man flicked through them and glared at my father and me, and for no reason I could understand made me feel guilty. My father looked the official in the eye and glanced away. He tousled my hair, winked at me and smiled at the man, who stared back with a blank face before returning our documents. In the evening, we got off at a town whose houses trickled down a steep hillside – pooling together at the bottom, with the lowest teetering on the edge of a river that buckled and kicked. We camped beside it, fell asleep to its fussing, and the next morning my father made a list of the things we needed to buy:

Bread
Rice
Dried beans
Salt
Cheese
Coffee
Pellets
Tea
Matches
Sugar
Wine
String
Rope
Shampoo
Soap
Needles and thread

Toothpaste
Candles
Knife

When we had bought and crossed off everything, we passed a hardware shop and, seemingly on the spur of the moment, my father said we should take a look around because there might be things we had forgotten. We stood at the counter and he produced a list I hadn't seen before. A man in an apron served us by fetching the items my father pointed at, until laid out before us was a trowel, many packets of seeds and a brown paper bag of potatoes which were so old they were already sprouting. My father didn't look at me whilst he paid.

'What?' he said when we were outside again, even though I hadn't said anything. 'They're presents for Mutti,' he continued.

'She hates gardening,' I said.

'I'm sure we can make her change her mind,' and again, just like on the train, he tousled my hair. I shook him off, angry about the lie but unable to work out the truth.

In the afternoon, we caught a bus with half a dozen schoolboys in short trousers and a woman carrying a basket covered with a tea towel. The bus was even hotter than the train, and piteous cries came from the basket as the bus swung around corners. When the boys got off, my father let me approach the woman. She frowned and spoke to me; a long stream of words were born in the back of her throat and rolled off the front of her tongue.

'Can Phyllis and I see the baby?' I said, enunciating every word. 'Please.'

I tucked my doll under my arm as I steadied myself against the seat, and the woman lifted the tea towel. A tabby cat, scrawny and balding, shivered in the bottom of the basket. My hand went in to stroke the top of its head, but the cat pulled back its gums and hissed, and I jerked my fingers away. The woman spoke again, abrupt, jagged words this time. I looked at her blankly so she shrugged her shoulders, covered the cat with the cloth and, still swaying with the rhythm of the bus, turned away from me to look out of the window. The cat began to wail again.

'Bavarian,' said my father, when I went back to our seat.

'Bavarian,' I said, without knowing what he meant.

He had unfolded a map I hadn't seen before, and draped it over the rail of the seat in front. In the map's creases the paper had worn thin, and in the centre there was a hole where the land had been rubbed away entirely. Phyllis and I sat next to him, looking over his arm. The blue snake of a river twisted through flat green, interrupted by spidery lines as if a shaky hand had tried to draw circles across the paper. The water flowed off the side of the map, and as my father flapped it, for an instant I saw in the top-right-hand corner a small red cross, inside a circle. He packed the map away, looked out of the window, then at his watch and said it was time to get off the bus and walk.

At first we had stuck to the narrow roads, dusty with a strip of grass growing down the middle. We had seen distant farms, but we met only one other person – an old woman in a headscarf who gave me a cup of milk. She held her cow, brown and docile, on a length of rope. The teacup, missing its saucer, was delicate, the china almost translucent, but most of the handle had been broken off, leaving two sharp horns which stuck out from the side. A stripe of green around the rim had been worn away in places by the hundreds of lips and teeth which must have pressed up against it. The milk in the cup was still warm and smelled of farmyards. The old lady, the cow and my father watched whilst I turned the cup so I could drink from a spot opposite the horns. The milk swilled around the inside. As I hesitated, I could see a tightness come in my father's face, the muscle at the side of his jaw bulging as he clamped his teeth together. Inside my head I said, 'If I drink this milk, Papa will say it's time to go home.'

I tipped the cup and the clabbered milk filled my mouth, washing over my teeth and settling inside my cheeks. The cow mooed as if encouraging me to swallow. I swallowed, but the milk didn't want to be inside me. It rushed back up, bringing with it all I had previously eaten. I had the good sense to turn away from the old woman's sandalled feet, but when I retched, my long hair caught in the fountain spewing from my mouth. Later that night in the tent, I ran my fingers through the matted strands and my stomach heaved once more from the smell.

My father apologized again and again to the old woman in English, but she didn't understand. She stood with her lips pressed together and her hand held out, beside her cow. My father dropped a pile of foreign coins in her leathery palm and we hurried away. I had no idea this wind-worn woman, creased and bag-eyed, standing outside her barn with her cow on a rope, would be the last person I would meet from the real world for another nine years. Perhaps if I had known, I would have clung to the folds of her skirt, hooked my fingers over the waistband of her apron and tucked my knees around one of her stout legs. Stuck fast, like a limpet or a Siamese twin, I would have been carried with her when she rose in the morning to milk the cow, or into her kitchen to stir the porridge. If I had known, I might never have let her go.

7.

At the beginning of our journey, I had been pleased it was just the two of us again. I forgot all about Oliver Hannington, the argument and the smashed glasshouse. But I was tired of walking and bored of how all the meadows and forests merged into one long deer track. Already I couldn't remember if we had camped for two nights or three after we got off the bus. Now, we were walking downhill, using the edge of the trees to take us into the valley. My stomach was hollow, and under my rucksack my shirt stuck to my back. My legs were so heavy they might have been lumps of stone.

From inside my bag, Phyllis said, 'I wonder if die Hütte is actually real. Do you think there is a Fluss so full of fish they can jump straight out of the water into our outstretched arms?'

'Of course there is,' I said.

I let the song come back to me, singing it loudly to drown out her voice. And even though he was ahead, my father joined in, clear and bold:

'And I told him that I will, oh alaya bakia,
When the river runs uphill, oh alaya bakia,
And when fish begin to fly, oh alaya bakia,
Or the day before I die, oh alaya bakia.'

At an unexplained distance from the haystacks, my father decided it was safe enough for us to rest. We sat side by side with our backs against the bark of a pine tree, our feet warming in the sun. I prised Phyllis out of my rucksack and bent her plastic legs so she could sit beside me. Now we were further down the hillside, I could see into the valley. At the bottom was a river, snaking like it had done on the map, and catching the light where it jumped and tumbled over rocks. The meadow grew into tall grasses and bushes along the banks, and I thought that this must be the river that flowed past die Hütte. My father tore at the last loaf of dark bread we had brought with us from the town, and pared strips of yellow cheese with his knife. The cheese was warm and sweaty and, although I was hungry, it reminded me of the milk I had regurgitated, but I didn't want to say anything to change my father's mood. When he sang he was happy. My father ate with his eyes shut whilst I made a hollow in the soft dough, pushing the cheese inside, so that together the two became an albino vole in a mudbank. Then the piece of bread and cheese became a brown mouse with a yellow nose, which ran up and down my leg and sat on top of my knee, twitching its whiskers. I offered it to Phyllis's pouting mouth, but she didn't want any.

'Just eat it, Peggy,' my father said.

'Just eat it, Phyllis,' I whispered, but she wouldn't. I looked at my father; his eyes were still shut. I picked at the crust, nibbling a few dry flakes.

Then, with an effort, my father said, 'I bet you didn't know that there *are* fish that can fly.'

'Don't be silly, Papa.'

'Tomorrow at the Fluss I'll catch a flish for our flupper,' he said, and laughed at his own joke.

'Will you teach me to swim there too? Please?'

'We'll see, Liebchen.' He leaned down and awkwardly kissed the top of my head, but both the 'darling' and the kiss were not right. Those were Ute's things.

He wiped the back of his hand across his mouth.

'Come on, Pegs. Time to get moving again.'

'I'm tired of walking,' I said.

'Just a little bit further.' He tapped his watch and shaded his eyes at the sun. 'We'll camp down at the Fluss tonight.' With a noise that came from the very bottom of his chest, he hoisted his rucksack on to his back. Whilst he wasn't looking, I stuffed the bread with the piece of cheese still inside it between the roots of the pine tree.

The next morning when I woke, my father was already up. I liked to wake without moving my body to see if I could catch myself in that empty place between sleeping and waking, just as I became conscious of the world and the position of my body. My arms were flung above my head, and in the heat of the night I had pushed my sleeping bag to the end of the tent. Looking up, I could see the dots of flies that had gathered, bumping against the ridge pole, hoping to find a way out.

'They should crawl through the holes you made with the fire,' Phyllis said in my ear. She lay beside me, her rigid hands digging into my shoulder. My nightie was sticking to me and there was sweat around my forehead and the back of my neck. Whilst we had been away from home I had taken to wearing the blue balaclava at night, despite the heat. It had been the first thing I had packed when I had heard my father's whistle back in London. Omi had knitted it and a pair of matching mittens from a blue jumper that I had when I was a baby. She had unravelled it, pulling at the live and wriggling wool, and with German words I couldn't understand she showed me how to hold my hands out so the wool caught and wound around them. Omi was my grandmother, and for a long time I thought she was only that. I remember the moment when I realized she was, or had been, other things too – a daughter, a wife and, most difficult to comprehend of all, Ute's mother. I couldn't imagine Ute having a mother, or any relations – she was too complete. Ute said that Omi was angry because I didn't know any German and couldn't speak to her.

'She blames me,' Ute said.

'Eine fremde Sprache ist leichter in der Küche als in der Schule gelernt,' said Omi, winding the wool.

'What did she say?' I asked Ute.

She sighed and rolled her eyes, 'She says I should have taught you German in the kitchen. She is a silly old woman whose brains have shrunk.'

I looked at Omi, wrinkled and brown like a walnut. I imagined her brain, also wizened, rattling around inside her skull.

'In the kitchen?' I persisted.

Ute huffed. 'She means I should have taught you at home when you were young, but it is not her business and it is a good thing you don't know German. Omi tells lies and because you cannot understand her, you cannot understand them. I told her that she tells too many stories.' Ute put on a wide smile for Omi, but the old lady frowned and I thought perhaps she wasn't as stupid as Ute believed.

I liked to watch Omi's face whilst she worked and talked to me. Sometimes she grew wistful and the wool slackened.

Then something in her story would agitate her. She would repeat a phrase over and over, staring me in the eyes as though that might make me understand. If Ute was passing, I begged her to translate, desperate to know what my grandmother thought was so important. But Ute would just roll her eyes again and say Omi was only telling me not to trust the stranger in the woods, or to be sure to always carry breadcrumbs in my apron pockets, or to stay away from the wolf's teeth.

'Ja, stay away from the wolf,' Omi would copy in halting English, and the hairs on the back of my neck would rise at her warning.

My grandmother moved my hands apart, so the wool could be wound fast and tight against my skin, making red tracks on the backs of my hands. When the jumper was gone, eaten away by a ball of wool that grew fat on its blue food, Omi reknitted it into a hat that I could pull down over my face so just my nose, mouth and eyes looked out. My grandmother sewed two small black ears on top and embroidered three lines of whiskers, radiating out from each side.

In the forest, I crawled to the end of the tent and stuck my head out. The world was muted beyond the blue wool. My father moved like a man in a silent film, on his hands and knees, blowing, without a sound, at the fire to coax a flame from the embers. I came out like a woodland animal and watched him pour water into a billycan; when a few flames started to lick upwards, he nestled the can amongst them. A stick cracked under my knee, but still he didn't turn around. I was a deer, a mouse, a mute bird creeping up to take my revenge on the hunter. I lunged at his back, launching myself forward, talons out and clinging on around his neck. My father didn't even jump.

'What do you want for breakfast, pipsqueak?' he asked. 'Stew, stew or stew?'

'My name isn't pipsqueak,' I said, sliding off him. My voice sounded like I was underwater.

'What is it today then?' My father sat back on a log he had put beside the fire the night before, and lifted a metal plate which covered another billycan. He fished something out from the stew with a fingertip, an insect or a piece of leaf, and flicked it away into the grass. He stirred the meat and set the billycan beside the boiling water.

'Sleeping Beauty?' my father asked, and turned to look at me. 'Little Blue Riding Hood?'

I sat beside him on the log and poked at the fire with a stick. He pulled the balaclava off my head by its ears and flung it behind him towards the tent.

'Rapunzel!' my father exclaimed. 'Rapunzel, Rapunzel, let down your hair!' He was suddenly loud, as if someone had turned up the volume. There were birds and wind in the trees, and in the distance I could hear the river, a never-ending chatter, like a crowd of faraway people.

Even with the hat off, my long hair stayed bunched in a wild and static-filled tangle against my head. My father hooked his fingers in it and tried to draw them downwards, but my hair remained nested, refusing to move.

'I can't believe you forgot to pack your comb,' he said, like he had said every morning for the past few weeks and, like all those times, I was instantly alert to the change in his tone of voice. 'Damn,' he continued, 'why didn't we just buy one?'

'It doesn't matter, Papa. Look, I can do it myself.' I dragged my fingers through my matted hair and patted it flat against my head. I could feel that it was only slightly better. I opened my eyes wide and tried to look my most beguiling. 'See, I don't need a comb.'

'No, I suppose we can get away with it.' He didn't sound convinced.

I relaxed and let out a breath. My father stirred the stew and dished it up on to plates. He made tea in two mugs, putting a pinch of leaves taken from a tin into the billycan and swilling the water around until it became brown. We had no milk, so we drank it without, each of us staring into the fire, lost in our own thoughts.

The river wasn't blue like the map had shown; it was a silver ribbon threaded through a green blanket. My father stood on the pebbles at the very edge, the toes of his shoes damp. He shaded his eyes, scanning up and down, assessing the best fishing location. I stood beside him, half his size, also shading my eyes and watching the water. I tried to hide my disappointment. I didn't dare ask where all the fish were, or why my father was having to catch one with a rod and line rather than just leaning in to grab a trout. He looked over his shoulder at the trees behind him; I looked over my shoulder too. On one of our evenings by the campfire in London, my father had told me about a fishing trip he had taken with his father in Hampshire. He said that they had fished in streams so clear he had seen the chalk at the bottom and trout hanging in the current with open mouths. I had imagined white sticks of blackboard chalk swimming in the clear water underneath the fish, but now that image seemed as impossible as the animals flying. My father said it was important to always look behind before you cast, because on that trip he had caught his father's eyebrow with the hook as he flicked the line over his shoulder. The barb had gone in above the eye, emerging from a fold in the lid. My father said that Grandpa had held his hand over his face and sworn a great deal, but the hook refused to go forwards or backwards, and when he shouted for the metal to be cut, my father, responsible for packing the equipment, realized he had forgotten to bring the wire cutters. My grandpa had made my father cut through the skin of his eyelid with the fish-gutting knife to remove the hook.

By the river, my father unpacked his fishing rod and slotted it together. I watched him for a while, but it took so long – feeding the line along the guides, tying on the artificial fly and attaching the reel – that I got bored. I wandered upstream and crouched at the water's edge, turning over stones, absorbed by the tiny creatures running for their lives.

My father whistled a tune I recognized from home, something I often fell asleep to. I caught the melody and hummed it whilst I squinted at him. With the sun behind him, he stood in front of the water as if he were conducting it, commanding it to flow. He pulled the line from the reel so that it lay in unravelled loops at his feet. In rhythm with his music, he flicked the rod up and over his head, craning backwards to watch the fly streak out behind him. He twitched the rod forward and the coiled line whisked up and through the guides, catapulting out to a patch of sunlight. I looked up and followed it, etching an arc over the blue sky. As the hook touched water, my father jerked his arm up and back, the line and fly following gracefully, and forward again so that they dropped further out. He repeated the movement once more, until the fly swam in the middle of the current and floated downstream.

He carried on casting backwards and forwards; a mesmerizing fluid action, something his whole body performed until the rod was an extension of his arm and hand. I walked upstream so the *swoosh-whip* of the line, cutting through the air, could have been the cry of a bird. The bank was lower where I was, eaten away by the river when it was in full flow. I untied my shoes and took them off. My father had bought them for me at the start of the summer. They were boys' shoes, dark blue with a white stripe and a leaping cat on the back of each heel. I removed my socks and tucked them inside the shoes.

The water flowed fast through the middle channel, but where I stood it had pulled back from the bank and left behind a strip of silt. I stepped down from the grass into brown mud which oozed between my toes, cooling my blood.

Out of the corner of my eye, I could see my father cast the line again. The day was hot and the water inviting; there would be no problem with wading up to my knees, even though my father still hadn't taught me to swim. Hopping on one foot, then the other, and in the process smearing mud over my legs, I removed my trousers. Mud caked their insides, but I flung them behind me on to the bank and took a step into the water, gasping with shock at the cold and the pain of the stones on the soles of my feet. I stood in the water up to my knees, churned mud swirling around my legs whilst the current tried to suck me away. It was the deepest I had ever been in and still my father didn't notice.

I gave up willing him to turn around to look at me; he was focusing all his attention on the artificial fly out on the water. I came out of the river and sat on the grass, prodding and picking at my numb legs, already changing to grey elephant skin. It wasn't fair to be the warmest person in the world, sitting next to the coolest thing, and not know how to swim. I wanted to ask my father whether he could teach me right away, but didn't dare. He cast – up, back, forward, up, back, forward, up, back, forward – until the fly rested on the water. Then the line tightened and he let out a long, low 'Wowyaa' as he pulled the line through the guides with his hand. There was a flash of heat in my head when I saw how much he cared for the fish. I might have been in the middle of the river, drowning, and if he'd caught me on the end of his line he would have been disappointed. I watched him for a bit longer, battling with the fish, pulling it in without letting his rod bend too far, allowing it to swim out a little and pulling it in again. A tired and docile trout was dragged through the shallows, whilst I walked into the woods and sat down in the long grass.

'Rapunzel! Rapunzel! Einer kleiner flish!' My father shouted like a winner.

It was as if I were in a cinema, watching the action on a big screen. What would happen next? When would the hero realize the heroine had disappeared? My father prised the hook out of the trout's mouth and laid the fish on the ground. He had already selected a heavy rock from the bank, and now he picked it up, lifting his arm high in the air, aiming at the fish's head. I narrowed my eyes in preparation but didn't look away. Before the rock came slamming down, my father glanced over his shoulder – to search for me, I supposed. There was a sourness in my chest; I wanted the fish to be beaten and I wanted my father to be shocked that I was no longer on the riverbank. He stood up, letting the rock fall beside the trout. Between the stalks of grass, I could just see the flapping of its tail whilst it drowned in the summer air. My father went to my scattered clothes and picked up the trousers. He looked underneath them as though I might be hiding there. I put my hand over my mouth to stifle a giggle.

I saw his lips form a word that may have been 'fuck'. Then, looking around, he called, 'Peggy? Peggy!'

I didn't answer, but sat still like a creature of the forest, a shadow.

My father gathered up my clothes and held them to his chest. The mud on the trousers marked his shirt with a brown streak; he put them back down and stared desperately out across the water.

'Peggy!' he shouted again, and he waded in, without even taking off his shoes. I winced for him because of the cold. He strode straight in, up to the top of his thighs, so he could look beyond the bushes which hung out over the water. I worried about how wet his shoes and shorts would be and how angry that would make him later. I was no longer quiet because I was hiding, but because I needed to hide. He stood in the water where I had been ten minutes earlier and scanned the banks upstream, shading his eyes against the sun. He turned and stared downstream, cupped his hands around his mouth and shouted with real worry in his voice, 'Peggy? Peggy!' and 'Shit!'

I looked where he looked, but there was nothing to see except the rippling shadows of branches and clouds, and the occasional bubble. He came back to the bank and ran in a short burst against the current, then ran back, all the while looking at the water. He reminded me of a Labrador whose stick has been thrown into the middle of a pond and who hesitates for a second before leaping in. Hopping and tripping, my father pulled off his boots and his shorts, now a darker shade of blue. He yanked his shirt over his head, leaving his clothes in a pile on top of mine. His torso was startlingly white against his brown forearms and calves, as if he were wearing a flesh-coloured tank top. He hesitated on the bank, then strode in again, as though he had dismissed the thought of diving into the shallows. I was really scared; scared he would plunge into the river and not resurface. And then I would be the one running up and down the bank, shouting. I wouldn't know what to do, where to go for help, how to get home. I wouldn't know how to swim or catch fish, or what to eat. My mind ran on as I watched him. I might be wandering around the forest on my own for years. I would have to sleep in the tent by myself, supposing that I could even put it up; and there would be rustling and howling and small animals scurrying around in the night. Something might be in the woods. That thought made me turn around from my position, hiding in the grass, and look behind me. A mass of trees and darkness loomed.

'Peggy!' my father shouted once more.

'My name isn't Peggy,' I called out.

He froze, up to his waist in the water. He appeared unsure of what he had heard. He turned his head one way, then the other, trying to work out where my voice had come from. He waded back to the bank.

Louder, I said, 'It's Rapunzel.'

My father looked towards where I was sitting and ran forward, almost tripping over himself in his anxiety. He bent over me and put his face, which changed from white to red, very close to mine. He took me by both shoulders and dug his fingers into the hollows between my bones. And he shook me.

'Don't ever, ever do that again,' he yelled into my face. 'You must always stay where I can see you. Do you understand?' My body was jerking backwards and forwards in the opposite direction to my head. Tears of pain and terror came, and I wondered if it was possible for my neck to snap from so much shaking.

His underpants were wet, leaking rivulets of water down his legs. He let go of my shoulders and, instead, held me by my wrist and pulled me upright. My father was a tall man. He lifted my wrist as high as he could, raising my arm over my head, so I had to stand on tiptoe in order for my body to follow after it. I started to cry – whimpering at first, then much louder. In bare feet, hopping over the twigs and stones, my father pulled me back to our pile of clothes and scooped them up. He carried on dragging me, howling, down the bank to the fish, which was still giving an occasional weak flap of its tail. He picked up the rock and held it up above my head. Against the bright sun, it was a meteorite spinning towards me. He brought it down fast. I tried to pull away, but his grip on my wrist increased. I kicked against the ground, knocking the slippery fish with my bare toes – turning it over on to my trousers. The hand with the rock whipped past my face by a couple of inches and landed on the trout's head, destroying it. My father let go of me and hurled the rock into the water.

'Fuck!' he shouted as he threw it. I curled into a tight little ball beside the trout, my fingers locked together over the top of my head, still expecting the blow from the rock to land on me. We were both silent; all the world was silent for a moment.

'I want ... to ... go ... home.' I struggled to get the words out between choking sobs. I tried to not look at the fish with its mashed head.

'Get dressed.' My father gave my shoes a kick towards me. He picked up his own clothes and put them on with fierce movements as if they too had misbehaved. He took his fishing rod apart in angry bursts.

Almost under my breath, I repeated, 'I want to go home, Papa.'

'Get dressed!' My father pulled my trousers out from under the fish as though he were performing a magic trick with a tablecloth. He flung them at me. Pieces of crushed fish flesh and skin stuck to them. Still crying, I put them on, then my socks and shoes.

'We'll go home when the fucking fish begin to fly,' my father shouted. I tried hard to swallow my sobs and talk in a way that would reach him.

'I miss, I miss,' I stuttered. I wanted to tell him that I missed Becky and school and Ute, but the words wouldn't come.

His anger was like a popped balloon – all the rage gone in an instant. He sat on the bank with his head in his hands.

'We can't go home, Rapunzel.'

'Why not?' My voice was reedy.

'Mutti, she just isn't there any more.' My father rushed the words without looking at me.

'She'll be back from Germany soon though.' Even as I spoke, I knew that couldn't be right; already more than two weeks and three days had passed since my father and I had sat beside the fire in London and he had told me that was how long it would be before Ute came home.

'No, that's not what I mean. She's gone, Punzel. She's dead.' He still looked at the ground.

I remembered what I had told my headmaster and Mrs Cass, and was frightened that, in saying it, I had made it happen.

'No, Papa. She's just in Germany,' I said. 'You're wrong.'

'She's gone. I'm sorry.'

'Gone where? Where?' My voice was a rising wail.

'I'm sorry.' He leaned in towards me, and I flinched as he held the upper part of my arms to my sides. My trousers were pinned against my thigh and I felt sick thinking about the fish brains soaking through the cloth. My father looked into my eyes and away. He pulled me to him, trapping me between his knees and burying his face in my hair. My head was squashed between his arm and his chest. His heart was loud, but his voice muffled. I thought I heard him say, 'The wolf took her, Punzel.'

'No. No, Papa. No.' I struggled against him, but he held me too tight.

He made a noise similar to the one I had heard in the glasshouse, the night before we had left, but worse – like one of our rabbits caught in a wire trap, wretched and unnatural. He said something else into my hair which might have been, 'The whole fucking world,' but I wasn't sure. I stopped struggling and went floppy in his embrace and the awful choking noises subsided. Without a word, and without looking at me, he stood up and walked off into the trees, leaving me in an odd crouch between the decapitated trout and the river. I wanted to call after him to ask him why we had bought the seeds for her if she was dead, but I never did.

Although eventually the stench of the fish on my trousers blended with every other smell, to become one big stink that we stopped noticing, the red stain in the shape of a duckling never faded from them. It was high up on the right thigh, so even when I had to slice them into shorts much later, it stayed with me.

8.

We followed the river as it wound through the landscape. Sometimes we had to make a detour into the woods, and once we waded through the shallows when our path was blocked by fallen trees. We started to cross marshy land, jumping from one grassy hillock to another, but my father wobbled and only just stopped himself from toppling into the boggy water. He said it was too dangerous and we'd have to turn back and go around it. We rested at the top of a hill, with the water unravelling below us. The clouds were heavy over our heads, and the air thick like the fug in a steamy kitchen. The sky threatened a downpour which didn't come.

My father unfolded the map and tilted it one way, then the other, matching the wooded landscape surrounding us with the features in front of him. I lay on my stomach, with my arm out and my palm upwards, as steady as I could make it, waiting for the grasshopper sounding its scratchy rattle in the grass nearby. I told myself that if I caught the insect, Ute would not be dead and soon we would turn around and start going home. I was tired of walking and camping and catching squirrels. I wanted a bed and a bath and proper food. A quick green flash from nowhere and the grasshopper landed on my hand. It sat there like Joan of Arc in its armour and helmet, large amber eyes downcast and saintly.

'Can we eat grasshoppers, Papa?' I whispered, so that the insect wouldn't be alarmed and jump away. My father still stood looking at the map and tapping his compass as though he would have preferred north to be in a different place.

'Papa,' I hissed, 'can we eat grasshoppers?'

'Yes,' he said, concentrating on the map and not looking down, 'but they're better boiled because of the tapeworms.'

'Do they taste nicer when they're boiled?'

'What?' he glanced at me, and the grasshopper launched itself back on to the battlefield, just as my fist closed around it. When I opened my hand, the creature was gone. My heart sank. I rolled on to my side and stared up at my father – a giant, holding back the heavy sky with the width and power of his shoulders.

'The tapeworms,' I said.

'Tapeworms? What?' He was still distracted, putting the map back in his rucksack pocket.

'How about grass? Is that nice to eat?' I picked a blade and put it in my mouth. It tasted the same as its colour.

'Come on, Punzel. Time to find die Hütte.' He lifted his rucksack on to his shoulders. Tied to the bottom was a dead rabbit, dangling from its hind legs.

'I wouldn't like to eat snails.' I stood up. 'That wouldn't be right, taking them out of their houses.'

My father picked up my rucksack, helped me into it and moved off in the direction of the glittering water.

'Papa? When can we go home?' I said in a voice so quiet he didn't answer. I followed on behind him.

The sky pressed down on the land, leaving us walking in a narrow strip of air, charged with electricity. With one more check of the map my father said we had gone far enough. We sat down, high above the river on a shelf of rock, looking over a gorge which water, although colourless and insubstantial when cupped by hands, had worn through stone. On our left, the water forced itself through a narrow gap so that it burst out, roaring and rushing over rocks and boulders, falling to a pool far below our feet. There, the water was still for a time until it moved onwards, widening, spitting and foaming through more boulders. I sat beside my father, my chin in my hands, watching him from the corner of my eye, trying to sidle inside his head without him knowing. On the other side of the river, stringy trees and bushes jostled for position between slabs of rock similar to the one we sat on.

'Maybe there's a bridge a bit further down, Papa,' I shouted over the noise of the roiling water. He gave me a sideways look that meant I had said something ridiculous.

'No, we have to cross down there,' he shouted back, standing up on the slippery rock. I crawled away from the edge on my hands and knees, and the two of us picked our way downstream until the bank was level with the water. In the middle, the river was a deep green, scattered with rocks poking their noses up for a breath. The water charged around them, creating eddies and whirlpools. Closer to the bank, the current dragged lengths of weed along with it so it seemed that long-haired women swam just under the surface, never coming up for air. My father selected a strong branch from under the trees, broke a stick from it, tossed the stick as far as he could into the river and, for a second or two, we watched it speed downstream, dance around the rocks and vanish.

'You should have taught me how to swim,' I said.

My father took off all his clothes, except his underpants, then put his boots back on and told me to do the same. He crouched down beside me and looked me straight in the eye and made me promise I would sit where I was and not move so he could see me at all times. That was the only reference he ever made to the fish incident. He had behaved so normally afterwards that, later, I wasn't sure it had ever happened.

My father stuffed our clothes into his rucksack and held it tight to his chest. He walked into the water without noticing the cold; there was just a slight shudder when it came above his thighs. Every now and again he glanced back to check I still sat where he had left me. I rested my head on my knees and watched him. The water came up to the top of his chest and he moved the rucksack higher, holding it above his head, feeling his way across the rocks. My father staggered, and when the water came up to his chin he had to tilt his head towards the sky. He forced his way forward until more of his torso emerged, until he reached the far bank and dropped the rucksack on to the stony edge. He came back towards me and did the same thing with my rucksack. Finally, back on my side of the river, my father took the branch he had found, held it horizontally and tied me to it, looping a length of rope once around my waist and around my wrists. He stood beside me and we both gripped the branch, as if we were holding on to the front bar on a fairground waltzer.

If we make it across, we can go home, I said to myself.

Side by side we stepped into the water.

'When it gets too deep for you to stand, keep holding on with your hands and let your legs float out behind. I'll be beside you, remember. It will be fine,' said my father. It sounded as though he was reassuring himself as much as me. I didn't like the way the weed women wrapped themselves around my ankles. We were stepping into the unknown; anything could have been under there with them. The water was colder than the day before, perhaps because of the oppressive heat in the air, or maybe because of the swirling speed of it. And it was noisier. Once we were past the vegetation, stones prodded under my shoes, and the shifting, restless riverbed tried to trick me and tip me over.

'That's a good girl. Nice and careful. We'll be at the other side in no time,' he said, and I wanted to believe him.

Icy inch by icy inch we crept in; the water chilled my knees, a thousand bees stung my thighs, and a cold, deep pain rose between my legs, until I was waist-deep, and then chest-deep, standing on the tips of my toes. The river treated us like boulders, its flow buffeting us, splitting and regrouping beyond our bodies.

In the middle, the noise of rushing and churning was overwhelming. My father shouted, 'Keep close to me! Keep close!' and something else, but the water snatched away every other word and spat them out far downstream. I could still touch rocks with my shoes, but the river, greater and stronger than me, picked my feet up and took them away. They didn't float behind me like my father had said they would; instead they were pulled and jerked as if they were a rag doll's. I gripped the branch so tightly I could see white knuckles. I was lifted off my feet and the stick came up to meet my face, or my face went down to the water. It filled my mouth and throat. I could taste it at the back of my nose, dirty and coarse. I tried to cry out, to let my father know, but more water choked me. My legs twisted. My father's eyes were wide and his mouth was open, but I was already under the surface when he shouted for me to hold on.

The current lifted my legs forward. My wrists were still bound, tied to the branch. My hair became the weed, dark strands whipping across my face, dragging with the flow. I went under and my father let go of his end of the branch. For an instant, his hands were on my waist, but I slipped away and it was just me and the angry river. It took me and played with me, turning me over and over, around the rocks and so fast that time slowed, and under the surface all was quiet. I could see whirlpools down there, where the disturbed liquid lifted and shifted the pebbles on the bottom and each time they moved a spurt of silt moved with them. I danced with them, was held by them, let go and became the water, flowing with it.

My father shouted, a small voice from far away. 'Peggy! Punzel!'

I opened my eyes to the roaring water, slamming me between rocks. My hand was full of pain, trapped between the branch and stone. And my father was holding me around my waist again, whilst he tried to untie me. The water was still struggling to take me, slapping my head forward. My father gave up with the tangle of rope and lifted me, still attached to the branch, over to the bank. He laid me on my back with my arms outstretched and I moved my head to the side, coughing and spewing water.

'Fuck, fuck. Peggy!' His nails were bitten down to his fingertips and my father found it difficult to pick at the knots in the rope, which had tightened around me when I had been tossed and turned in the water. He worked at them until they loosened, then he shifted me on to my side and slapped

80

my back. And picked me up, floppy, and held me in his arms.

'Oh, God, I'm sorry. I'm sorry. Where does it hurt? Here?' He pushed my hair out of my face. 'Does it hurt here?'

Realizing that I was on the bank and still alive, I cried, dry choking tears. My father, misunderstanding, began to check me all over, bending my knees and elbows and wiggling my fingers. One knee was grazed and oozed watery blood. The other was already swelling and changing colour. My wrists were sore where they had been rubbed between the rope and the branch. When my father had examined me all over and was satisfied that my injuries were superficial, he opened my mouth to look at my teeth.

'About eight years old, if I were to hazard a guess,' he said in his army voice. It made me laugh, and he laughed with me and kissed my forehead and kissed my cheeks, his face wet, but not from the river.

'I lost one of my shoes,' I said in a whisper. We both looked at my feet – a wet shoe on one foot but only a sock on the other. My chin began to wobble again.

'I promise, Peggy –'

'Rapunzel,' I said.

'I promise, Punzel, that we will come back and look for it and I will teach you how to swim.' He was solemn, as if he was making a very serious vow. 'But we're nearly at die Hütte. We need to reach the cabin before it gets too late.' He carried me up to the rucksacks and dressed me and dressed himself. He wrapped my shoeless foot in an empty canvas food bag and secured it to my ankle with a piece of string. Inside my head I made a vow too – that I would never go in the water again.

The walking was slower after that. I hobbled along behind

him, my grazes stinging and my foot feeling all the stones and roots in the ground through the bag. My father used a stick again to beat an uphill path through the undergrowth. He held back branches for us to pass beneath, but he hurried, excitedly urging me on. He didn't get his map out again; we just walked away from the river, and after another ten minutes the bushes thinned and we came into a space where the trees were much less dense. Ahead of us in a small clearing was a single-storey wooden cabin.

9.

After breakfast, I lay on the sofa as I often did, my eyes shut, drifting off in the overheated sitting room. There were so many possibilities for activity, but all were optional and all seemed pointless when our lives didn't depend upon any of them. I could watch television, try to read a book, write down my thoughts and draw pictures of what I remembered, as Dr Bernadette urged me to do, or I could listen once more to *The Railway Children*; I had checked and it was still in the sideboard. Ute had given up trying to encourage me out of my lethargy and was simply happy that I was downstairs, where she could keep an eye on me. She didn't understand that because there was so much choice, I chose to do nothing. I preferred to lie still, with my mind empty.

But today, I let a few of the memories in: singing 'La Campanella', my voice echoing off the high rocks; lying under the trees, watching summer midges dance; sheltering from the rain in the lee of the mountain, my back protected by its massive presence. Still half asleep, I heard the music and recalled it spilling from the cabin, mixing with birdsong and wind in the grass. I remembered being sure that the last summer would never end. On the sofa, in

London, the music became louder, richer. It was no longer just one or two voices, but chords and harmonies, layers of sound we had never achieved in the forest. I woke fully and understood that actual wooden hammers were tapping real metal strings, which in turn were reverberating against a soundboard. Ute was playing the piano. It was a lullaby I had heard often when I was in my bed as a child, when she had forgotten to come upstairs and I had taken comfort from the music, as if it were tucking me in and kissing me goodnight.

Resting on the sofa, I kept my eyes closed and pretended to be sleeping. For a long time I lay still and let the music caress me whilst I thought about the last time I had heard Ute play – just before she had left for her concert tour. No one had thought to tell me she was going; one day I had come home and she was gone. That *is* what happened; that is how I remember it. But the doctors say my brain plays tricks on me, that I have been deficient in vitamin B for too long and my memory doesn't work the way it should. They have diagnosed Korsakoff's syndrome and prescribed large orange pills, which Ute makes me take with my first sip of black tea in the morning. They think I've forgotten things that really happened and have invented others. Two days ago, after I had swallowed the pill and Ute was watching me gobble my porridge in the glasshouse, I asked her why she had left so suddenly that summer. She looked down at the plate of toast balanced on her lap and said she didn't remember. I knew she was lying.

When Ute had finished the piece she was playing, through my half-closed eyes I saw her get up from the piano. She came and stood over me, stretched out on the sofa. She reached out a hand as though to brush hair from my fore-head, but recoiled when we both heard a car pull up outside. A car door slammed, and the front door opened. Oskar rushed down the hall and into the kitchen.

'Mum!' he called. 'Mum, I'm starving!'

I heard the suction noise of the fridge opening. Ute left the sitting room and I rose to follow her, watching her pick up Oskar's trail of discarded coat, gloves and scarf. I passed the thermostat in the hall and turned the wheel until I heard the heating click off. Oskar stood in the kitchen, with a yogurt in his hand. He had taken the top off and was licking pink gloop out with his tongue. I wanted to do it too, but instead I stood watching with my back pressed into the kitchen counter, amazed and enchanted by this creature that was my brother. With his clothes over her arm, Ute tut-ted and held out a teaspoon she had taken from the cutlery drawer.

'How was your morning at Scouts?' she asked, but he was too excited to hear or to notice the spoon on offer. Instead Oskar wheeled his arms about, demonstrating his friend Henry Mann having an epileptic fit – 'a real-life epi' – whilst clutching a half-empty beer bottle the boy had found in a flower bed during litter-picking duty. Henry, his limbs twitching, had sprayed the beer over himself and everyone who had been crowding around him. Oskar's yogurt tilted inside its pot, close to slopping over the edge. Ute grabbed it from him as he flung himself on to the kitchen floor and did an impression of Henry – blond hair flopping, kicking his legs and jerking his body across the tiles. Ute told him to get up right away and stop being so silly, but I stood by the kettle, looking down at him, laughing.

His limbs went still and Oskar said to me, 'Your teeth are really rotten.'

I hid my mouth behind my hand.

'Oskar!' Ute said.

'It's true,' he said. 'And she has half an ear.' I pulled at the hair on the side of my head. Every morning I spent an hour or so in front of the mirror, wetting and combing it down, hoping it had grown longer overnight.

'Get up,' Ute said. 'Get up. Go at once to change those muddy clothes.'

When Oskar had gone upstairs, Ute put the kettle on and I sat at the table.

'The dentist, he will mend your teeth, Peggy,' she said from behind me. 'And I promise your hair will grow. You are still my beautiful girl.' She laid her hand on the top of my head.

I tucked my chin into my chest, but I let her hand stay.

The kitchen was hot even though, outside the window, a rime of frost lay on the garden. Ute placed a cup of tea in front of me and instinctively I curled my hands around it.

'You haven't forgotten that the police are telephoning today?' she asked. 'And Michael and your friend Becky are coming this afternoon?'

I thought 'friend' was an odd word to use about someone I hadn't seen for nine years.

Ute sat down opposite me, cradling her own cup. 'But maybe it is all too much for one day. Perhaps I should cancel,' she continued, almost to herself.

'The police?' I said, and gave a short laugh. She was about to say more when we both looked up at Oskar standing in the doorway. In his hands was a box, which he held out like a gift. His eyes were round and his brows raised. I wondered if he had been practising an apologetic face in his bedroom mirror.

'I thought we could all do a jigsaw together,' he said. He came forward to put the box on the table. 'I found it in the cellar.' The picture was an illustration of a thatched cottage in a wooded glade. A rabbit sat in the foreground beside a meandering stream, and a haze of bluebells spread under trees dotted with brilliant green. Ute made noises that suggested she didn't think it an appropriate image, but we had nothing better to do, so we tipped the pieces out and sorted through them.

'These trees are wintereyes,' I said, turning over each piece so that colour showed on every one.

'Wintereichen,' said Ute. She picked up a scrap of green, peered at it intently and put it face down, in a different place.

'They're oak trees,' said Oskar, grouping all the blues together.

The three of us raised our heads at the same time and smiled at one another. I kept my lips together.

'Can you speak German?' I asked Oskar, looking down.

'Sprechen Sie Deutsch?' he said in a very poor accent. 'No, Mum couldn't be bothered to teach me.' He teased her in a way that I had never been able to.

'This is not the reason,' said Ute with a pout. 'There are always so many other things to be getting on with.'

'What about the piano? Did she teach you to play the piano?' I asked.

'She says it's her instrument.'

I smiled at that, behind my hand. 'She said the same to me.'

'It is only because I do not think the Bösendorfer is suitable for children to be learning on,' she said. 'You do not learn to drive in a Porsche. It is the same thing, exact.'

'It was nice to hear you play,' I said. I found a piece of the edge where the stream flowed out of the picture, and locked it into another fragment of silver. 'We had a piece of piano music with us,' I said.

'I know,' she said. 'The Liszt – I searched for it much later and found it was gone. It was a very old copy, from Germany.'

'I'm sorry. There was a fire. It got burnt.'

'It doesn't matter. I don't worry about the music now.'

We both stopped doing the jigsaw and looked at each other, whilst Oskar continued to match the pieces.

'It was the music I played when your father and I met – the piece he turned the pages for.'

Oskar stopped concentrating on the jigsaw too and watched us, as if hoping for a revelation, but neither Ute nor I said more. The Liszt played itself in my head, fluttering and rippling, and something unravelled inside me; a stitch I had once believed was firm came loose – a tiny thread waiting to be pulled.

We gave up on the puzzle after that, and Ute started making lunch and an Apfelkuchen for the afternoon visitors. Oskar wanted to go into the garden to stamp on frozen puddles, so he put his coat back on.

'It is too cold, Oskar, to be outside. It is the coldest November in London since time began,' Ute said, already busy with the flour.

'Records,' I said.

Ute scowled at me. 'What?' she asked.

'Since records began,' I said, but she still frowned. I caught Oskar's eye and we both laughed. 'I think I'll go outside too,' I said, getting my coat and scarf from the hall.

The cold, fresh air was a relief after the stuffy house. Our breath came out in clouds and the bricks on the terrace glistened, waiting to slip up an unwary foot. White dust lay along the top of the box hedging. Oskar jabbed the heel of his boot into the ice that had formed in the bottom of a flowerpot saucer, then tried to pack the dust into a snowball, but it fell in crumbs from his hands. I longed for a chilly blanket of real snow tucked around the naked and shivering wintereyes.

Oskar rapped his knuckles on the thick ice which had risen like a soufflé out of a bucket hanging on a nail beside the back door. I recognized it; it was the bucket my father and I had used, with a tap attached to the bottom so we could brush our teeth with running water. In the frozen garden the tap dripped an icicle.

'Would madam like something to drink?' Oskar laughed and turned the handle, twisting it hard; his mouth twisting too, with the effort. The tap snapped off. And for the first time since I had come home I cried – for the music, for Reuben, but most of all for the waste of a bucket.

IO.

'Die Hütte,' said my father as though he were starting a prayer.

I could say nothing. At that moment, with just one shoe, my hair still lank from the water, I knew, even more than when my father had smashed the fish head, or told me Ute was dead, that something had gone wrong with our holiday. I stared at the cabin with my mouth hanging open. In my imagination it had been a gingerbread house with roses around the door, a veranda with a rocking chair, and smoke puffing from the chimney. Exactly who was there to tend the roses and light the stove hadn't been clear, but even seeing Oliver Hannington would have been better than the tumble-down witch's house that stood before us.

Its walls were hung with wooden shingles, and where they were missing, dark gaps grimaced like a mouth with knocked-out teeth. The front door hung open at an angle, and the single window had warped and popped its glass. The only thing to remind me of home was the bramble that scrambled across the roof and dropped in loops through the gaps in the shingles that were nailed there too. Searching for light, the bramble had reached the window and now stuck its blind tendrils out, beckoning us to join it inside.

Saplings sprouted unchecked against the walls, so it appeared as if die Hütte, ashamed of its dishevelled appearance, was trying, and failing, to hide behind them. I half expected a trail of breadcrumbs to lead off into the trees that pressed in from both sides.

'Die Hütte,' my father said again. He took off his rucksack, dropped it and walked towards the cabin. I followed him up the slope, wading through the grass.

Up close, the cabin seemed even more dilapidated. The wooden door frame was spongy where I leaned against it, the hinges had rusted and the bottom one fallen away. It took a few seconds for my eyes to adjust to the interior darkness, illuminated by shafts of light from the holes in the roof. The stink, an animal smell, musty and rank, like a dog's damp bed, hit me before I could make out any proper shapes. My father had already pushed his way inside and was sifting through the mess, kicking at the broken things that might have once been furniture, all made from the same rough timber as the inside walls. With each item he found – a stool with two legs, a rusty spade, a broom with a few twigs clinging to the end – he cursed under his breath. In the middle of the room a table leaned drunkenly with one leg bent beneath it. My father pulled it straight, so the surface became horizontal, gave it a shake to check its stability and started loading it with things from the floor: the prongs of a garden fork, a kettle without a lid, pans, heaps of dirty cloth which fell apart as soon as he lifted them, and other unidentifiable pieces of metal and wood which were strewn around. I glanced behind me, down the slope to the trees, worrying that maybe a bear had made this mess, but the line of dark trunks stared back without giving anything away. Inside the cabin, the wall to my right had been splattered with what looked like icing, stuck with feathers. It had dripped over the shelves, coating a metal box which was raised off the ground on four small feet. My father picked up a wooden bowl from the floor and plonked it on the table.

'Fuck,' he muttered, and, 'fuck, fucking liar. It must be ten years since anyone's been here,' he said to himself more than me. 'Humans, anyway.'

I didn't want to go in; the smell scratched at the back of my throat. I stayed in the doorway, watching my father frowning at every broken implement he found. He picked up pieces of pipe that appeared to have dropped out of a hole in the roof. He shook his head and ran his fingers through his long hair. A bit of the white icing stuck above his ear.

'How the hell did they manage to get this all the way up here and over the Fluss?' my father said, giving the box a kick with his foot.

'Where will we sleep?' I said.

My father looked around as if he had forgotten I was there. His mouth smiled, but his eyes didn't.

'If I can get this going, we'll be as warm as toast,' he said. He picked up another piece of metal pipe and tried to slot the two together. I knew he was pretending to be happy.

'I don't like it. It smells.'

'You'll get used to it,' he said.

The Railway Children and the house with the three chimneys came back to me, and how the children had been frightened when they had first arrived. Perhaps I should try being brave. 'It's only the rats,' I said to my father in a northern accent. He looked at me as though I were peculiar.

'Out of the way, Punzel.' He squeezed past me and pulled the table into the middle of the room. He tested it again and gingerly put one knee and then the other on to it. Nudging all his found objects out of the way, he stood up. His head was just higher than the three beams which ran crossways below the roof. He stretched on the tips of his toes and craned his neck. 'Damn,' he said, running his hand over the beam closest to him so that a shower of white flakes came down, making me cough. He jumped off the table and pulled it to the other end of the cabin, climbed up again and examined the other two beams. Dust swirled in shafts of light.

'What's the matter?' I asked.

He got down and did his pretend smile again. 'Nothing for you to worry about,' he said, sitting down on something that might have been a bed, which leaned against the opposite wall to the shelves. He bounced once or twice, and something cracked and gave way beneath him. He got to his feet without comment and stamped on the floorboards.

'There should be a root cellar under here somewhere,' he said. 'And the roof is going to need work.' Using a rag that was crusted into a stiff block, he grasped one of the loops of bramble hanging from the ceiling and gave it a tug. It resisted. My father carried on moving things around, pushing junk with his feet, picking up objects, examining them and putting them on the table. 'Where are the damn jerry-cans? He said there were jerrycans.'

I backed out, into the long grass, as my father dragged the table towards the door, before realizing it was too big to fit through.

'Must have made it inside,' I heard him mutter.

'It's only the rats,' I said again, but this time he didn't even look at me. I walked back down the slope. The thick air weighed heavy on the top of my head as I sat on my father's rucksack and stared at die Hütte. It looked back with a piteous face but was perhaps pleased that it now had company. The land rose steeply behind it; wooded on the lower slopes, then a few trees clinging to rocks until, craning my head backwards, I saw sheer cliff and, beyond that, sky, the colour of a bruise. Far behind me, if I concentrated, I could hear the river's never-ending rumble. Either side of where I sat in a small clearing were tangled bushes, which gave way to dense trees. I was aware of them watching me, shoving against one another to get a better look, but when I whipped my head around, as if I were trying to catch them out in a game of What's the Time, Mr Wolf?, they were still.

I sat for a long time, my chin in my hands, gazing at my father working and sorting. When he came outside, he sang snatches of opera, changing the words, singing about living in the open air and what fun we were going to have. I scowled at him, refusing to smile. Just outside the door, he made a pile of usable objects: three buckets, an axe, a fire poker. Another mound, of broken items, grew faster. When he went back inside, the singing stopped and instead he grunted and swore as he worked. I wondered whether, if he couldn't see me, he thought I wasn't there. I stumped back up to the open doorway and stood on the threshold.

'My knees hurt and I'm hungry,' I said into the gloom. The hut was clearer now; I could see the floor, and the narrow bed had been emptied so that its wire mesh, which had lain flat under the debris, had sprung back on itself. I didn't see how we would be able to sleep, curled up like dry leaves.

My father didn't stop. He had found a large chest and was taking out tools from inside it, one at a time: the head of a hammer, dislocated from its handle, a saw with missing teeth, a rusty file, a paper bag of nails. As though he had discovered a box full of treasure, he examined each item, looking at it closely and placing it with care on the floor beside him.

'Papa, I'm hungry,' I said again.

'What?' he said, still not looking up.

'I'm hungry.' This time quieter.

He carried on working.

I turned and went down to where we had dropped our bags. The rabbit was still tied to my father's rucksack. It needed to be skinned and cooked. At the edge of the clearing where the bushes and weeds started, I pulled up tufts of hairy thatch and collected twigs and larger sticks, every so often lifting my head and daring myself to glare at the forest. Back at the rucksacks, I searched through my father's, pulling out packets of dried beans, his coat and two of Ute's winter dresses. I dropped them quickly, as if at any moment she might discover me at her open wardrobe, fingering her clothes with my sticky hands, but then I held one of them up to my face, inhaled comfort and security and put the dress over my head. Ute had called this one her camel dress, and it was scratchy around the neck like I imagined camel hair might be. The bottom of the dress pooled on the ground, even when I tied the belt as tight as it would go, but I liked the feel of it against my legs. I dug through my father's rucksack until I found his char-cloth tin, and the flint and steel, and then tugged at the long grass to make a clear patch for the fire, but it clung to the earth and ripped through my fingers; so, holding up the dress, I trampled the stalks, flattening a small area. My father would have made a stone circle for the fire to burn in, but there were no stones.

Red welts had risen on my wrists from the rope, and the backwards and forwards motion of the steel and flint made me wince, but I was able to produce sparks with just a few strikes, and I thought how proud my father would be that I could light a fire without using any of our emergency matches. The dry kindling caught quicker than I had expected, the flames gobbling up everything I fed them. The smoke hung heavy above the fire and drifted off towards the river, away from die Hütte.

Once the fire was going well, I dug into my father's rucksack again and found his skinning knife in a side pocket, still in its leather sheath. I wasn't supposed to take it out – it was too sharp and dangerous for little girls – but, clumsy from the dress, I carried the knife up to the cabin in both hands, my wary eye on it, and stood in the doorway again.

'Papa, can I use the knife?'

'Not now, Punzel,' he said, without turning around. He was chipping the white stuff off the metal box with a spade. I stepped back outside. On top of the pile of salvageable items was an axe. I considered it whilst putting the skinning knife in the pocket of my dungarees. The axe was long-handled and heavy-headed and, grasping it in two hands, I pulled it from the heap. Its shaft was polished from years of sweat and oily hands. I ran my thumb along the pitted edge of the blade without any idea of what the action meant. Attempting to skin the rabbit with a forbidden knife would get me into trouble, but my father had never warned me about using an axe. Holding it near the head for balance, I carried it through the clearing and laid it beside the fire. The grass smouldered in places; I stamped the patches out with my one shoe.

I untied the rabbit from the rucksack and tried to arrange him on his tummy with his legs tucked underneath so that he may have been nibbling the grass. But his head kept lolling forward at an awkward angle – his neck clearly broken. I laid him on his side with his hind legs stretched out, so that he could have been springing over a grassy mound, and tilted his head upwards; his ears were still alert and soft, even in death. Only his eyes had changed – blinded by a thick fog.

The trees whispered and watched me whilst I arranged the rabbit. I thought about the trout and how easily and swiftly my father had changed it; with one blow to the head he had brought flapping, slippery nature under his control. Glad that the rabbit couldn't look at me, I kneeled up beside him and lifted the end of the axe shaft in both hands. 'Sorry, little Kaninchen,' I whispered. I hefted the axe into the air, where it wobbled, deciding whether to tip me over backwards, but my shoulders tilted and the axe took over, swinging itself forward with terrifying violence – taking me with it. I shut my eyes; the axe was in charge. With a life of its own, it cleaved the air and I felt the crunch as steel met flesh and bone, and it buried its blade into the earth with the downwards force. It pulled me in its wake, my forehead slamming into the handle.

'No!' my father shouted from the cabin, and I heard him racing down towards me.

I opened my eyes and up close saw a mangle of blood, fur and bone where the rabbit's neck had been. The beautiful ears were severed, halved and pulped by the blade so that the animal had bloody copies of my balaclava's furry tips. My father yanked the axe from my hands.

'What are you doing? What the hell are you doing?' He gripped the handle with the head hanging down, hopping around me and the rabbit and the fire. 'That could have been your fingers! Your hand! Why can't I leave you alone for just a minute?'

I stayed on the ground, trying to make myself as small as possible. He came towards me, but I flinched and he must have realized he still had the bloody axe in his hand because he flung it away into the grass.

'I wanted to make us dinner.' My voice was thin. I touched my forehead and could feel an egg-shaped lump already forming under the skin where I had hit the handle.

'Can't you do what normal girls do? Go and play. Go!' He pointed at the cabin and shoved my rucksack into my arms. 'And take that bloody dress off.'

I untied the belt and shrugged off the dress, leaving it in a pile on the grass. I ran crying up the slope and, without any hesitation, into die Hütte, and squeezed into a corner between the metal box – now recognizably a stove – and the bird-pooped shelves, my arms around my knees. I pushed my hair out of my face, repeating the action again and again until my crying hiccups subsided. My back was pressed against the wall, and it felt good to have something solid behind me after weeks of living under canvas. I opened my rucksack, pulled out Phyllis and cradled her into my neck.

'There, there,' I crooned. 'Ssh, Liebchen, don't cry,' I said, brushing the hair out of her face too. She hopped around me on the dirty floor and on to the shelves, then jumped along them, scraping up the white droppings with her pretend shoes. I tucked her in behind the stove, and my fingers touched something in the wood of the cabin wall, under the bottom shelf. When I crouched to look I saw that a word had been carved there, gouged into the wood with the point of a knife. I traced it with my finger: 'Reuben'.

II.

During our first few days at die Hütte, every sunny afternoon blended into each warm evening. I spent my time
playing outside with Phyllis, washing all the small things we
had found – metal plates, a few pieces of cutlery, wooden
bowls – in buckets of water my father hauled up from the
river. Although he had made me a shoe from a hessian bag
with a carved shingle for the sole, I mostly ran around barefoot, and naked apart from my pants. In the evenings we
rolled plants into rope and told stories around the campfire.
At odd times I would remember with a jolt that Ute was
dead, and Phyllis and I would crawl inside the tent to cuddle,
until she stopped crying.

On the third day of camping outside die Hütte, my father
climbed on to the roof with the mended hammer and the
nails, and worked on repairing the shingles. At first he made
me stand inside and direct him to where I could see sunlight
sneaking through, but after a while he didn't seem to need
my help and I wandered outside into the sunshine.

'Make yourself useful,' my father called, his words man-
gled by the nails he held between his lips. 'Take the traps
and catch us some dinner.'

I still hadn't been into the forest on my own; the thought
made me nervous and excited as I hurried to put on my
clothes and my odd shoes, and to collect the nooses. I hesitated on the edge of the clearing, then took a few steps

forward into the trees. Gnarled and mossy roots spread like giant's fingers amongst ferns that came up to my chest. There were as many trunks fallen and rotting as there were upright trees, fighting for the patches of green daylight that filtered down through the leaves. The forest smelled earthy; moist, like the cemetery. I pushed my way through the plants until I came to a massive trunk which must have come down years before, its decaying wood spongy and dark. I stepped up on to it, and the rotten bark gave way, tipping me off so that I stumbled, only just catching myself before I fell. A shiver ran through the trees as though they were laughing, and I had to fight the urge to turn and bolt. At my feet was a thick branch, newly fallen, and I picked it up to whack the trunk with it and beat a path through the ferns and damp plants until the way became clearer and the ground peaty. Looking back at where I had come from, the ferns closed around something quick and low and grey that ran through the undergrowth.

'Wolf!' a voice hissed inside my head. My heart thumped in my throat, but I stood my ground. The forest was testing me. I growled, deep in the back of my throat, and hunkered down with my branch held out, ready to spring forward and fight, but the ferns didn't twitch again, so I sat on the forest floor and then lay back, spreadeagled. The cool, damp earth penetrated my clothes and chilled my skin. I let the trees encircle and lean over me whilst I looked up through the canopy as if I were staring through a fisheye lens. They checked me for one of their own and turned me upside down so that the faraway blue sky, hidden behind their leaves, became the land and I floated free.

When the feeling had faded, I rolled over on to my

stomach, my eyes in line with the mossy forest floor. Spread out in front of me, for as far as I could see, was a forest of giant chanterelles. At ground level they were transformed into exotic trees with egg-yolk-yellow gills, towering over me. I stuffed them in my pockets, cupped them in a hammock made from the bottom of my T-shirt and ran back to die Hütte.

My father and I walked all of the land on our side of the river. Our southern boundary was the water, and our northern, the slope of the mountain. East of the cabin was a forest of deciduous trees.

'Oak trees, or Wintereichen,' said my father. 'The acorn is one of the most nutritionally complete foods, the only food in this forest that contains carbohydrates, protein and fats. What is the acorn?'

'The acorn is the only food that contains carbohydrates, protein and fats,' I said.

'And what's the name of the tree?'

'Wintereye,' I said.

The wintereyes, beech and the occasional hoary yew spread downhill towards the river, until a horseshoe of tall pines then scrubby bushes filled the gap between the mostly deciduous trees and the bank. Through this forest was the gill – a deep channel of mossy rocks which had long ago tumbled down the mountain and settled on top of a gurgling stream that we could hear but couldn't see. We didn't cross it; not far beyond, the mountain rose in crumbling scree, which looked impossible to climb. To the west of the cabin was a smaller area of forest, also bounded by the river and the mountain. We named this the rock forest, because whilst the east side had the gill to funnel the boulders that the mountain threw down, on the other, huge rocks had slammed into the soft earth and lodged there, half buried, amongst the trees. Every day, I walked the same route, checking our nooses for their grisly harvest. If they were empty, there would often be a rabbit in a snare, more mushrooms, as well as leaves and roots, edible berries, fish my father caught, the provisions we had carried with us. We were never hungry that summer.

Each morning since we had arrived, my father had cut notches in die Hütte's door frame, but when he got to sixteen he decided to stop.

'We're not going to live by somebody else's rules of hours and minutes any more,' he said. 'When to get up, when to go to church, when to go to work.'

I couldn't remember my father ever going to church, or even to work.

'Dates only make us aware of how numbered our days are, how much closer to death we are for each one we cross off. From now on, Punzel, we're going to live by the sun and the seasons.' He picked me up and spun me around, laughing. 'Our days will be endless.'

With my father's final notch, time stopped for us on the 20th August 1976.

My father showed me how to hone the knife against a stone to keep it sharp; how to put a nick in the fur behind a rabbit's head and pull off his jacket so that he was left with just his socks on; how to pull his grey insides down and out, but save the heart, liver and kidneys; and how to put him on a spit to roast. In the forest, we used every part of the animals we killed – saving the bones for needles, trying to form thread from the guts, and making poor attempts at curing the skins. We were busy, too busy for me to question why our fortnight's holiday was slipping into three weeks and then a month.

After a week, my father said we could move out of the tent and into die Hütte. He had pulled out the bramble, patched the holes in the roof, screwed the door back on straight and got the stove working. He stood outside the cabin and cheered as smoke appeared from the metal chimney that poked through the shingles. I jumped up and down and clapped too, without knowing why it was so exciting. The sun shone from a sky so shiny it hurt my eyes to look up into it, whilst the rising wind whipped the smoke away.

'There's still lots to do, but tonight we sleep in die Hütte,' my father announced with his chest sticking out and hands on his hips. 'We should celebrate,' he said, and slapped me on the back as if I had mended the stove. 'What shall we do, Punzel?' He looked at me, laughing.

'Celebrate!' I said, and laughed too, although I wasn't sure at what.

'Let's make a kite. We can fly it from the top ledge.' He shaded his eyes and looked high above the cabin. 'Fetch me the string; I'll cut some sticks.'

I ran into die Hütte and my father went to the woods.

By the time I had found the ball of home-made cord, which was stuck on a peg behind the door, my father was down by the tent, kneeling with his back to me, working away with the knife. I ran to him, holding the ball in the air: 'Papa, I found it!' But here my memory slows, like watching an old cine film, jerky, with all the colours too bright. My father spoke to the camera but no words came out. He was in front of the tent, slicing it with the knife. Stabbing and jabbing at it, slitting it open as if he were preparing a carcass. He looked over his shoulder at me, smiling and chattering, but all I could see was the gaping hole in the tent's side. And then the sound cut back in, as though I had shaken my ears free of water and I heard him say, 'The wind will be strong up the mountain.' He made a sawing action with the blade, so that a flap of canvas came loose. Watching him made me double over, holding my stomach. 'We can make the tail from these little bits of canvas,' he said, busy working. 'God, this would be so much easier with scissors. There must be scissors somewhere in die Hütte.'

I sat on the ground, tears falling. It was too late to stop him.

'How will we get home, Papa, without a tent?' I said to his back. He turned around and looked at me, confused for a second, but then understanding.

'We are home, Punzel,' he said.

It took him an hour or so to make the kite. It was a blue diamond – patchy, where the sun had scrubbed away at the colour – and the length of my father's outstretched arms. He tied pieces of string to three of the four corners, and where these met he attached the ball of cord. We didn't talk whilst my father finished it, but I could tell he was trying to be happy.

'Come on. Let's go.' We hadn't been up the mountain before, but where the land rose behind the little house, when I squinted, I could see a slab of bald rock, high above the treeline. I dragged behind him whilst he followed an

animal track through the ferns – a path no wider than my
shingle-bag shoe – a groove in the layer of last year's fallen
leaves. From down in the river valley, I heard the wind
coming up through the wintereyes. Like approaching rain,
it raced towards us, shaking the canopy, an infectious palsy,
passing the shake from one tree to the next, until it was
over our heads, fracturing the light on the forest floor.
Then it was gone, racing ahead up the mountain. Eventually the peaty ground became rock, the trees thinned and
we had to scramble on our hands and knees. My father had
tied the kite to his back so he could use both hands to pull
himself upwards. As I followed behind him the diamond of
blue canvas mocked me, the awful knowledge staring me
in the face whilst I climbed that we wouldn't ever be going
home.

The rock platform was much bigger than it had appeared
to be from below, where the foreshortening of the view up
the mountain changed it to a narrow ledge. In reality, it
stretched back to a near-vertical cliff-face a way behind us,
whilst from the edge we could see down over the tops of the
trees to our cabin and the patch of green surrounding it.
From that high vantage point, the limits of our land were
obvious: die Hütte sat towards the back of its small clearing,
bordered below by the pines and the river, glinting in the
sunshine. To our right the mountain curved around the rock
forest until it met the water. And to our left was the forest
we had climbed through, but beyond that, the mountain
again, sloping down to the water in a tumble of giant boulders, as if long ago half the mountain had slipped off for a
swim which had lasted centuries. Die Hütte was held in the
mountain's embrace: two arms wrapped around us, pulling

us back from the river like an anxious mother, whilst we hid in a crease in her skirts; an insignificant wrinkle in a mountain range that spread as far as the horizon. Beyond the river the wooded land rose again to another ridge, and after that I could see only blue sky.

My father had been right: the wind was strong. It tugged at our bodies and whipped my hair into a frenzy, wrapping it around my head and flinging strands of it into my mouth. It sucked the breath from me and made my heart race, even though inside I was still angry. My father stood with his arms out at the edge of the slab and shouted, a long tailing 'Weeeeaaaay' that the updraught caught and carried away.

He untied the kite from his back and immediately the wind wanted it. The tail uncurled, flicking. My father checked the tightness of the knot and, holding the ball of cord in his fist, he let the kite go. Instantly it was airborne. Demanding more and more string, it jerked at the line in frustration. Even I had to admit it was a beautiful thing. It soared over the wintereyes, becoming a blue bird in a blue sky. It took all the string my father fed it, until one loop remained, tied around his palm. We both stared up; our necks craned back until they ached and our eyes blurred.

'Do you want to have a go?' he said.

I nodded, and he put the loop over my fingers and closed them around it.

'Hold tight,' he said, and smiled. The kite tugged at me, nagging for attention. My father was looking up as I straightened my fingers and let the kite jerk the string from my hand. The blue diamond got even smaller, the string sailing off below it. For a moment my father was confused; he looked down at my empty hand and back up at the string.

'No!' he shouted into the wind. And as I watched the kite fly away over the river and the trees, towards home, I felt an instant of real and absolute happiness.

That night, our first in the cabin, the weather broke and my father's roof-mending skills were put to the test. The rain pounded on our little house in the woods, dripping through the holes in the shingles he had missed. He had tacked a square of tent canvas over the empty window, so when the first lightning bolt flashed, the stove, the table and the wooden walls all flared an electric blue. The wind pulled and pushed at the canvas and shrieked through the gaps around the door. We lay curled together in our sleeping bags on the single bed, a mattress made from ferns beneath us, and whilst the thunder rolled over the forest in angry waves, my father told me stories. He whispered them into my hair as he held me, but much later I wondered whether the stories and what happened in the morning were my punishment for letting go of the kite.

'Once upon a time,' he said, 'there was a beautiful girl called Punzel, who lived in the forest with her papa. They had a little house, with a little bed and stove to keep them warm; in fact they had everything they could have ever wished for. Punzel knitted her long hair into two plaits, which she curled into seashells, over her ears.'

I thought of Becky sitting in the front row in our classroom, not a hair out of place.

'And with her coiled plaits she could hear all sorts of things: the deer and the rabbits chattering in the forest, her father calling to her from a long way off, and all the people of the world shouting at once in their different languages. When her hair was curled around her ears, Punzel could understand every one of them.'

'What were they saying?' I whispered back as the room flashed. I clung to my father, afraid that the wind would lift off the roof above our heads and whip up all the things in the cabin so that he and I would be whisked around and around with the bed and the stove and the tool chest, until we were sucked up and away.

'Well, mostly she heard the people of the world fighting with each other.' The thunder rumbled right on cue. 'They couldn't live together happily. They lied to each other and when people do that, in the end, the world they have built will always come tumbling down. Punzel hated hearing the people of the world lie and argue. But one day she woke to find that the angry planet was silent; all she could hear was the sound of her father chopping wood for the stove and the animals asking her to come out to play. And Punzel was the happiest girl in the world.'

It took me a long time to fall asleep that first night, even after the storm had passed and with my father's arms holding me tight. In the morning I woke alone. I listened for the animals and the sound of my father chopping wood, but I could hear only a few birds and the wind rising up from the river. The cabin was cold in the early morning, but I got out of bed and opened the door in my nightie. My father was trudging up through the clearing, walking through the leaves and twigs that were strewn about. His pyjamas were wet and his hair stuck flat to his head. He was crying and shivering, and he scared me even more than the thunderstorm had.

'I couldn't do it,' he said, curling into a ball on the doorstep, hugging his knees and making horrible noises. 'I couldn't do it.'

I knew he wanted me to ask what he couldn't do, but instead I backed away from him and crouched in the corner beside the stove. I reached out and let my fingers touch the letters gouged into the wood under the bottom shelf. *Reuben*. After a while, my father gathered himself together and came inside. His pyjama bottoms were muddy and the knees ripped. He wiped his nose on his sleeve and opened the stove to put a log on the embers, then he removed his pyjamas and hung them on the length of rope that we had strung up to dry our clothes.

'I went over to the other side of the Fluss,' he said. Steady drips of water punctuated his words with a hiss each time they dropped on to the hotplate. 'To see the damage from the storm. It's worse than I imagined.' He sniffed. 'The rest of the world has gone.'

That's how he said it; just like that, matter-of-fact. And I continued to sit in the corner with my hand under the shelf and my insides hollowed out. He changed into dry clothes and neither of us said any more about it.

In the afternoon, my father gave me a present of a comb. He had carved it from a slither of wood, filed and sanded it and given it half a dozen teeth. He made me sit on one of the mended stools and combed my long dark hair. Where he found the knots too difficult to draw the comb through, he cut them out with his knife. When my hair was as smooth and sleek as it had ever been at home, he divided it with a centre parting and made me plait it. He tied the ends with string and we coiled them around my ears, sticking the loops in place with twigs. When it was done, he looked me in the eyes, holding my shoulders.

'We'll be all right. It's just you and me now, Punzel,' he said, and gave me a crooked smile.

I wanted to ask him if the Russkies had done it, but was too afraid to make him cry again. He picked up the buckets and said that he wouldn't be long and that I should keep the stove going, but I stood at the door and watched him go, holding on to the door frame, terrified he would disappear into the trees and not come back. I stood there for a long time, just waiting. And almost too late, I remembered the stove. I opened its little door to a billow of smoke and prodded its red insides with the poker. The pointed end turned over a small charred book which lay amongst the embers and, as I watched, a flame caught it and curled it open as if an unseen hand flicked through the pages. I stared at my passport photograph whilst it blistered in the heat and my face melted away into the fire.

12.

'Where's the piano?' It was the first thing I said when I opened my eyes on our third morning in the cabin. I think my father had been waiting for the question, maybe since we had arrived.

He didn't flinch; he was over by the stove, boiling a pan of water and fiddling with the flue. He twisted a section of tube to stop the smoke from seeping out, but it escaped from a different gap. He twisted it again, creating a new hole. A grey cloud loitered in the roof space.

'Papa! The piano,' I said, sitting up. 'You told me die Hütte had a piano.'

I tried to imagine having the one from home inside the cabin. We would have to remove the roof and lower it in. An upright piano did not occur to me. In front of the single bed we shared, a dirty rag rug lay on the floor, one quarter torn off or eaten away. The table stood under the window, laid with forks and metal plates; the three-legged stools were stored underneath. Up against the opposite wall was the tool chest, with the remains of the tent rolled on top; and facing me was the stove, tucked into its wall of shelves. It had taken us a whole day to clean the bird poop and feathers off them – droppings stuck so hard to the planks we had to chip them off with a chisel my father had found in the chest. He carried bucket after bucket of water up from the river, but we had nothing to scrub with, so we improvised with grit, rubbing it under blocks of wood until the planks were sanded clean. Odd nails and hooks had been hammered into the sides of the shelves, and it had been another of my jobs to hang up the billycans and assorted saucepans and utensils we had unearthed as we cleaned. There was no room for a piano.

'I'll make one,' said my father, putting two cups of weak tea on the table. We were already rationing the leaves.

Behind me on the bed, Phyllis made a noise which suggested she was tired of stories and promises.

'Oh, Papa,' I said. I sounded like Ute, and perhaps he noticed that too, because he looked at me with a sorry face.

'Maybe not a whole piano. I could just make the keys, find some wood, work out the mechanism. It shouldn't be too difficult.' My father was fired up at the idea, running his hands through his hair, already planning.

I sat on the edge of the bed, feeling sceptical.

'I'll make you one, Punzel, wait and see, and you can learn to play. Your mother might not have taught you, but I will. And I brought some sheet music with us.' He was like a child in his excitement. He stood on a stool to reach up into the rafters, tugging down his rucksack, which was stored there. 'I wasn't sure about showing it to you because I knew it would make you remember, about the piano.' He handed me a faded green booklet, the paper cover rubbed to felt from years of handling. 'It was out on the piano when we left, so I took it. Your mother would have wanted you to have it.'

The cover had the word 'LISZT' in black, and underneath, 'La Campanella'. Above a line of writing that was probably German, a beautiful winged lady sat reading music and holding a small harp-like instrument, as though she had all the time in the world to choose what she wanted to play. Her face was serene, and she seemed to be untroubled by the fact that a baby was struggling under the weight of the book which he held open for her. All around them was an abundance of produce: grapes, pears, apples, flowers, leaves. I would have stepped into that world if I could, and swung on a drape of ribbon, whilst the lady played and the baby dropped grapes into my open mouth.

Impatient for me to look inside, my father took the music and laid it open on the table, the white paper shaded blue in the morning light that struggled through the canvas windowpane. In the white spaces between the lines were handwritten words and numbers in green biro. Ute's hand-writing: 'beschleunigt!' – underlined three times; 'achten'; and, many times, 'springen'. I imagined her leaning forward at the piano to write something, biting her bottom lip, and I remembered with a lurch that Ute, the piano, the room she sat in, had all gone.

The dots, sticks and lines blurring in front of me meant nothing. Ute had never taught me even one note. Some-times I had been allowed to stand beside her whilst she practised, as long as I didn't fidget, but I never understood the translation of the cryptic symbols into the jumps and ripples she made with her fingers, and the sound that came out of the piano. Like the German language, Ute had kept the music for herself.

My father put his index finger under the first three sticks along the bottom line and sang three identical notes, the third one a fraction shorter than the others. His finger moved along, and there were three answering chimes from the high notes. He didn't hesitate; he didn't have to search around for the right pitch, but sang them as though he were the instrument, and the sound that came out of his mouth was pure and sweet. He repeated the low notes, and the highs followed along behind them.

'This chord,' my father held his finger under two black circles, clinging to a single stalk, 'is encouraging the high ones to take over. Listen.' He sang the refrain from the beginning, low then high, low then high. 'But just when you think they've got the hang of it, there is the tiniest of pauses, as if these – on the treble clef – are nervous.' My father held his right arm in the air, his thumb and forefinger pressed together and his lips pursed. Wait, just wait, he seemed to be saying. 'And suddenly they find their courage.' He forgot the sheet music and sang a few bars of the melody from memory, fast and rippling, his arms conducting.

'Can you hear the little bell? A hand bell made of china. It rings over the top, like this.' He was silent for a moment, and I strained to hear the bell amongst the noise of the wind and the creaking of the roof and walls. My father sang a high trilling tune and went back to the sinuous melody.

I recognized the music from home, from lying in bed and hearing Ute play it. I thought it sounded more like a trapped bird fluttering against a window than a bell.

He dropped his arms and stopped singing. 'Perhaps it's too difficult. Your mother . . .' he paused, as if this was the first time since we had been away that he had thought about her at the piano; his voice sounded strained. 'Your mother used to say it was one of the most difficult pieces. There are two separate tunes that tease each other, so many trills, and it's so fast. It was a stupid piece of music to bring.'

I was worried that already his mood was changing.

I sat on the stool, my feet tucked under my nightie to keep them warm, and looked at the music. I ran my finger along the fine horizontal lines, remembering the sound of it flowing through the floors of our London house – soaking into the wood, coursing up the white walls, swelling against the windows, creating a backwash which flooded up the staircase to my bedroom and lifted me out of my bed, so that as I drifted off to sleep I was held aloft by a salty sea of music.

'I really want to try, Papa,' I said, attempting to sound eager but still examining the notes and the green writing. I spread the fingers of my left hand as wide as I could and placed them on the table beside the pages.

'Like this,' my father said, leaning over me and stretching my fingers even wider, to place them on imaginary keys. 'Hang on,' he said, and fetched the pen, which hung by a piece of string from a nail. Shooing my hands away, he drew piano keys – fifty-two large and thirty-six small – along the edge of the table. The lines wiggled where the pen nib caught in the grain of the wood, and the keys tapered towards the low notes. Later, we tried colouring in the black keys with charcoal from the fire, but although it made the table look more like a piano, the soot coated my fingers and smudged across the white keys until they were all a uniform grey and we had to wash the table and start over again.

We moved the cups of tea out of the way and sat side by side on the stools.

'It's going to take a lot of practice, Punzel. Are you sure about this?'

I knew it was a warning he thought he ought to give,

rather than a challenge he wanted me to back down from. There was an enthusiasm bubbling inside him, like he hadn't had since he started work on the fallout shelter. My father always needed to have a project.

'I'm sure,' I said.

'Maybe we should start with scales first, or at least the names of the notes.' My father took my right hand and touched my thumb on one of the large keys in the centre of the table. 'This is middle C.' He sang the note, a long, strong 'laaa'. What's this?'

'Middle C,' I said, singing it with him.

'C, D, E,' he sang, his hand moving to the right. He tucked his thumb under and continued, 'F, G, A, B, C,' then rolled his hand back down again.

By the end of the morning, I could play and sing the C major scale, up and down the table, my fingers rolling in a jerky crab across the wood. He chose one of the long sticks propped in the corner by the stove, ready for snapping into kindling, and used it as a metronome, tapping out the rhythm on the wooden floor whilst he paced from bed to stove and back again. We practised until my fingertips were sore from the friction against the table, and until hunger made us stop and we realized it was the middle of the afternoon and none of our jobs had been done.

Every day I practised, starting with scales and arpeggios with both hands until my wrists seemed thicker and the tendons on the backs of my hands stood proud. Eventually, when the leaves outside die Hütte showed a tinge of yellow, my father said I was ready to start playing 'La Campanella'.

'Begin with the most difficult part,' he said, hovering in the same way that had made Ute snap at me whenever I had hung around her when she had played in London. He leaned over the piano and put his hands on the keys, playing a bar or two and humming.

'Papa! *I'm* meant to be playing, not you.'

Reluctantly he went back to binding more sticks on to the twig broom whilst I flicked through the music and returned to the first page.

'Don't start at the beginning,' he said, standing up again and coming over. He plucked the music out of my hands. 'Every time you sit down at the keyboard, you'll want to play the bit you know the best and that part will get the most practice, so you should always start a piece of music with the most difficult section.' He flicked through the booklet and stopped at page nine, where a run of notes formed the steady upward slope of a mountain, reached a peak and fell away to a series of small hills. He propped the pages in front of two saucepans to keep them upright. The music slipped and he moved it up again, tutting. 'I need to make a music stand.'

'Papa, it's fine. Stop fussing.' I elbowed him away.

'Here's the pen,' he said, handing it to me. 'This is your music now, you must add to your mother's annotations.'

I put my fingers on the keys, waiting, nervous. I thought about the beautiful music that had flowed from Ute's hands and how, when she had played, everyone stopped to listen. I remembered a line from a review that had been framed and hung in the hall of our London home: 'Ute Bischoff turns the music in on itself with the gentlest of touches.' When I was younger I had thought it meant that Ute sat at her piano with a sheet of music, folding the dots and the sticks inwards with dexterity and precision, scoring creases until the page was a delicate piece of origami sitting in the palm of her hand. Taking hold of two corners, she pulled them in opposite directions so the sheet blossomed into a paper flower.

'How will I know if I'm doing it right, if I can't hear the music?' I said.

'Beethoven was already deaf by the time he was my age,' said my father. My face must have shown that I wasn't sure I believed him. 'Really,' he insisted. 'But he still played and composed.'

'But I'm not Beethoven,' I whined.

'Just hear the notes inside your head and watch your fingers – you'll know when they go wrong.'

'But I need to read the music at the same time.' I pressed a silent chord with my left hand.

'You'll work it out.' I could hear his impatience building, but when I glanced around, he had turned away to take the broom between his knees and carry on with his work.

My right hand started in the foothills, white and black notes rolling over each other as the piece climbed. And whilst it climbed, I sang. Sharps and naturals flowing under my fingers and out of my mouth. The need to breathe was frustrating. I had to gulp air even when there was no pause in the music. When my fingers didn't match my voice, or my voice was too fast for my fingers, I started the run over again. I came to understand Ute's green notes – when to be steady and which fingers she had used for the most difficult sections. I liked to think they were messages written for me to find, in the middle of a forest on a piano that made no sound.

When I played, my father would sometimes sing the bass line whilst I was the bell, or the bird; or one of us sang the treble clef with the other joining in on the high notes to create the chords. By page six, the bird was joined by a cat, and the fluttering became more desperate. The bird circled higher and higher, trying to escape the open maw that followed its flurries at the window. When the bird tired and swooped too low, the cat jumped, feathers were lost, and I despaired for the creature. In the final refrain, as if sounding an alarm call, the bird began to fight back. The animal I had taken for a sparrow or a wren became a fiercer creature, showing its talons and curved beak so that fur flew as well as feathers. By the time we reached the closing bars of the music the window was smashed, one of the animals had gone and the other was dead, but whether it was the cat or the bird, I could never be sure.

'La Campanella' was the first thing in my head when I woke in the mornings and it was the song I collected kindling to, the tune I found I was singing without realizing when I checked the traps, and what I hummed whilst I stuffed handfuls of wood strawberries into my mouth when they should have been going into my basket – a mouthful of pips and a sharp burst of bitter forest.

When my father realized I wasn't going to stop, that every day I would play without him having to remind me, that already music was as much a part of me as breathing, he decided it was time to make keys that moved. As the summer turned, my father drew his design on the inside covers of the Liszt: measurements, materials and equipment. We had no idea that the making of the piano was likely to kill us.

My father planned the piano without hammers or pedals, strings or a soundboard. It had only keys, and the sound it made was the sound we made ourselves. Even once he was happy with the design, making it wasn't simple: the tools he had found in the chest were blunt and rusty, and most of them were too large for making piano keys. Still he went at it in a frenzy of creation. He forgot to bring up water from the river or to chop wood for the stove. He barely stopped to eat, and I had to drag myself away from the pen-drawn keyboard to go into the forest to check the traps and pick plants and berries so that we had food.

His first decision was what wood to use. He tried roof shingles, but they were too thin; fresh-cut wood was too green, the keys splitting as soon as they dried. The only spare planks we found were disintegrating in the long grass behind the cabin. When we picked them up they crumbled wetly, leaving behind a muddy negative and thin pink worms lying flaccid against the soil. In the end, my father prised a plank from one of the interior walls so that die Hütte's insides were exposed – grey daub and smooth tree trunks. When I looked away, almost embarrassed, as if I were seeing something indecent, he promised me we would pack the gap later with moss and clay.

My father rose with the sun to carve the keys into shapes that would meet his exacting requirements. He was an obsessed perfectionist. He worked until dusk, when he could no longer see the chisel without danger of slicing something other than wood. We had brought with us one torch and four candles, which we kept on a shelf alongside the few stubs of wax we had found when we moved in. The torch must have been cheap or else the batteries had got wet, because it petered out after a week or so. Even though my father might have wanted to work all through the night, his rule was that candlelight was for emergencies only. When it got dark we went to bed.

He cut each white and black key to a template with the saw and worked at them with the chisel. He cursed our lack of sandpaper. On the table my father nailed two blocks of wood far enough apart to lock all the keys together in a row. From the plank, he cut a long strip of wood into a square piece of dowelling, which he tacked the length of the table between the blocks. Each key had a corresponding shallow groove cut in its underside at a quarter of its length so that when the key was placed in position, over the dowelling, it could be rocked backwards and forwards. He then had to weigh down the top end of each key so that when I pressed and released them they would return to rest with their front edges higher than their backs. The only things we could find in the cabin to use as potential weights were a handful of worthless coins we had arrived with, but there weren't enough for eighty-eight keys. Whilst he mulled over this final challenge my father continued to work at the rect-angles of wood, scraping and smoothing each key so they would sit packed in together but still be free enough to move without grating against their immediate neighbours. We found the solution for the weights at the bottom of the water buckets.

The one job I refused to help with was fetching water from the river. My father had tied a bucket to a tree which had tucked its roots around a slab of rock sticking out above the pool we had seen from the other side of the river. Every day he lowered the bucket down and drew the water up. I could never get close enough to the edge without the world spinning and my stomach churning like the white water, so that I had to turn away. He had tried to teach me to fish lower down the river, where we had emerged, but even the noise made my legs weak. After we had arrived, I never again asked him to teach me to swim. My task each day was to walk through the forest to check the animal traps and gather whatever edible plants I could find.

Once a day, my father staggered up the slope to die Hütte with a bucket in each hand; twice a day if we wanted to wash. He would set them down beside the stove and use a billycan to ladle small amounts into the saucepans. A thick sediment smelling of pondweed settled at the bottom of the buckets. And in the mud there were white and grey pebbles, which for centuries had rubbed against the river rocks until they were smooth. Within a week I had collected eighty-eight pebbles of a similar weight and size from the bottom of the buckets. Using the corner of the chisel, my father dug a hole in the top of every key and tapped a pebble into each one.

For the remaining days of the summer, my father worked on the piano on one side of the table and I learned to play on the other.

When the weather changed, the piano was finished. The long hot days and thundery showers had been replaced with mornings that smelled of autumn, and mist that hung about the river. Many of the ferns were curling and changing to the colour of straw. But we had no idea of the date.

The piano was clunky and crude, but I thought that maybe it was the most beautiful thing I had ever seen. Despite all the whittling, many of the keys stuck together and continual playing gave me blisters and splinters. Several times my father took it apart to shave off a sliver and pack it all together again. And yet I could press a key and hear the note it made; release it and the key would pivot back to a resting position and the sound would stop.

The creation of the piano had taken the summer and the best days of the autumn. We should have been gathering and storing food and wood for the winter and, too late, we discovered that music could not sustain us.

13.

'There's a tennis court at the bottom,' said Oskar, pointing to the far end of the garden. 'I wanted a swimming pool, but Mum said tennis would be better exercise.' He said 'Mum' as if she were a woman I had just met. Perhaps he was right. I wondered what it had been like for him, having Ute to himself for eight years and not knowing his father or his sister – family he thought he might never meet or who might already be dead; strangers he would never bury. When Oskar heard I was alive, what had he wished for?

'Can you play tennis?' I asked.

Oskar, in contrast with Ute, was skinny and long-limbed. His shaggy hair hung over his Scout neckerchief – in the end he hadn't changed out of his uniform when Ute had sent him upstairs.

'Only a knockabout,' he said, and smiled. Too young to be called handsome, he was sweet-looking, with a wide mouth that carried on in an upwards curve even after the ends of his lips had finished. It wasn't like mine – small and pursed, with a disapproving pout.

Oskar had at first ignored my tears over the broken bucket and had continued to pick up lumps of ice and smash them on the terrace so that splinters flew all around us. I had turned my face away from him, and when the choking heaves had subsided, Oskar had asked if I wanted his hanky. I took it from him, rather grey and certainly used, but I wiped my eyes and my streaming nose and put it in my pocket.

My brother didn't seem cold, even though the day hadn't yet seen any sun. In his coat and khaki shorts, he jumped about me, chattering, his breath misting. He twirled and threw his arms around whilst he pointed out a new bird bath and the pile of leaves where a hedgehog was hibernating. I wondered what he would say if I told him that Reuben had shown me that the best way to cook hedgehog was to bake it in a coat of clay.

I dug my hands deeper into my duffle-coat pockets and shrank my chin down into my scarf. The cold air came through my tights and under my dress. On the terrace, my brother suggested a tour of the garden – *his garden*. I resented that he didn't acknowledge the fact that it had once been mine, that I had played in it, camped in it, before he was even born.

'There used to be a swing seat next to the house,' he said. 'It was great fun. Me and my friend Marky made it go really high. But the cushions got left out in the rain and it stank and Mum had to throw it away.'

'The one with the hole in the awning?' I said, my words clipped.

Oskar sized me up from under his eyebrows, his chin tilted downwards, creasing over his neckerchief.

'Was the material dirty white with large blue flowers?' I said. 'Did it have a squeak that sounded like a duck laying an egg, and a frill around the bottom that made the backs of your legs itch?'

For a second he was confused, as though he was trying to work out how I knew so much about a seat that was his seat and had always been his seat, but a flush rose in his cheeks and I realized I had gone too far. We walked down on to the lawn, flanked by tidy borders, brown and crisp with winter plants.

'Can you still walk straight through to the cemetery at the bottom of the garden?' I asked, to make amends.

He didn't answer, just carried on walking. All day the frost had stayed, riming every stalk, every leaf, every blade of grass. Oskar's shoes left shallow prints across the lawn. I trod close behind him, matching his stride and placing my feet where his had been.

If I can fit inside every one of his footsteps, I said to myself, my brother and I will be friends.

I averted my eyes as we passed the tennis court, constructed on the patch of ground where once my father and I had pitched our tent and built our campfire. Instead I looked beyond it, where the brambles and thistles had been cleared and there was more lawn and a summer house. It seemed to take only a few moments to reach the bottom of the garden, whereas in my memory the walk down from the house to the cemetery took five minutes or more. A high chain-link fence now separated the lawn from the trees, but I recalled their outlines as soon as I set eyes on them, like the furniture and ornaments in the house – unremembered until seen once more, and then familiar. Ivy was creeping its way back into the garden, reclaiming old territory.

Oskar approached the wire as though it might open up and let him through, but instead he bent down, hooked his fingers through the holes and pulled it upwards. It lifted high enough to make a gap, just big enough for an eight-year-old boy, at least a skinny one, to crawl through.

'Mum doesn't like me to go into the cemetery. She doesn't let me go out alone,' Oskar said, when he was on the other side. He pushed up the fence and turned his head away from me when he spoke. 'We drive a lot. She even takes me in the car to see Marky.'

We both looked back at the house, the white cube blending into a sky which threatened snow.

Oskar raised the fence higher, for me to crawl under, before the tension in the metal flicked the wire back into position. From the garden the trees had seemed like old friends, but as soon as I was amongst them they were full of menace and the air underneath was even colder. It took me a second or two to get my bearings, but Oskar must have come often without Ute knowing, because even in the dim light he found the narrow paths that wound around the graves without trouble. The undergrowth and ivy were denser than when I had been there last, the ground a green lake with treacherous rocks sticking out of it at obtuse angles. Even in the frost, the cemetery smelled of decaying vegetable matter. The ivy still clung to the trees and the graves, dripping like liquid plant from everything. Determined and persistent, it had wrapped its vines, many as thick as a wrist, around stone – breaking and lifting with its grip, so it seemed to be prising the lids from the tombs, to peek with its leafy eyes at the human remains inside.

I followed Oskar over undulating ground to one of the main paths. Slabs of fallen stone buried under years of leaf fall had created small mounds, whilst dips had formed where the underground world had shifted and settled. At the edges of the path, someone had been at work, hacking back the ivy, leaving a heap of greenery for composting or burning. They had revealed an angel, risen up out of the green waves which lapped at her plinth. Hairy tracks crawled over the folds of her drapery where the ivy had been ripped away, and her arms were raised in supplication, but they both ended in the stumps of her wrists.

We sat side by side on her bare feet. Below us the inscription read, 'Rosa Carlos, born 1842, died 1859. Lost to all, but memory.'

'Lucy Westenra was buried here,' I said, remembering one of my father's stories.

'Who's she?' asked Oskar.

'The girl from *Dracula*. She became a vampire and sucked the blood from children.'

'I'd drive a stake through her heart before she could do that to me.'

'Aren't you frightened?'

'What of?'

'Being here on your own.'

'I'm not on my own,' he said.

And I looked up at the angel, her stone cheek merging into the sky, and wondered if he meant Rosa.

'You're here,' he said, and I was suddenly, ridiculously, pleased. 'Anyway, I like it in the cemetery, it's peaceful. I brought Marky here once, but he threw a rock at an angel's face and broke off her nose.'

'Have you ever climbed the Magnificent Tree?' I asked.

'Which magnificent tree?'

'It was over there, I think.' I waved my arm in the direction the path led. 'Papa and I used to climb it.'

'I don't think there is a kind of tree called a Magnificent Tree.'

'Yes there is,' I snapped.

We sat in silence for a while, looking out over the snaggle-toothed stones and crooked crosses.

'Did you come here then? With Dad?' It was the first time Oskar had acknowledged the man had existed.

'Sometimes,' I said.

'Why did he have to go away?' The question burst out of him, surprising us both. His cheeks went red again and he picked at the lichen which grew across the stone toes like badly painted nail varnish.

'I don't know,' I said honestly.

'Marky says that Dad thought the world was going to end. He says Dad was crazy and ran away to join a cult in the woods. But the world didn't end, did it?'

I almost smiled, but instead I said, 'Marky doesn't know anything.'

'Why didn't he come back for me, or take me too?'

I could tell he had asked himself this question over and over.

'Why did you get to go and not me?'

'You weren't even born. Maybe he didn't know about you.' I shuffled my bottom on the cold stone to get more comfortable.

'Well, Mum could have gone with you too.'

'She was in Germany when we left. Anyway, it was all a spur-of-the-moment thing.'

'That's not what Mum says.'

'What does she say?' I was interested, now that I might get information from Oskar that I wasn't able to ask Ute about.

He continued to look down and scratch at the lichen with his dirty fingernails.

'Oskar?' I prompted him.

'She says Dad left a note, but she won't show it to me until I'm old enough to understand. She says he wrote that he was sorry but he had been thinking for a while that he needed to go on a journey, and that he would always love me.'

'Note, what note?' I said, standing up.

'I don't believe her. She's always lying and forgetting what she's told me. I know she's only trying to make me feel better, and he probably didn't write anything like that at all.'

'What note, Oskar?' I said again, speaking over him, my voice bouncing off the stones around us.

'I don't know and I don't care!' Oskar climbed on to the angel's feet so he was taller than me.

'Where's the note?' I demanded.

'I don't know! None of it's true anyway.' He jumped down from the plinth. 'I wish it was Dad who had come back instead of you,' he said, and pushed past me, running back along the track into the trees.

'Oskar!' I called after him. At first I heard him tearing through the undergrowth, twigs cracking, but then he was gone and the cemetery was silent. Gradually, I became aware of the rustle of leaves, something falling from a tree, way off, and the frost cracking and re-forming. There was a scrabbling noise behind Rosa Carlos and a steady *drip, drip, drip* across the path from where I stood. My breath came in little puffs in front of my face. The cemetery bulged in towards me, the stones ballooning and flattening themselves again. The face of my father, which was still stuck under my breast, was scalding. Half crouching, I put my hand under my dress and took the circle of photographic paper out. I couldn't look at him. With my left hand, I clawed at the earth beside Rosa Carlos. I could make only a minute pit in the frozen ground, but I placed his head in it, face up, and pressed the soil down on top of him.

I4.

It wasn't until the piano was finished that my father looked up from his work and realized the autumn was almost over. One morning he set out with his rucksack to the forest of wintereyes to collect acorns. He was excited at the possibility of flour and described in great detail the flatbreads, porridge and thick stews we would soon be eating. But when he returned he lay on the bed with his back to me and wouldn't speak, even though I stopped playing and begged him to tell me what was wrong. Without fully turning around he threw the rucksack across the room so that a handful of acorns flew out, pinging off the shelves and table and scattering over the floor.

'There are no acorns,' he said.

I gathered a few together. 'There are. Look,' I said, holding out my hand, not understanding.

'Not enough to even make one dumpling,' he said.

'But where have they all gone?'

'The fucking squirrels got there first,' he said.

'We can eat the squirrels then,' I said, which made him laugh, but he wasn't happy for long. As the weather changed his mood worsened. I still played the piano every day, but my father rarely joined in and instead of encouraging me he complained if I lingered on the stool in front of the table. He worried that the season had turned without us. He wrote detailed lists and calculations on the gun-pellet boxes, flattening them out into fat crosses, and on both sides of the map – the only paper we had left in the cabin apart from the sheet music. He pressed down hard with the pen so his writing would be legible over the green valleys and pale mountains:

Increase the woodpile
Collect and dry mushrooms
Bulrush roots
Dried meat
Dried fish
More wood
Daub cabin
Check shingles

I woke in the night to the glow of a candle on the table and my father bent over the map, chewing the end of the pen, the creases in his forehead ploughed into furrows. I worried about what kind of emergency we must be facing.

'What is it, Papa?' I asked the halo of light.

'Winter's coming,' he said tersely, even though it seemed to me that the sunny autumn was lasting for ever. When I got back to sleep, I dreamed of two people frozen to death in their single bed, locked together in the shape of a double S. When the spring sunshine crept under the door, the bodies defrosted and melted. An unknown man came upon the cabin, hacking his way in with an axe through the stems of a thorny rose which bound the door shut. I saw his hand, rough and hairy, reach out to pull back the sleeping bags, revealing faceless pulp, like the slippery guts of fish. I woke sweating and terrified at the image and the feeling I was left with, but even worse was the realization a few seconds later that no man would ever fight his way into die Hütte to find our decomposing bodies; there was no one left in the world but the two of us.

My father made me stop playing the piano and together we carried the bow saw, which lived on a hook in the rafters next to the scythe, into the forest. My father had tensioned its wooden frame and sharpened its teeth with the file until they shone with vicious intent. When he balanced it on end, the saw stood as high as my shoulders. We worked on cutting the forest's fallen branches into manageable sizes – running the full length of the blade through them, moving the saw backwards and forwards between us. We talked about all sorts of things whilst we worked. But often my father used our time together in the forest as a lesson.

'Always use the full length of the saw.'

'Always use the full length of the saw,' I repeated mechanically, without waiting for his question.

'This blade has ten teeth per inch, but there are others in the chest for finer work if you ever need them,' he said.

I was concentrating on our rhythm, comforting in its regularity. I breathed in the autumn smells of humus, fern and fresh wood sap. I watched the sun freckle the forest floor, and when a patch of warmth found me I lifted my face up towards it.

'Punzel! Pay attention. This is important for you to know.'

'Why?'

'In case I'm not here and you need to cut wood.'

I laughed. 'But you'll always be here.'

He carried on sawing whilst I sat on the thin end of a

branch to steady it and to keep the cut open, so the blade would move without snagging.

'What if I have an accident? Retreaters need to know these things.'

'I'd rather be a survivalist,' I said. 'In a bug-out location.' I rolled the words around my mouth to see how they sounded. I hoped they would make my father smile, but there was just the slightest of pauses in his sawing and he didn't look up. 'That's what Oliver said,' I continued.

'What else do you know about Oliver?'

'Nothing,' I answered, remembering the conversation in my bedroom just before he had slammed the front door.

'Oliver said a lot of ridiculous things.' My father pushed and pulled the blade faster, head down. 'He said he was a Retreater, a survivalist, but it turned out Oliver Hannington was interested in other things and too pathetic to even try it.'

'Not like us, Papa,' I said, but he couldn't have heard me, because he continued speaking.

'He liked to talk the talk, Oliver, but he didn't walk the walk.' On every 'talk' and 'walk' my father pushed forward, hard, so the saw ate deep into the wood and I had to grip tighter to keep my balance on the bouncing end. 'The cabin is in the perfect location,' my father said in an accent which copied Oliver's disturbingly. 'Fully equipped, James, stores of food for the winter.' He stopped imitating Oliver's voice and continued speaking. 'He showed me die Hütte on the map, told me about the fresh running water and herds of deer; it was even supposed to have a root cellar and an air rifle tucked out of sight on one of the roof joists. He told me that all I would need would be the gun pellets. So I bought boxes of pellets, boxes and boxes of pellets, but no bloody gun.' My father was panting and his words came out breathless and jerky. He wasn't talking to me any more. 'Oliver had never bloody set eyes on the place.'

'But if we hadn't been here when the rest of the world disappeared, we would have died too. So really, we should be grateful,' I said.

My father stopped sawing, his expression vacant as if my words were taking a while to go in. He turned his face away from me just as the branch complained and split apart, and I landed on the ground with a bump.

For the rest of the day, my father pulled and rolled branches to the cabin so we could chop them up with the axe. I collected bundles of kindling, which we tied together with home-made cord and my father attached to my shoulders. I staggered back, remembering an illustration from a book of Christmas carols: a ragged man bent double under his load of winter fuel.

The day after, outside die Hütte, my father balanced one log on top of another and gave me a lesson in how to use the axe.

'Watch, Punzel: right hand near the head, left hand at the bottom of the handle. Swing up,' he hoisted the axe above his head, 'let the weight take it forward, and your right hand will slide down to join your left.' The blade flew, its own momentum cleaving the top log in two. He crouched behind me, and with four hands on the axe we tried it together.

Remembering the rabbit, I shut my eyes as the tool swung crookedly and wedged itself in the bottom log.

'Keep your eyes open,' he said, and I wondered how he knew when he had been standing behind me. 'Try again.'

Over and over we swung the axe together until I thought my arms would dislocate from my shoulders.

'I think I can do it by myself now,' I said, although I didn't mean it and just wanted the job to be over so I could go indoors to play the piano.

'Show me,' he said.

I gripped the axe tight with both hands and, tightening my stomach, swung it up over my head, shut my eyes and let it fall forward. When I opened them, the top log was still in place, and the axe head was again deep in the bottom log. This time I couldn't even wiggle it loose.

My father laughed. 'Maybe next year,' he said.

We stacked hundreds of logs around the exterior walls. By the time we had finished sawing and chopping, they covered all four walls, right up to the eaves; only the door and the window with its tent curtain were left uncovered. My father put me on his shoulders for the last two rows, passing up one log at a time. He was delighted with our second layer of insulation.

When we had as much wood as my father's calculations said we needed, we worked on gathering food to store for the winter. We smoked fish, squirrel and rabbit meat over an outdoor fire which we kept alight day and night. And then we hung the pieces, as brown and flat as old kippers, from the rafters, between strings of dried mushrooms and berries and upside-down bouquets of herbs, until the roof space was swathed with macabre decorations. Near the river we found a boggy area where a bed of bulrushes grew. We pulled them up, eating the stalks and storing the roots in the tool chest, hoping they might keep like potatoes. We spent days raking through the leaves in the forest, searching for mushrooms, until at bedtime, when I shut my eyes, patterns of brown and orange leaves danced behind the lids. My father had an eye for mushrooms, and whilst I was bored after twenty minutes, he returned with oyster, hedgehog, ceps, chanterelles and beefsteak. There was too much food for us to keep up with the preserving, so we ate the rest fresh. Every meal was a feast, as though we were fattening ourselves up for hibernation, and all of it was delicious. We were healthy, plump and well fed. I lay in bed, looking up at the dark shapes dangling from the ceiling, thinking about the hard work it had taken to gather and preserve them, and I was sure my father must now be satisfied.

When the chest was full of food instead of tools, and the rafters appeared to have a colony of roosting bats, the early winter wind came to slap us in the face and tell us it wasn't enough. We weren't supposed to be eating the food we had preserved until well into the winter, but the temperature dropped so fast that the fish and the animals ignored our hooks and traps, and we often had to eat from our stores. My father's calculations were out by at least a month.

Drips hung from our noses, turning to ice in my father's moustache when he went outside. Indoors, we huddled beside the stove, one side of our bodies always freezing, the other burning. In the mornings I woke curled inside my sleeping bag, my hands tucked into my armpits. A thick skin of ice grew over the water bucket in the night and the tooth-paste froze in its tube. We wore as many layers as we could, and were so round and padded that on the occasional days when it was warm enough to reveal a leg, a bottom or a bit of chest to wash, it was a shock to see how thin and white our bodies had become. I dragged the piano closer to the stove so my finger joints would still flex and I could practise my scales with the heat on my back. We stacked logs in the window space and packed all the gaps in the walls with damp mud and moss. We lived in the dark.

'It's too cold to snow,' my father said, but it seemed he didn't know everything. One morning, we woke to a different sound. Our normal noises – the kettle on the stove, the brushing of teeth with a dot of toothpaste and our singing – were deadened. I heard them like I heard the rumbling of my stomach, distant and muted. But it wasn't until I pushed against the door that we realized it had snowed. My father wrapped me in all the clothes I owned, including the blue mittens and the balaclava, which had already lost most of its whiskers. On my feet I still had my oddly matched leaping-cat shoe and the shingle-bag. He worked at the snow with the spade until he was able to push the door wider and we could step outside.

Our world had been transformed. Instead of a tumbledown cottage where the witch lived, die Hütte had changed into the woodsman's cabin, snug and inviting, with smoke puffing from the chimney. The snow had been pushed up the clearing by the wind, and lay in thick drifts against the trees and the cabin's walls. My father and I ran about, whooping and laughing, falling backwards into soft piles, lying down and making snow angels, rolling two balls into a snowman. My father's face even lost its worried frown in the hour or so that he played like a child, with no concerns about the next meal or that one day we would run out of toothpaste for ever. The snow melted and refroze into clods of ice around my shingle-bag shoe, so that my foot grew heavy and I lost all feeling in my toes. Only then did I agree to go back indoors.

The best thing about the snow was having as much water as we needed right outside the door. We scooped it into the kettle and pans, and kept a constant supply of warm water on the stove. We had never been so profligate with the water my father had to lug up from the river.

In the afternoon we treated ourselves to a standing-up bath. Outside the cabin, we took it in turns to balance naked, shivering with one foot in each bucket, to have warm water poured over us. The last time I had washed all over had been in a communal campsite shower, its floor slopping in dirty water from a drain blocked with short dark hairs. I looked at our view now, with the bare branches of the trees standing out spidery and black against the snow like the lungs of the world. And I thought about the view that Becky had had from her bathroom window: a brick-and-concrete London.

'Do you think it's snowing at home?' I asked. I stood drying myself in front of the stove, rotating by a quarter of a body-turn at a time, so that one narrow strip of me roasted to pink, whilst the opposite side chilled.

'We are home. London has gone. You know that, Punzel,' said my father, arranging our piece of soap on the shelf. It was already thin enough to see light through it when I held it up to the sky.

'I forgot.'

'I know it's hard. But you have to remember, none of it is there any more; the garden, the house, the cemetery, school – they're all gone.'

'What about Germany?' I said, bending over to dunk my head into a bucket of warm water. 'And Omi, has she gone too?' I scratched my scalp and tugged at my hair. We had finished the shampoo at the end of the summer.

'All of it,' he said.

I jumped up, flinging my head backwards and throwing out water droplets, which hissed on the stove. My father twisted my hair, squeezing out a trickle.

'But there are still hills over the Fluss.'

'Come on, I'll show you.' My father helped me into a jumper and my dungarees, which had been warming above the stove. He put on his coat and, picking me up with one arm, wrapped me inside it with him.

I clung on to him with my arms and legs and we went outside. It made me feel strange to think there was no one left to see us emerge from die Hütte into the snow; no one to wonder at this new double creature – a PapaPunzel. Our two-legged, two-headed body lumbered into the clearing.

'This whole wonderful world is yours and mine, Punzel. Everything you can see is ours. Beyond the Fluss, over the hill,' he pointed in that direction, 'there's nothing. If you carried on over the top, you'd fall off the edge into a never-ending blackness. Ptarrr!' He loosened his grip on me.

I shrieked as I felt a lurch with the drop of my body, before he caught me again.

He laughed at my fright and then became serious. 'And the same with the mountain.' He turned, running his out-stretched arm in a semicircle, taking in all the places I knew: the forest, the clearing, the cabin and the rocky slope up to the summit. We both looked up to the sharp line slicing through the white sky. 'On the other side there is only emptiness, an awful place that has eaten everything except our own little kingdom.'

'What's it called?' I asked in an awed whisper.

He paused, and I thought it was because even the name must be too terrible to speak. At last he said, 'The Great Divide. And you must promise never to go there. I couldn't survive without you. We're a team, you and I, aren't we?'

I nodded. 'We're the PapaPunzel,' I said.

'Do you promise not to go there?'

'I promise.' I clung to him.

'What do you promise?'

'I promise never to go there.' I was deadly serious.

He carried me back into the warmth, rinsed out our grey underwear and hung it near the hotplate, where it steamed and singed. I sat next to the fire and imagined our microscopic white and green island adrift in the blackness – an overlooked crumb, left behind when the Earth was gobbled whole by the Great Divide. My father told me many times that winter that the world ended beyond the hills, and he often made me repeat my promise.

Later that same afternoon, when we had eaten mushrooms stewed with ground elder, I persuaded my father to let me use his boots to go out on my own. The traps needed checking, I said, and I had set them on my own nearly every day, so a little bit of snow wasn't going to worry me. I put on my anorak, two pairs of socks, my father's boots, wadded with more socks in the toes, then tucked a couple of stove-warmed rocks into my mittens and went high-stepping through the snow drifts. The clearing was trampled and dirty, but further away from the cabin the snow was untouched, and I understood my father and I really were the last two people in the world.

Although I knew which branches caught the most

squirrels and which holes yielded the most rabbits, I followed my usual route in order to check them all. It took
me first down to the river; but no animal tracks showed in
the soft meringues heaped over the bank. I trudged into
the trees. They stirred their sleepy heads to see who was
coming, then settled back. I had expected the ground
under them to be clear of snow, but even here I had to
wade through it. The wind had blown it in drifts against
one side of each trunk, making the forest flash black and
white. Deer and birds had been there before me, and I even
saw tracks that might have been wolf, but I didn't find any
squirrels or rabbits – dead or alive. Every trap was either
covered in snow or empty. I imagined the animals tucked
up asleep in their beds for the winter, and wondered what
we would do if they didn't come out again until spring. In
my head, I counted the number of animals still hanging
from our rafters, and worried about my father's scribbled
sums. Perhaps I could eat slower so we would have enough
food to see us through.

Each empty trap made me think about how angry my
father would be when I returned without any food. He'd
shout and throw a billycan across the room. I'd ducked but
it would clip the side of my head, bouncing off and clattering on the floor. I went back to the traps that were buried
in the snow and uncovered them in case there was a creature I had missed. The forest was more handsome than I
had ever seen it, but all I could think about was returning
empty-handed. Many of the snow drifts came up to my
knees, and my feet became wet and numb; I was cold and
trembling, but still I walked. I hummed the last bars of 'La
Campanella' and played the notes within my mittens, but

it didn't take my mind off the panic that was building inside me.

When I neared the place where the wintereyes sprouted from the rocky soil, I remembered a noose I had tied to my favourite tree, higher up the mountain, in the summer. It had never caught anything, but now I wondered whether the acorns that we had forgotten to gather because we were too busy with the piano might have attracted a squirrel into my trap. In desperation, I continued up through the trees.

The wintereye, crouched in the rocks, had been kept squat and crooked by the wind which raced up the mountain. Its roots clasped the stone with giant claws, and below the branches the snow was patchy, the flakes scattered by the wind. From a way off, I could see that the noose was not there – perhaps it had rotted or been nibbled by an animal. But as I drew closer, under the wintereye, I saw footprints. Feet, in man-sized boots, had shuffled around under the tree and walked off across the rocks. They had made the same kind of movements my father had when we played outside die Hütte, as if this person too had hopped around. I stepped into one footprint, from heel to toe – it was the same size as my father's. For an illogical moment I wondered if he had been there before me, but we only had one pair of boots, and I was wearing them. A breeze came up through the trees, sprinkling snow, and when the wind reached the wintereye I was standing beneath, the tree shuddered and in a scratchy rattle the branches said, 'Reuben!'

I ducked low against the trunk, scanning the rocky outcrops above me. There was no movement, no shadows unaccounted for. I looked at the footprints I crouched

amongst and wondered if I could have remembered incor-
rectly: perhaps I had been there already to check the trap;
maybe the prints were mine. In my head I reran the route I
had taken – from the river up through the pines, zigzagging
between them, out the other side to the wintereyes and
here. I was sure I hadn't made them. When my thumping
heart had steadied, I hurried back to die Hütte, jumping and
turning at every whump of falling snow. Each creak of my
father's boots through the drifts made me look around, suspicious that the man who had carved his name in die Hütte
was following me.

I smelled the smoke from our stove before I saw the cabin,
and I ran, bent over, across the open ground, as if a sniper
might have been raising his gun to take aim. My father's
tracks in the clearing were already turning to slush, and the
snowman we had made had shrunk as the day had warmed.
In front of the door, lying on the snow, was a squirrel. A
dead squirrel. I couldn't see any blood on it. I looked at the
roof and wondered if it had been up there and had lost its
footing, falling conveniently on to our doorstep. But the
snow on the edge of the shingles was dripping and it was
impossible to tell. I glanced around. The feeling of being
watched made me nervous, but the relief of returning with
even a single animal was enormous. I picked up the squirrel
by the tail and went inside. My father, who was sharpening
tools, glanced over his shoulder.

'I was starting to wonder if I should send out a search
party, but there were no volunteers. Only one?' he said,
looking at the squirrel. 'They're probably all keeping warm
in their dreys, sensible creatures.'

Our room was cosy, safe. I stood by the stove, warming

through, feeling the bite of blood flowing again through my veins. My father carried the squirrel outside to gut and skin it. And I wondered whether Reuben was watching him too.

15.

Although I loved the snow, every morning I hoped it had melted, so my father's mood would lighten, but each time I woke I could tell from the muffled sound that more snow had fallen. My father and I re-counted our stored food and he reworked his calculations; his writing becoming smaller, filling in all the gaps on the map, so that undersized numbers even floated down the river.

'One thousand calories a day,' he said, more to himself than to me. 'Or eight hundred? There's no fat on a squirrel. How many calories in squirrel? Two hundred? Two hundred if we're lucky. Four squirrels a day each, for how long?' He threw down the pen and put his head in his hands. 'How can I work out how much food we need if we don't know what the date is?'

I stopped humming, my fingers still, on the keys.

My father looked up at me, his face white and drawn. 'It's not enough,' he said. Until that winter I had always thought my father had a solution for everything, that he had all the answers, but I learned soon enough that I was wrong.

We began rationing the food we had stored. Every day, packed into my father's boots, I trudged through the snow to check the traps, but many days I came back with my rucksack empty. I never lost the feeling of being watched, but I didn't see any more footprints except ours. When I stayed indoors, my father wore the boots down to the river to fish, standing with the falling snow coating his head and shoulders, until he said he could no longer see to cast. I wasn't sure which was worse: tramping through the cold and finding nothing, or sitting by the fire with all the food surrounding me and not being allowed to eat any of it.

Within a week or two, any remaining summer plumpness had gone. My father's face became gaunt and his ribs showed through his skin when he lifted up his shirt to wash his armpits in front of the stove. All I thought about was food and music. If my father had the boots and I was indoors, I used 'La Campanella' to measure the time from one meal to the next. I calculated that playing the piece sixty times from start to finish would take me through from breakfast to lunch. I ate my food in morsels, sipping at our thin stews – a few scraps of meat floating in grey water – licking the spoon clean between each mouthful. We had smoked the squirrels without removing their bones, simply crushing them with the hammer, and so at mealtimes the room was full of the sound of crunching bones as we ate everything in front of us.

We were always tired, always cold and hungry; it became difficult to remember a time when it had ever been any different. I thought less often about Ute and our old life, but sometimes a particular memory would pop up out of nowhere to remind me.

'Is it Christmas yet?' I said one day when I was plaiting my clotted hair into the coils which helped to warm my ears; it no longer needed sticks to keep it in place.

'Christmas! I hadn't even thought about it,' my father said, putting a log on the stove fire. 'It might have been and gone already or it might be Christmas next week.'

'But how will we know?' I whined.

'How about we decide that Christmas is tomorrow?' He jumped up, at once animated by the idea.

'Really? Tomorrow? But that means I missed my birthday,' I said.

'But it also means that today is Christmas Eve,' he said, laughing. He grabbed my hands and spun me around, crashing against the table, tool chest and bed. His excitement was infectious; I was amazed that it was so easy to name the days in any way we chose. My father sang:

'O Tannenbaum, o Tannenbaum,

Wie treu sind deine Blätter!'

'I haven't got you a present,' I said, my head spinning.

He thought for a second, then clapped his hands. 'Wait here and I'll get us both one.' He made me face the wall whilst he got ready, saying, 'It'll be the best present you've ever had.'

When he had gone, I sat on the bed, chewing my nails, worrying about how my father was too happy and how long it would be until his happiness left. And then I thought about food. And because it was Christmas, I thought about Christmas food. The rich smell of roasting meat; the fug of vegetable steam in Ute's kitchen; her smack on the back of my hand when I stole a piece of crisp, salty skin from the turkey, cooling on the blue and white serving plate which came out once a year; the gravy spooned over layers of white meat because it was too thick to pour; Brussels sprouts, boiled for so long I could squash them in a burst of bitterness between my tongue and the roof of my mouth. At that moment I would have eaten a whole pan of overcooked Brussels sprouts without complaint. I shut my eyes and tried to ignore the growls in my stomach. I tasted the fried oiliness of roast potatoes and the sweet crunch of undercooked carrots. Tears came when I remembered home-made trifle: soggy sponge fingers spread with raspberry jam – picking the pips out of my teeth later – set in a red jelly which my tongue washed through my mouth, transforming it back into liquid. Next, a layer of cold custard, gloopy and best swallowed in one gulp before there was time to think too long about the texture. And finally, the multicoloured sprinkles – leaching their colour into the whisked cream, like something bad spilled on to fresh snow. My spoon reached right to the bottom and, with the noise of a boot being pulled from wet mud, brought out a strata of Ute's trifle.

Half an hour later my father beat on the door of die Hütte.

'Surprise!' he called.

I opened it, and he stood there smiling, one arm around a tall fir tree, as if he were introducing me to a rather lanky girlfriend. Disappointment overwhelmed me.

'No, no, no!' I kicked at the door, so it swung towards him faster than I had intended and there was just time to register the shock on his face before he was shut out. I backed myself against the far wall as he shoved the door inwards, man-handling the tree into the room.

'What's wrong? What is it?' He pushed the fir into the corner beside the stove, where it leaned sideways, embarrassed at overhearing our family Christmas argument and trying to act as if it wasn't listening.

'I wanted a proper present, like normal children get.' Even whilst I said the words, I felt guilty.

'Oh, Punzel,' my father said, bending down to my height

and holding my shoulders, 'you knew there wouldn't be any other presents.'

'Or food. I don't want to eat stupid squirrel any more.' I reached up to bat one, but it was too high above my head. My father's eyes narrowed.

'You ought to be grateful to be alive.' He stood up and backed away from me.

'It's Christmas Eve. We should be eating Kartoffelsalat and Wiener!' I shouted. Tears were coming again.

'It's always about you, isn't it?'

'I want turkey and trifle.' I couldn't stop. 'I don't want a stupid Christmas tree.'

The tree slid sideways and thumped against the floor as though it were trying to avoid being dragged into giving its opinion.

'This is all there is,' my father shouted, his veins standing out on his bony temples. 'If you don't like it you can leave.' He held the door open and a swirl of snow came in.

'I'd rather live in the forest than here with you.' I ran to the door. I was only dressed for inside – jumper, dungarees, my three pairs of socks – and the cold in the doorway took my breath away. I hesitated.

'Wait, Ute!' My father reached out and grabbed my wrist.

We stopped like that, both of us taking in what he had just said. We were frozen in a tableau, me half out, my father pulling me back in. He let go of me and I came inside and shut the door. He sat on the edge of the bed and gave himself a kind of hug, wrapping his arms and hands around his shoulders and over his head. I picked up the tree and wedged it into the corner, pushing the buckets in front so that it wouldn't fall again.

'It's a lovely tree, Papa,' I said, looking down and flicking off water droplets where the snow had melted. I was overcome by a wave of homesickness brought on by the smell of the pine in the room. Facing the corner, I let my silent tears fall because Ute was dead and because my father was sitting on our bed crying too, for something I didn't understand.

We ate well that Christmas Eve: four squirrels in the pot with a handful of mushrooms and dried herbs, and a couple of bulrush roots baked in the stove.

'Sod the calculations,' said my father.

For two or three full moons after Christmas, we eked out the smoked and dried food, supplementing it with occasional wild finds. As our stores decreased, each meal was smaller than the previous one and I was always hungry. Our empty stomachs dragged us out of bed, muscles shivering. Borrowing my father's boots, I would clear the snow from the traps and reset them with clumsy fingers. Once or twice I came back with a rabbit, which we made last for days. We ate every bit except the fur. We even washed out the intestines and stomachs, and boiled them. 'Chitterlings' my father said they were called. When they had all gone and the pan had been scraped clean, we sipped at plain water, boiled in the same saucepan, my father trying to convince me that there would still be some goodness left. Until, one day, the only stored food remaining was four bulrush roots in the bottom of the tool chest. We cut them in half and found brown veins lacing through them, each with a grub inside. My father stumbled to the sluggish river to use the fat bugs for bait, but no fish came. We dug through the snow under the trees, looking for a frozen mushroom or two we might have missed, and scrabbled around where the bulrushes grew, searching for more roots. Under the snow, the earth was like rock, the trowel bouncing off it when we tried to dig. Every day we stayed out less and often came back with just a handful of pine needles, which we boiled into a tea and drank.

We stopped playing the piano or even singing and spent a lot of the day sleeping or lying in bed with all our clothes on, listening to the snow creak and stretch, waiting for it to fall from the roof. Sometimes I imagined a squirrel was playing up there, and I would go to the door, hoping to find another lying on the doorstep. I begged my father to let us eat the sprouting potatoes he had bought, or a pinch of the carrot or cabbage seed. Once, when he was out fishing, I searched die Hütte for them, going through all the pockets of the rucksacks and balancing on my tiptoes on a stool on top of the table, so I could see along the joists, but I didn't find them.

'We'll get through. Just wait,' he would say. 'We'll need those seeds when the spring comes.'

Hunger flowed over me in waves; bedtime was the worst, when I would feel that my stomach was devouring itself from the inside and I would sit up in bed, holding my cramping muscles, looking around the cabin for something I could eat. My father boiled anything he could think of: a putrid pap he collected by re-scraping the animal skins we had discarded and even once, in desperation, his leather belt. I sipped the foul liquid and lay back down on the bed, holding Phyllis's hard little body against mine.

Mornings were easier. When I woke I was always able to convince myself that this would be the day we would find food. I remembered when my father and I had sat at the top of the meadow and he had cut some cheese and given it to me with a hunk of brown bread. The cheese and the bread might still be hidden in the roots of the tree we had stopped to rest under. I made a plan to go and find it and packed my rucksack with Phyllis and a toothbrush, but when I stood at the edge of the river I realized that not even starvation could make me cross it.

Two mornings later, I woke to the scream of the wind, shrieking through the gaps in die Hütte, shaking and rattling the roof shingles and sending invisible icy streams across my face. Outside, the noise from the forest was of crashing and whipping, as if the trees were being uprooted and flying through the air. My father stirred beside me, mumbling something but not waking. I squeezed closer into his side and buried my head under my sleeping bag, trying and failing to ignore the sound of the storm. Finally, I wriggled my way out, scrambled over him and pulled the door open. It was only a chink, but frenzied snow blasted me in the face through the gap. It took the weight of my body to push the door closed. I shook my father's shoulder; he groaned, although his eyes remained shut.

'Papa, Papa, a blizzard! A blizzard has come.'

He moaned again, bringing his knees up to his chest inside his sleeping bag. 'I need to go to the loo,' he said. His breath was sour and the corners of his mouth cracked open when he spoke.

'I'll get you the bucket,' I said.

'Outside.' His voice was a whisper.

'You can't go outside, Papa, there's a blizzard.' I stroked his hair back from his sweaty forehead. Shivering, he pushed

155

his sleeping bag down and swung one leg and then the other off the bed. A rank smell rose from him as he moved, and I stepped backwards. He was wearing his cardigan and, over that, his dirty coat. He also had on his trousers with patches across the knees, and a pair of socks – nearly all his clothes except for the boots. I wondered how he had managed to get up in the night and put on everything without me hearing him.

The cabin was dark, but I could see the shape of him on the edge of the bed, doubled over, clutching his stomach. When the spasm had passed he said, 'Fetch me the rope, Punzel.'

The masses of the table and the stove loomed at me, but I found the bucket and took it to him, together with our loops of home-made rope, and put them on the floor in front of him. He had his head in his hands, and when he lifted them away I saw that in the night his eyes had shrunk back into purple sockets, or else the bones of his face had come forward, to press against his stretched skin.

'Tie the end of the rope on to the door handle and get me my boots,' he said.

I hoped he might already be feeling a little better if he had so many instructions for me. I did what I was told and he put the boots on. He leaned on me as he staggered up, and I was strong, full of a strange energy, my empty stomach forgotten.

'I have to go outside to use the loo,' he said.

'But the blizzard will come in if we open the door, Papa.'

'It's just windy. I'll be back in a moment. Quickly, help me.' We stumbled over to the door and he opened it. Outside, the snow was a snarling white beast, clawing and biting at our faces. It blasted straight through my dungarees and the jumper I had worn to bed.

'I don't mind if you use the bucket indoors.' I was sure going outside wasn't the right thing to do. 'Please, Papa, don't go.' I clung on to the back of his coat, but he shook me off.

He took hold of the rope and, turning back towards me, he said, 'You can eat the seed potatoes now. They're under a loose floorboard, near the stove,' and he stepped out into the storm.

The whipped-up snow stung my eyes, and after a couple of paces my father was a blurred grey shape and after three he was gone. The rope, attached to the door, spooled out slowly, stretched tight, then slackened. I couldn't bear to shut the door after him, so I stood in the opening, shivering, with my teeth chattering whilst snow blew inside, piling up and melting on the floor.

'Papa!' I called, but the wind flung the name of my father away. For a long time I stood at the door with the snow beating against me, grit in my eyes, the front of my jumper caked and stiff. Eventually, I shut it and went to the stove, stomping on the floor until I heard the rattle of a loose board. Tucked under it was a hessian bag full of wrinkled potatoes and the packets of seed that my father had brought with us. I looked at the pictures – carrots, cabbages, leeks, beans in garish colours – then I put them back in the bag, laid it under the floor and replaced the board. I shoved a log on to the embers of the previous evening's fire and moved a pot of snow water to the other side of the stove. I went to the bed and tidied our sleeping bags. I went back to the stove and moved the pot again. I bent to check the fire, but when

I straightened I couldn't remember if it needed another log or not. I went to the door and peeped out into the storm, shielding my eyes. There was just wind and blasting snow. The rope was still slack.

'He'll return in a minute,' Phyllis said, but muffled, because she was under the covers.

'By the time I get the rest of my clothes on, he'll be back,' I said to her. I put on my anorak, balaclava and mittens, which were kept warming on a nail above the stove. I got Phyllis out and together we sat on the edge of the bed, watching the door. I pulled on my shoe and the shingle-bag. 'Wait here,' I told her, and I went out into the snow after my father.

The noise of the storm was a tremendous roar, a shriek of fury. I crouched low, my face down and my arm across my eyes. Each breath was an effort. With my mittened hands I held the rope, the whipped snow freezing the wool, so my fingers became fixed into the shape of hooks. Doubled over, I shuffled along, hand over hand. The end of the rope tapered to the thickness of string and, as I reached it, the wind almost whisked it away from me. My father was not there. I looped the rope twice around my hand.

'Papa!' I called again and again into the white noise, but my words were taken so quickly, I wasn't even sure I had said them aloud. As if playing Blind Man's Buff, I stretched out from the end of the rope as far as I could, groping for someone I couldn't see. I prodded the drifts around me, terrified the rope would unwind from my fist and I, too, would be lost. Without the rope, I might crawl back in the direction I thought was right and miss die Hütte by inches.

Using the rope to guide me, I circumscribed the snow for

a shape, a sign to show that my father had been there. And then I nearly tripped over him. Hunched like a rock, with his head and arms tucked underneath, my father was white, snow piling up against the sides of his body. I brushed it off his head.

'Papa! Please!' I cried into his ear, my voice shaking, desperate. 'Take hold of the rope.'

'Ute?' He lifted his head from his white pillow.

'Papa!' I tugged again and again at the collar of his icy coat until he got to his knees. I saw that his trousers were undone and drooped around his hips. The flesh on his bottom hung slack and empty. I looked away. 'Take the rope,' I repeated.

Hand over hand, we crawled forward as if we were following a trail of breadcrumbs. Finally the shape of die Hütte came out of the white – solid, substantial. I pushed my father through the door. Outside the storm howled its frustration. I shook the worst of the snow from our clothes and with effort got my father back on to the bed and laid the sleeping bags over him. I stoked the fire and made a pan of pine needle tea. As I held the mug to his lips, I could taste the thick tomato soup that Ute used to spoon-feed me when I was ill in bed, and the sharp tang of it rasped the back of my throat. There was nothing else to give my father, so I lay behind him, trying to warm his body with mine.

I lost track of how many days or nights we lay there, but on the last of them, whilst the blizzard blew itself out, I dreamed of Ute's Apfelkuchen, plump and warm. I woke to a phantom smell of cinnamon and apples, which teased me out of bed to check inside the stove and sniff in each of our pans to find the source. I could still smell it when I opened the door to determine whether it was carried on the wind, only to find that the snow was receding and a brown forest reappearing around us.

I checked on my father, who was still sleeping, put on his boots and went out into the new day. I walked between the trees and they parted to allow me access. At each trap, I bent or stretched on legs that I thought might not bear my weight for much longer. I trudged up to the wintereyes, making fresh tracks on my usual paths. I rested there, trying to ignore the hollowed-out feeling inside me. When I removed my mittens and held my hands up in front of my face, my fingers shook. I curled up on the hard ground and imagined I was a small animal, a rabbit in its burrow, a hedgehog in a pile of leaves, a downy blackbird in its nest, and I shut my eyes, thinking that if I could sleep, when I woke, everything would either be better or just be gone. Instead of her cake, I dreamed of Ute. She was swimming in the Great Divide. She floated in the blackness, her pale body lit by the moon, and gave a little flick of her legs, which had become a fish's tail. There was a steady drip as the Great Divide filled up, and I knew that, soon, Ute would swim away. The water rose higher and there was a flash of iridescent scales and then only Ute's face until a wave took her. The noise of the water woke me, and I saw that the snow was melting and dripping from the trees.

Instead of returning, I followed the footprints of an animal, a wolf or a fox, that had trotted along one of the mountain trails. It took me in a loop around the back of die Hütte, but not as high as where we had flown the kite in the summer. When I could look down on the rock forest far below me, I came across mounds of heather tucked amid the south-facing boulders; perhaps the stony overhangs above had protected them from the snow, because they were flowering – purple bells studded the twiggy stalks. An insect had found the plant before I had and amongst the blooms had laid its grubs in gobs of spittle. I picked one up and, without inspecting it, put it in my mouth and swallowed it whole. The next one I bit down on. There was an instant, like eating an overripe berry, when the flesh gave way with a burst of thick liquid. It tasted of almonds. I ate the larvae until I was full. The rest I plucked from the heather, put in my pockets and ran back to die Hütte, slipping and sliding down the icy mountain.

16.

As the food came back to us, so did the music, as though the fish and the squirrels and the green buds of spring nourished not only our bodies but our minds too. I read 'La Campanella' like a book I couldn't put down; one that, in the end, I was able to recite by heart.

In the lighter evenings my father worked with the rabbit and squirrel skins to make me a pair of moccasins. They were warm and dry, but it took him many goes to get the curing process right. We no longer noticed the smell of our bodies, the unwashed stink of our clothes or the reek of our hair, but the rotting animal odour of the first few pairs of skin shoes my father made was truly disgusting. At night I often left them outside die Hütte and fell asleep thinking of the leaping cat on the back of my missing shoe, jumping off on its own dangerous journey towards the Great Divide.

My father and I settled into a routine: a pattern of rising at daybreak; an hour or two of work – chopping wood, collecting kindling; breakfast; an hour of piano; my father's trek to the river and back up for fresh water; gathering food and eating it if we were successful; an hour or two of free time; more work and food and piano; and when the sun set we'd get ready for bed. The rhythm of our days cocooned me, reassured and comforted me. I slipped into it without thought, so that the life we lived – in an isolated cabin on a crust of land, with the rest of the world simply wiped away, like a damp cloth passed across a chalked blackboard – became my unquestioned normality.

My father created a vegetable garden in front of the cabin, carrying bucketfuls of the rich forest soil and digging it into the earth. As soon as the ground was warm enough, we planted the seeds and the seed potatoes, in neat rows. Every morning my father asked for rain so that he wouldn't need to make so many trips down to the river, and every evening I asked if the vegetables were big enough to eat yet. We fought a constant battle with the birds and the rabbits and deer, which were drawn to the young green shoots of our first plants. In the following years, my father built a fence around the garden and we made complicated devices, involving trip-wire and stones which fell into tin cups, to scare the animals away from our precious crops.

In my free time I continued to map the forest and the mountains. I explored every spot; there wasn't a tree that I hadn't stroked or stood beneath, gazing up into its canopy and making myself dizzy with the sky passing by. Like a big cat in a zoo, I paced out my territory in the half-hour's walk from the riverbank to the sides of the mountain that protected die Hütte in the curve of its hand. I sat on boulders, looking down on our cabin or across the river to the edge of the world, my stomach churning at the thought of the black void that lay over the hill.

On the far side of the forest, towards the gill, I built a secret place. I bent thin saplings into an arch, weaving and tying them together. I interlaced these with reeds and sticks, and laid fresh ferns over the top so that my father could have walked past and not noticed my green bower. Inside, it curved over the top of my head when I sat upright, but most of the time I lay on more ferns covered with moss that I had prised from the rocks. I stretched out on my back, with my head sticking out of the opening, watching an upside-down world of branches and leaves and blue sky. I was a weaver bird and it was my nest.

One morning, as spring changed to summer, I woke with 'La Campanella' singing in my head. The room was still dark – just a dim light shone around the edge of the window, which we had unblocked and covered again with tent canvas. I had dreamed of the music and a bird, tapping with its beak on a windowpane. It had cocked its head and peered at me sideways, its eye ringed in blackbird yellow.

I had been struggling with the last musical notes on page five, where a fermata hung over a rest. My father had explained that the symbol meant that my fingers could pause for as long as I pleased. I had played it over and over but was never satisfied. I was cross with Ute and with Liszt for not giving clear instructions on how to play it, for leaving the decision up to me. In the grey-blue light of early morning, I needed to read the music and I needed to do it immediately. I climbed over the sleeping bulk of my father. It was still too dark to see the notes on the page; even putting a new log on the fire didn't cast enough light for me to be able to sit at the table and play.

Above the stove, melted on to a shelf, was the stub of our last candle. My father specified when we were allowed to light a candle; it turned out that it wasn't just emergencies after all. On Christmas evening, when we said something approaching a prayer for all those who had died, we had lit one. And we had stuck one in the middle of our joint birthday cake, made from mashed bulrush roots. Although my birthday was in wintertime, we had picked a warm spring day to celebrate it and I was allowed to blow the candle out and make a wish. It was a wasted wish; I had asked to have a chocolate cake with buttercream icing for my next birthday. And one night, my father had lit another candle when we had heard scrabbling noises coming from the tool chest full of food and had suspected rats. The light from the candle had flickered when he chased a shrew around the cabin and out the door. Another time, I was sick in the night and missed the bucket, and there had been numerous other incidents and accidents when he had decided that a candle was necessary. Now we had one stump remaining.

For me, that morning, the need to read the music was as urgent as any of the other occasions that had required light. I pulled at the candle, snapping it from the shelf, and lit it from a feathery twig that I poked into the fire. I melted a drop of wax on to the piano table and stuck the candle in it. I propped open 'La Campanella' and sat at the piano, humming the trills under my breath in the guttering light. The next moment I heard a roar, as if a bear were standing on its hind legs behind me, its claws raised, ready to fight.

'Punzel!' the bear shouted.

I cowered on the stool, cringing and waiting for the bloody slash of a claw across my back.

'What the hell are you doing?'

The candle stuttered and went out.

'Candles are for emergencies,' he yelled. 'What is it that you don't understand about living here? Once this candle,' he yanked it off the table and shoved it in my face, 'has gone, there are no more. No more. Do you understand?'

The smoke from the dead wick made my eyes water.

'Do you understand?'

I nodded. 'I'm sorry, Papa,' I said. 'I was just trying to work out a trill. I didn't think about it.' The tears were welling; they would overflow with my next blink.

'That's your trouble – you never bloody think.' He stormed about the room, making it even smaller. 'I knew I shouldn't have brought you with me. You're too much of a liability. I should have let you die like the rest of them.'

I took the corner of the front cover and closed the music, a pain in my chest at the reminder that we had been spared.

'You don't deserve to be here, wasting things without thinking. If there was only going to be two of us, it should have been me and Ute.' He whipped around, but I couldn't bear to look at his purple face. I pulled on a moccasin as quietly as I could. He saw and he shouted, 'Yes, just go! Get out of my sight. Don't come back until you've thought about wasting things for your own pleasure and gratification.'

I pulled on my other shoe, grabbed my anorak and ran out into the morning. I ran across the clearing, leaving tracks in the dewy grass and skidding under the cover of the trees. I ran along the deer tracks into the forest until the ferns and the cow parsley grew up around me and I was running blind. Without thinking, I found myself at my nest and I crawled inside. My legs were bare and cold. I lay curled on the damp moss until the sun came over the mountain and found its way in through the gaps in the twigs and leaves, creating shadows that waved over me. I stretched out on to my stomach, my head propped in my hands, and let the tears dry on my cheeks whilst I stared out of the entrance into the forest.

That's when I saw the boots, ankles, thick socks. They strode past my hidden doorway with a purpose. They knew where they were going. Blood pounded in my throat, but my body was frozen in place. In two or maybe three paces they were gone from my view and I wasn't sure that I had seen them at all. I let my breath out, very quietly, very slowly. I lay in the same position for a long time until my bony hips ached against the hard ground and the damp seeped into my joints. I sat up. The boots I had seen go past were not my father's.

His I knew well, his I still often wore when the weather was bad. These were black and had come up higher around the ankle and had more laces and rounded toes. They were splattered with mud and looked wet, as though the person wearing them had waded across the river. Folded over the top had been cream-coloured socks and, striding in them, a pair of muscled legs. A man's boots, I said to myself; definitely a man's boots. Reuben's boots. The thought thrilled and terrified me. I had been told over and over that all that was left was a scrap of land floating in the dark of the Great Divide, so this man couldn't just be passing through. Instead of two, there were three.

After maybe an hour of hiding in the nest, looking out, waiting in case the boots came back, I needed a wee, I needed to eat, I needed to go back to die Hütte and warn my father that we were not alone. I shuffled to the opening and stuck my head out, looking right and left along the forest tracks; they were empty. The ground wasn't wet enough for the boots to have left any prints. I came out and scuttled into the ferns which huddled over me, where I squatted to pee, splashing over feet and ankles. I was a sparrow in a bush with one eye on a worm, the other on the bird of prey circling overhead. Through the undergrowth I went, avoiding the paths until I could see die Hütte in the clearing. I raced across it, like I had the previous winter, head down, feeling exposed and vulnerable. The cabin was empty. I sat on the edge of the bed and picked at my fingernails and ate the food my father had left straight from the pan. Eventually, I heard him whistling outside and the door opened. He came in with two buckets of water sloshing over his boots.

'Papa!' I jumped up from the bed, breathless, wanting to get everything out at once. 'I saw a man –'

My father interrupted me. 'I don't want to hear anything from you today.' He held his hand up in a stop sign, palm towards my face.

'But, I saw –'

'No.' He cut over me again, his hand still out but now with only his index finger pointing skywards. 'Nothing,' he said forcibly, as if he had been thinking about my punishment all morning. 'There will be no playing the piano today. No singing. Today you will work and you will say nothing.'

I sat down on the bed, my news spoiled. After a moment's thought, I clamped my lips together and went to the corner by the stove and picked up the axe. I carried it outside with the sharpening stone. I was powerful with the tool in my hands and angry enough with my father to use it. I stroked the blade with the stone until the sun caught its edge. I placed a small log on the block, as my father and I had done last autumn, and holding the axe shaft halfway down, I lifted it over my head and let its weight slam into the wood. The little log split clean in two.

★

The boots never passed by my nest again, or at least I never saw them. Our second summer in die Hütte was even hotter than the first. My father worried about everything that year: forest fires, not enough rain for the vegetables, missing the acorn harvest again. But we doubled our autumn stores, cramming the shelves with dried and smoked food, and even though the snow was heavy and the winter cold, it was never as desperate as our first.

As I grew and the years blended one into the next, there was a rhythm to our lives; we let the seasons and the weather dictate when the seeds should be planted, when the acorns should be gathered and when to celebrate birthdays and Christmas. I still sometimes thought of Omi, and if she were alive to knit her winter gifts, how grateful I would be for them in the forest. The thoughts of her and Ute no longer caused a sting of pain inside me, but instead a bittersweet memory.

When each long winter had passed, my father sometimes decided on an activity that would consume him like constructing the piano had once done. One spring, he worked on diverting the gill so we would have a stream running past the cabin. For weeks he levered boulders with branches and dug in the rocky ground, but when the next storm came the mountain ignored all his efforts and carried on channelling water where it had always done – down the gill. When these plans and schemes failed, my father would sink into despondency for days, until another idea came to him and he was excited all over again. Keeping up with his moods made me irritable, but sometimes when I was alone in the forest I would think about Becky – what she had smelled like, how she had sounded, what she might have said to make things better: 'You ought to be happy. You won't know how happy you are, till your pretty life in die Hütte is over and done with.'

17.

On my bed, Ute had laid out a purple top and a skirt for me to change into – three tiers of fabric with white dots sprinkled across them, and each finished off with a circle of lace. They might have been selected by a fourteen-year-old shop assistant.

When I had arrived back in London, Ute had bought me new sets of everything. She went shopping without me, leaving Mrs Cass downstairs, flicking through a magazine in the sitting room whilst I sat by the open window in my bedroom. I had tried to imagine the two of them becoming friends, sharing confidences and mopping up tears, but the images wouldn't stick.

Mrs Cass had, of course, been too curious to stay downstairs. Later, I overheard her saying to Ute that she thought she had heard me crying, but I knew that wasn't true. She had poked her head around my bedroom door, in her hands two cups of tea.

'Do you mind if I come in?' she said in a stage whisper but she was already through the door. She hadn't altered since I had last seen her that day at school; she might have been born plump and grey-haired. Her lipstick was too red and her eye shadow had settled into the folds of skin across her eyelids. She tried to hide her shock at what she saw – the wound dressing still covering my ear, my stubble hair – but I caught the look on her face before she changed it to one of sympathy. 'I thought you might need some company,' she said.

I had shifted my furniture around, pushing the bed and the chest of drawers towards the door and moving the desk so I could open the window. I needed to lean out over the glasshouse and garden, towards the cemetery, to breathe in the smell of trees and green and the cool air of autumn. It took an effort to bring myself back into the room and face someone new.

'You look so like your mother, it's uncanny, even with your short hair,' Mrs Cass said. For some reason she seemed unsure what to do with the tea, and rather than pass me a cup, she sat on the edge of the bed and balanced them both on her knees. 'It must be nice to be back in your own bed,' she said.

'I had my own bed in die Hütte, in the cabin,' I said.

'Of course, but it's not the same as being home, is it? With all your old things about you.'

The two of us looked around the room – the books kept by Ute but too childish for me now; the empty wardrobe, waiting for Ute's return; the chest of drawers with its row of teddy bears and dolls on top, from which Phyllis was forever absent; and, across every surface and taped to the walls, the notes and cards welcoming me home. An uncle I had never met wrote me a long letter about the importance of family, a neighbour had put a postcard of a cat through the letterbox and said I could drop in any time, and children from the school I never went back to had drawn me pictures. And then there were the letters not on display, those that Ute tried to tear up before I could read them: complete strangers offering me their spare rooms in return for unspecified favours; people who wanted to write my life story; and others, assuming I had already sold it, asking for money. All of the things around us belonged to a different person, someone whose bedroom I had temporarily taken over until I could return to the forest.

Mrs Cass lifted the cups off her knees and we both saw that the bottoms had left circular marks on her skirt. 'And you'll have a whole new wardrobe when your mother gets home.' She looked at the clothes I was wearing: the checked skirt I'd been given, which I'd grown fond of but was still held around my waist by safety pins; and a blouse and cardigan that Ute had selected from her own wardrobe, both far too big. 'Teenage girls always find new clothes exciting. I know my granddaughter does – she's about your age – Kirsty, always down the shops buying something new. I'm sure she'd be happy to take you, when you're feeling a bit more up to it.'

I couldn't imagine ever feeling up to it. She rambled on, and I let my mind drift away, remembering the anorak I had left behind and my father's boots that I would never see again. Someone must have thrown them away without realizing how precious they had been to me, how much more cherished than all the things I had returned to. Only the balaclava remained, hand-washed and line-dried, hidden under my pillow. It was the one thing I had brought home, and Ute had allowed me to keep it.

'There must have been plenty of things you had to do without, though. I just can't imagine it, all those years alone in the wilderness.' Mrs Cass shook her head.

'It wasn't the wilderness and I wasn't alone,' I said.

She made a dismissive noise. 'That man. I never thought I'd say this about someone, Peggy, but maybe he deserved what happened. He took you away from your family, from the people who love you. It was wrong, Peggy. He was a bad man.' She stood up, the cups still in her hands.

'I didn't mean my father.' I turned back towards the window and leaned out over the sill, suddenly desperate for air.

I don't know what Mrs Cass thought I was about to do, but, alarmed, she cried out, 'Peggy!' and came towards me.

I was afraid she might touch me. I tried to take a breath, but my lungs wouldn't fill. 'I just need air,' I said, panting. 'There isn't any air in this house.' I grabbed at the window catch and we both heard the front door open and Ute shout something into the road. The door slammed.

'Yoo-hoo,' she called from the hall.

I couldn't catch my breath and the ends of my fingers tingled. Mrs Cass looked stricken, and she cast her eyes around the room as if she thought climbing into the wardrobe or hiding under the bed might be a good idea.

Ute appeared in the doorway, laden with shopping bags.

'That reporter is still outside,' she said, concentrating on squeezing between the furniture which blocked the doorway. It wasn't until she was past the chest of drawers that she saw Mrs Cass. 'Angela,' she said, surprised, but when she looked at me she dropped the shopping and clambered over the bed so that she could hold the sides of my head and make me breathe in time with her. We counted to five, in and out, until my breathing slowed.

'I was just seeing if Peggy would like a cup of tea,' Mrs Cass said, holding the cups out as proof.

'Peggy takes her tea black,' said Ute without turning around.

'Well, perhaps I'd better get off.' Mrs Cass and Ute manoeuvred past each other. 'Remember, Peggy,' Mrs Cass said, 'whenever you want that shopping trip with Kirsty, just let me know. It won't be any trouble.'

Ute had filled the wardrobe and drawers with my new clothes. She had guessed at the size of my waist and breasts and feet, but now, two months later, the skirts and trousers she had chosen were already too small.

I ignored the clothes she had left out on my bed and looked inside the wardrobe. I flicked the hangers and then opened the chest of drawers and rummaged through jumpers, T-shirts and jeans. Just like the toys and books, none of them were mine. Wearing the same dress I had put on that morning, I went back downstairs.

18.

One summer I found Phyllis lying face down in the dust under the bed I still shared with my father. I hooked her out with the broom. Her nylon hair stood up from her head in a tangle as if she had been struck by lightning, and she was naked apart from her painted black shoes, so I could trace the seams where her plastic body had been fused together in the mould that made her. The colour of her rosebud mouth was garish, and her eyebrows were crooked from where I had drawn them on when I was younger. I didn't understand how I had ever thought she was beautiful. I sat her on one of the shelves next to the stove.

I had other things to do than play with dolls. That year, the sunny days had started early – when I planted the carrot seeds – and it stayed warm right through to when I pulled up the first little finger-sized sticks of sweetness, which I ate with my back to die Hütte and my hand in front of my mouth. Everything about the heat irritated me: the flies which came into the cabin and wouldn't leave; the mosquito bites in the middle of my back I couldn't reach; the noise in my father's throat when he swallowed a cup of water; and the ants that marched along the shelves to our honey store. I swiped a fingertip through their advancing army, stopping the queue in its tracks, until the ants found another route. I watched them for a while and then picked through the stuff Phyllis sat with. We never threw anything away: the pen with its insides written clean; my father's compass – broken when he had dropped it in a bucket of water; the last pieces of the map, written and rewritten on, until there was no green left; the rusty spyglass; our toothbrushes – hairless sticks; and the empty tubes of toothpaste which we had sliced open summers ago and licked clean. I picked one up and sniffed it. In the corner of the folded metal was a memory of mint. In an instant I was back in a proper bathroom, in front of an open medicine cabinet, packed with a jumble of bottles and tubes; a grown-up's cupboard I had been forbidden to look in. Ute called my name from downstairs, and I swung the mirrored door shut, bringing my guilty, eight-year-old eyes into view. At night, in die Hütte, I would sometimes let my fingers wander over my features, the bump in my nose, the jutting cheekbones like my father's. Once, I took a full bucket of water into the daylight and looked down on its surface, but with the sun behind me only my silhouette was cast back – a thicket of dark hair over scrawny shoulders. I longed for a mirror.

My father was fond of saying, 'If you own too many possessions, sooner or later they start owning you.' So I had to make do with 'treasures' I had collected: rocks from the river in the shape of horses' heads; a fistful of crumbling flowers, dead within a day of picking because we didn't have a spare water container; jay and magpie feathers; a crisp snakeskin; pine cones of different sizes lined up like an opened Russian doll; acorn cups for a miniature tea party; a bird's nest lined with downy feathers and full of speckled eggshells which I had found cracked, under the wintereyes. Only Phyllis reminded me that once I'd had a different life from this one. I kneeled in front of the shelves, sorting through a pile of flints my father thought we could sharpen into spearheads. Every autumn he still hoped we would catch a deer. I took a flint and, crouching beside the stove, gouged 'Punzel' into the wood of the wall beside the word 'Reuben' that I had found all those years ago.

'What are you up to?' asked my father, coming in and setting down buckets of water.

'Nothing,' I said, jumping up, holding the flint behind my back.

'You should do your piano practice,' he said, as if he had been thinking about it whilst he walked up from the river. 'It's been a long time since I've heard you play.'

'It doesn't matter. It's not as though I'm going to be a concert pianist, is it?' I said.

My father looked over at me as he scooped water with the billycan. 'That's not the point. It's about commitment. Saying you're going to do something and then doing it. It's the worst kind of person who goes back on a promise, even one they made to themselves.'

'I never promised, and anyway there's no point.'

On the shelves, the ants were back in the honey.

'Come on.' My father pulled out the stool from under the table and nodded at it.

'If I were a concert pianist I would have something nice to wear,' I said, my arms folded. 'And I would be able to see what I looked like. If we didn't live in this horrible dirty house with ants in the food, then everything . . .' I trailed off.

'Sit,' he said. He moved a wooden bowl with the remains of breakfast crusted around the edge.

'I hate living here. I wish it would all burn.'

'Play!' He picked up the stool and thumped it down.

'I wish I was dead!' I shouted at him, my head pushing forward.

'Sit down!' my father bellowed, and slammed his fist on the piano table.

The wooden keys jumped and rattled against each other. I sat heavily, my hands in my lap, my head down, jaw clamped. He snatched up the bowl and threw it hard towards the wall. It bounced off the stove pipe and on to a shelf, scattering acorns across the floor.

I slammed the flint down on to the table, spread my fingers into claws and jabbed at the keys, growling. I stabbed at them again and again, making sounds no human should be able to make. Just as suddenly the anger left me and my fingers found the familiar comforting pattern of 'La Campanella', but after a moment they paused, and instead re-formed themselves into a different shape and I played 'Oh Alaya Bakia', humming it to myself. I couldn't remember the last time we had sung it. I made up some new words: 'In the forest there are trees, oh alaya bakia.'

And without hesitation my father, from behind me, sang, 'Deer and wolves that no one sees,' and we both laughed and the sour feeling which had filled die Hütte left.

After a few false starts, I added, 'There's no suitor left for me, oh alaya bakia.'

There was a pause whilst my father thought, and in a rush he sang, 'Still it's better to be free,' and laughed again. 'Hang on,' he said as I started to play the whole thing through. He snatched a stick of burnt wood from the fire and wrote our new verse on the wall above the piano table. We sang the whole song together, as loud as we could, until the sound

179

filled the cabin. I imagined the music bursting out of the door, bouncing off the mountain, flying over the river, spreading out through the trees on the other side and even crossing the Great Divide. If there was anyone else out there in all that blackness, a solitary note might flit through infinity and land on a shoulder to find its way inside that person's head.

I gave myself to the music as if it possessed me, consumed me, letting the tune go off in a different direction, my fingers running up and down the clunking keys. Singing with me in harmony, my father drew five long horizontal lines on the wall in front of the piano table, the treble clef, and five more lines below with the bass clef curled upon them.

'Key? What's the key?' he asked frantically, seemingly worried that if he didn't put it down fast enough it would be gone.

I stared at him.

'What key is it in? How many sharps, how many flats?' he continued.

'I don't know. I'm just playing.' It was like shouting over the roar the river made after the winter thaw, but speaking stopped my music. 'It just came out,' I said, slumping on the stool.

My father sagged too. We looked at the empty bars he had scrawled. The lines jumped and wobbled where the charcoal had followed the grain of the wood. They were unequal distances apart and sloped at such an alarming angle that any notes placed upon them would have tumbled downwards, bumping into each other until they formed a heap of sticks and balls at the bottom. My father rubbed the back of his arm across the charcoal, smudging the lines, turning the wall and his arm grey. He lifted the knife from his belt and scored the lines into the full length of the plank. He did the same to the plank below and the one above, carrying on up the wall as high as he could stretch. I sat and watched, fluttering my fingers in a trill, on the keys.

'OK, play it again.' My father listened with his head cocked.

He tried to catch the first few notes, scribbling them down on to the wall, but he couldn't keep up with my playing and singing as the music ran away with me again. In the end he sat on the bed and watched. This time I just kept going, singing and singing, until I stopped playing, picked up the piece of charcoal and leaned across the piano. I hesitated; I could play my scales and read 'La Campanella', but it was another thing entirely to translate the music in my head to black notes on a wooden wall.

My father came over and took the piece of charcoal from my hand. He drew notes until the stick broke. He filled up the bars with a music that he had in his head, and it was my turn to sit and stare. I fetched him another stick and he carried on filling up the wall with lines and dots, music that I couldn't follow, sounds that jumped and scratched and weren't music at all. I replaced him on the bed, watching the sweat trickle down his face whilst he drew manically, rubbing out, rewriting each note until the whole wall above the piano became grey. I bit my nails, worrying about the noise trapped inside his head.

I fell asleep to the scratch of charcoal on wood and my father's snatches of melody. When I woke in the night with him sleeping beside me in the airless room, I climbed over him, my old nightie sticking to me, and stood on the rug. The door was still open, and the light from a full moon illuminated the walls of die Hütte – all of them filled with notes, unintelligible words, lists, lines and arrows connecting passages, as if I stood inside the pages of 'La Campanella', rewritten by a manic hand.

Outside, our world was still, scented with warm vegetation and a trace of stove smoke. The moon showed the trees and the mountain and the grass in muted shades of their daylight colours. At the back of die Hütte I crouched over our toilet hole to pee. When I wiped myself there was a smear of dark blood across the moss. I held it up to the moon to get a better look, frightened that something had cut me between my legs without me knowing. At the same time I smelled the smoke again and understood in a rush which made my heart falter that the smell of smoke wasn't coming from die Hütte but from the trees. I walked towards the rock forest at the back of the clearing, sniffing, trying to follow the smell with my nose, but it had drifted away. Without warning, two huge rushing shapes jumped out from the trees, bounding in great leaps. I cried out, but just as soon as I realized they were deer, they had crossed the clearing and were gone into the forest on the other side. Then the smell came again, faint, but distinctive. Burning.

Dropping the moss, I turned and ran back to the cabin, aware of wetness between my legs, under my nightie.

'Fire!' I shouted as I ran. My father had rolled over on to his back but hadn't woken. I shook his shoulder. 'Fire!' I shouted into his face. He had black smudges across his forehead and I saw that his hands and his chest, too, were sooty.

He cracked open his eyes. 'It's the stove, Punzel,' he said, his words slurred with sleep. 'Come back to bed.'

'No, there's a fire in the forest. I smelled it.' I pulled the cover off him and saw that he was still wearing his trousers and socks. He sat up, yawning. I pulled on his hand to try to give him some urgency. The black rubbed off on mine.

'OK, OK,' he said. He was still pulling on his boots whilst I already had my moccasins on and was hopping in front of him, trying to hurry him up. We went outside and stood in the clearing where the land rose, our noses lifted, breathing in, and the smell came again. 'How full are the buckets?' he said.

'I don't know; one full perhaps, the other half full.'

'Get the spade.' I watched his face as he spoke, and in the moonlight I thought I saw the flicker of a smile cross it before he said, 'I'll bring the water.'

The dark line of trees was two dimensional, a silhouette, but we knew our way in. I walked behind my father into the forest, carrying the spade. It might have been like old times, but the man's back I followed was thinner, less jaunty. I imagined the bird's nest on the shelves in die Hütte crackle from a lick of flame which curled around the feathers, turning them brown, crumbling them to ash. The toothbrushes buckled and melted, dripping off the shelf, and Phyllis's hair fizzled and lit up around her head like a halo. I thought about going back to die Hütte and scooping all I could carry into my arms and running with it down to the river – horse-head stones in my pockets and pine cones tucked into my hair. But in my imagination I saw myself stop at the water's edge and look down into the dark, unable to go any further.

I carried on walking behind my father. 'What are we going to do, Papa?' I said.

The bitter smell in the air was stronger now, I could taste it, too, harsh in the back of my throat, but whatever we were walking towards was silent; the only noises from the forest were the sticks snapping under our feet. He didn't answer.

Where the trees thinned, scrubby bushes and grasses had claimed the ground but were dry from the weeks without rain. My father stopped and I came up beside him. The moonlight filtered through the trees, which cast long shadows, but in front of us I could see puffs of smoke rising from the ground, the earth smouldering. Whilst we watched, a flame flared up, illuminating the forest litter, consuming a fern and dying away. I looked further into the trees – the ground as far as I could see was smoking.

'Where's the fire?' I said.

'Under the leaves,' said my father in a whisper, and my feet inside my moccasins seemed hotter.

I stepped backwards. My father put one bucket down and threw the water from the other in an arc towards where the flame had erupted from the ground. The soil hissed and steam billowed. He threw the water from the other bucket in the opposite direction, with the same effect.

'Will that work, Papa? Will we be all right?' I wanted him to say that it would be fine, that we could go back to bed and in the morning we would wake up to have another normal day weeding the vegetable patch and going down to the river to fish. If he told me we could return to die

Hütte, I promised myself I would never complain about not having enough water, but again he ignored me. 'Should we go back now, Papa?' I tugged on his sleeve. 'Please let's go back. We could get more water.' As I said it, I realized how hopeless that would be, how far away the river was, and even if we could carry more, we only had two buckets – three if you counted the one tied up to the tree on the bank. For a long time my father stood watching and thinking, with me hopping around him, trying to get his attention or an answer, a plan. The smoke puffed closer. When I glanced over my shoulder, the trees were fading, blurred with grey.

'Pass me the spade, Punzel,' he said. I handed it to him. He thrust it into the ground and lifted out a pile of smouldering leaves. Fire leaped from the small pit at his feet and he moved back, to stand beside me. I could feel the heat and, whilst I watched, a stick lying across our path lit up, a tongue of fire passing along its length and jumping sideways on to other plants, the flames licking outwards. My father let the spade fall from his hand and in an automatic reaction I caught the handle before it fell into the fire. At the same time, my father grabbed my wrist and squeezed it tight, holding it towards the flames. I cried out and dropped the tool.

'Leave it,' he said. 'We don't need it any more.'

The spade lay on the earth, and the orange flames crept around it. For two seconds my father held my arm out over the fire – offering me up, whilst I struggled to get away from the heat. Then he let go of me and I backed away, rubbing my wrist.

'Yes,' he said, 'more water.' His voice was monotone, his

words drawn out. He picked up the buckets and turned back the way we had come.

I stared after him, trying to make sense of what had just happened. I looked back at the spade in the fire but its handle had already blackened whilst, ahead, my father swung the buckets as though he were on a stroll down to the river. I had no option but to follow him.

When we reached the clearing, my father went into die Hütte, but I hung back, staring into the dark trees, unsure about whether I could see a low flicker of fire. A lesson from school came back to me: a cartoon where a cat called Charlie had told us in a squeaky voice not to play with matches, and a talk afterwards by a real fireman about fire needing three things to burn – fuel, air and something else. I wished I had listened more rather than messing about with Becky.

I remembered a phrase – fire break – a circle around die Hütte that the fire couldn't cross. I fetched the trowel from the vegetable garden and tried to dig a shallow channel around the back of the cabin, but the ground was solid from where our feet had tramped across it and it was difficult to get anything more than the point of the trowel into the earth. I stopped and realized that the furrow I was cutting was too close to the wooden walls; if the fire reached it, the sparks would simply leap across. I went closer to the trees and started to work at the ground in a different place, digging the trowel in and tossing spoonfuls of soil behind me. The earth was softer but, just below the surface, a tangle of roots snagged and impeded me. Still I kept hacking and sobbing, glancing into the forest and back at die Hütte, hoping to see my father reappear. I dug with desperation, scraping at the earth, chopping at the roots with the side of the trowel. My palms grew blisters, which popped. I sat back, defeated. 'Papa!' I cried, but he didn't come. Throwing down the trowel, I kneeled on the ground and scrabbled with my hands at the earth between the roots. When I glanced around again, my father was standing a foot or two behind me, silent, clasping a bucket to his chest. In a crab-like motion, I scrabbled backwards across the ground, frightened by how he had appeared without me noticing. 'Did you get more water?' I said.

'Punzel, I've been thinking,' he replied, crouching down, so our eyes were level.

I saw that the bucket was crammed with things from die Hütte – a ball of twine, our tin plates, the hammer and other tools, with acorns rattling around loose – and I thought he must have had the same idea as me: to save everything he could.

'Perhaps it's time to let it go.' He spoke calmly. Tucked under his arm was a roll of animal skins.

'Let what go?' I scrabbled further backwards across the loose earth, my nightie getting dirtier, but he shuffled closer on his haunches. His face was dark, the sky behind him the colour of tracing paper.

'All of it.'

'We just need to get some water.'

'We don't need any of this stuff.' He pulled out the twine and tossed the ball away into the trees, where it unravelled, its tail still stuck in the bucket. 'Our time in the woods is over, Punzel.' He put down the bucket and the skins and picked out the tin plates. He clashed them together and lifted his head back, shouting, 'Say good-bye to the last human beings on the planet!' He stood up, beating a rhythm with the plates, and gave a kind of howl that ripened into a laugh. His eye sockets were hollowed out, and the tight skin across his skull shone where his hair was retreating.

I covered my ears, terrified by the animal my father had become in the few minutes I had been digging. He flicked the plates like Frisbees into the trees, picked up the bucket and the animal skins and set off towards the fire. I sat in stunned silence, then stood up and ran after him, following the trail of twine that he dragged behind him.

The fire was much closer to the clearing than before, but still it crept low across the ground, consuming all the leaves and twigs that lay before it, but only licking around the bottom of the large tree trunks, then moving forward. My father was dancing close to the edge of it – advancing and every now and again taking a leap backwards, away from the heat. As well as the smoke there was a fetid smell, and I saw he had thrown the animal skins into the flames at his feet. The fire sparked and fizzed through the fur. I made an attempt to pluck them out, but the heat was too intense.

'Please come back!' I shouted, my arm covering my mouth. My father turned to look at me, surprised to see me there.

'It's OK, Punzel,' he said, the flames flickering across the smile on his face. 'We'll go together. I would never leave you.' He bent down to the bucket, removed something else and flung it into the fire. I stood dumbly and watched the words 'La Campanella' curl and fold over themselves, and notes and staves and Ute's handwriting catch light and transform into ash. Leaving the bucket where it was, my father walked back towards die Hütte again. I picked up the bucket and once more followed him. Inside the cabin he was filling the second bucket with anything he could find, sweeping our belongings off the shelves with the side of his arm. I tugged on his sleeve, begging him to stop, but he shrugged me off. All the time he was talking to himself as if I weren't there, saying things like, 'This is it now, this is the answer. How could I have been so blind? Of course, we'll go together.'

He moved towards the piano table and started to pull at the wooden keys, prising them out of their positions. I walked towards him, formed my hand into a fist and punched him in the stomach as hard as I could. My father was still a strong man, so I think it must have been the surprise that made him double over, winded. He crumpled on to the floor, hugged his knees and cried. In between my father's wails I thought I heard the fire eating through the undergrowth, crackling, and for a second I thought maybe my father was right: it would be easier if we let it all go. I stood there wondering what was next, and a trickle of liquid ran down my thigh, the blood I had forgotten about flowing down my leg and around my ankle. At the same time, I looked out through the door and saw a curtain of rain move across the valley and up towards us and the fire. I went outside to greet it.

In my mind, the blood, the rain and the fire became associated with the change in my father. He was subdued for days afterwards, as though he knew he had been bad, and I often wondered if he had started the fire himself. But I became aware that his plans for what would become of us hadn't gone away, they had been clarified. He still often got up in the middle of the night to draw diagrams and unintelligible scribbles over the walls of the cabin. In the mornings he would try to engage me with them, jabbering and jumping on the table to point out a particular argument about survivalism.

'Oliver Hannington wouldn't be able to answer that one,' he would say.

'Oliver Hannington is dead; everyone is dead except us,' I would answer wearily.

The day after the fire, I walked through the burnt rock forest. I found the metal part of the spade, but the handle was sooty and disintegrated in my hands. One of our plates was in a tree, the other below it, in a skeletal bush – the enamel scorched. With a stick, I poked through the ash caking the ground, but not even a corner of the sheet music remained. The forest smelled heavy and dirty and sorry for itself. The leaves in the canopy dripped and most of the vegetation had gone; the ground was grey sludge. The fire had reached the beginning of the clearing and had gone all the way down to the river, but the rain had started before it had spread across the mountain to the forest on the other side.

I found only one tree that had caught fire. It stood alone, blackened and twisted. I sat on a rock and watched a crow return to it again and again. The bird couldn't settle; it was all wings and flap and rusty cawing. It must have had a nest high up where the limbs became distorted. But I had no sympathy for the crow; the feeling I had was jealousy. I would have given up everything – the music, my memories of London, the forest – to become that bird and to be able to fly away to make a new nest in a new tree. But I also acknowledged that if it *were* possible for me to wish hard enough to become that crow, it would be equally possible that long ago, something else – a fly, a rabbit, a bee – may have looked at me, Peggy Hillcoat, and been jealous of everything I had then and might have in the future. And if that creature had wished hard enough, it might have given up everything to become me.

19.

After the fire, when I had finished growing and was as tall as
I was ever going to be, I insisted on a bed of my own. I
pleaded for it, stamped my feet, turned my back on my
father, refused everything he asked for until he relented. My
bed had squat log legs and a warped frame cut from a pine.
We placed it against the back wall towards the stove, so each
morning when I woke, with my head warmed by the fire
and my feet chilly, the first thing I saw was my piano. I had
spent every spare five minutes rolling plant stalks along my
thighs to make rope thick and strong enough to criss-cross
the bed frame. On top, I laid a straw mattress – bundles of
dried grass stitched together with more rope – a layer of
furs, and over that I put the scraps of my sleeping bag. I tried
to hide my joy from my father, who sulked and predicted
that the rope would sag and that by the end of the first night
my bottom would be inches from the floor. I didn't care.

'Sleep tight, don't let the bedbugs bite,' he called out bitterly when we were both in bed.

He complained about being cold, about there being too
much space in his bed, but I lay in the dark, smiling up at the
joists. And when I was sure, from the sound of his breathing, that he was asleep, I put my fingers between my legs.

The first morning, it took a few seconds to orientate
myself – I woke to sunlight inching under the door instead
of an out-of-focus view of wood grain and splinters, my

head having been squeezed in the gap between the wall and my father's back. I jumped out of bed, opened the chimney damper, shoved a log on to the fire embers and climbed back under my furs, luxuriating in my own space. From my low position in the bed I saw the name again – gouged into the wood under the shelf next to the stove. I hadn't thought about Reuben for so long, I couldn't remember when I had last touched the letters or even seen them. And how many autumns had passed since I had watched the boots walk in front of the nest? Eight? Nine? The memory of them was connected to a different girl, naïve and new to the forest. I lay on my stomach in the bed and stretched my arm above my head to touch with the very tips of my fingers where Reuben had once carved his name, and I mine. Had he been in die Hütte before us and abandoned it? And where was he now? I was sure that if he lived on our side of the river I would have bumped into him, or seen more evidence of his existence, other than a pair of damp boots.

That day, whilst I played the piano, hoed between the rows of new carrot leaves and walked my usual route to check and set the traps, I wondered how the head and face at the other end of the boots might look. I gave him a clean-shaven chin, a flop of sandy hair and blue eyes. I gave him an American accent, but he reminded me too much of Oliver Hannington, so I started again with dark curly hair and a drooping moustache. I thought about him crossing the river without being frightened, striding through the rapids in his sturdy boots and thick socks and climbing up to the ridge on the other side. He teetered on the lip of the Great Divide, he gazed into the empty blackness and he wasn't afraid.

The spring afternoons were my own to do as I wanted. I sheltered from the rain in the nest whilst newborn ferns unfurled around me, and thought about whether Reuben might play the piano or the guitar. I dreamed of duets and recitals. Perhaps he lived in a brick house across the river, with a mirror and a bath. Or he was a famous Russian writer who didn't speak any English and was searching for his wife and children. Maybe he had been mistakenly arrested for spying, escaped to the forest and got stuck here after the Great Divide happened. When I found a patch of sunshine to lie in, I put my hands behind my head and remembered how his ankles had seemed particularly well fed. He must catch and eat deer, I thought, something my father and I had still never managed to do, or maybe there were boar across the river.

I watched for him when I walked amongst the celandines, their yellow heads paling into summer. I whirled around when I caught a movement from the corner of my eye, but the man was always faster. I studied the ground for footprints which weren't ours, but saw only the tracks of deer, birds and wolves. One day, I had the idea of climbing again up to the ledge where we had flown the kite, to see the very edge of our land through the spyglass. My father came into the cabin just as I was taking it down from the shelf.

'What are you going to do with that?' He seemed immediately suspicious.

'I'm going to see if it works. I'm going to climb the mountain.'

'There's nothing to see, just trees and the ridge.' He dropped the logs he was carrying in a heap next to the stove.

'I'll just look at the trees and the ridge then,' I said, gripping the spyglass behind my back, as if I could hide it from him.

'It's not a toy. You'll only drop it.' He held out his hand. I was a puppy, receiving obedience training.

'I won't. I'll be careful. I promise.' I moved to go.

'Punzel. No!' He reached behind me and pulled my wrist, squeezing. 'You are not allowed.'

'Why not? You can't stop me. The spyglass is mine.' I yanked my arm back, but he gripped harder, burning the skin.

'I don't want you playing with it.'

'I'm not going to play with it, I'm going to use it to look across the Fluss.'

'I don't want you to do that.'

'Why not?'

'I just don't. That's enough!'

'It's not up to you what I do!' I was shouting now.

'Give it to me,' he yelled back. I was the bad dog with a bone I had snatched from my master's table. 'The spyglass, Punzel.' The palm of his left hand was straight out, the fingers straining backwards and the tendons in his wrist quivering. That's when I knew Reuben really did live over the river and that my father knew it too.

'It's mine. It was a present, from . . .' and I realized I couldn't remember who had given it to me. There was a flash of a memory – tearing wrapping paper, seeing the frown lines on Ute's face magnified and encircled by brass, but no memory or name of the giver.

In that second of doubt, when I was shocked at how my previous life had disappeared so easily, my father grabbed the spyglass from my hand. Without thinking, just like after the fire, I made a fist and punched him; this time the blow was weak, pathetic, it glanced off his chest. But it was enough to make him strike back. The end of the metal tube clipped my eyebrow, splitting the skin. I cried out as blood flowed into my eye and down the side of my nose. My father stepped forward, I knew it was to say sorry, but I pressed my hand against my head and turned to run. I ran to the forest and kept going, even when he called after me. I scrambled blindly up through the trees, my tears mingling with the flow of blood, and climbed the mountain, smearing mucus over the tufts of grass I used to pull myself upwards. When I reached the platform where we had flown the kite, I shaded my eyes with my hands and stared across the river to the mountain on the other side. As my father had said, there were only trees; trees and dark clouds rolling in over the top of the ridge, which drew a line along the edge of my world.

I sat there for a long time, watching for a puff of smoke or the movement of a man, but there was nothing. The midday sun passed overhead, and as I stumbled back down the sky grew darker and the first drops of rain fell. By the time I was walking through the forest to the nest, the rain was falling in sheets, so that it was hard to see further than a step or two ahead. As I crawled inside, I heard my father calling my name again – his voice muffled and distant because of the rain. I curled up on the moss with an empty stomach, avoiding the water where it came in through the ferns, and hoped that I would die before morning, thinking how that would serve my father right.

I tried to sleep, but the rain grew even heavier and the moss spongy, and no matter where I lay, muddy water soaked into my clothes. There were few other noises apart from the constant pouring, just the occasional scuttlings and crawlings that kept my eyes and ears straining into the darkness. The rain continued to pound, and after a while I thought I could hear another noise, a rushing of water and trees creaking and complaining. There was a crash somewhere up the mountain behind me, one that shook the ground under my body, a second's gap of rain, and another thump and another, then wood splitting and breaking and a huge lumbering, trampling noise coming towards me down the mountain. There was a kind of breathless panting and I realized it was me. The blood pumped in my throat. I was ready to run or to face the thing coming. It was a monster about to pounce, claws out, teeth sharp. I scrabbled against the boggy floor and had just stuck my head out of the entrance when a final terrifying crash, travelling through the ground into my bones, came from behind and a boulder bigger than the nest dropped into the forest in front of me. It was followed by a shower of smaller rocks, which fell through the leaves into the nest, and all I could do was curl into a ball and cover my head. When the storm of stones had died away, the monochrome forest swayed, settled, and shifted in its sleep.

I walked for the rest of the night, shivering until the rain stopped. I was determined never to go back to my father. When daylight broke, I hid behind a tree and watched the smoke rise from our chimney into a blue sky and smelled breakfast on the stove. Eventually, the door opened and my father appeared. He looked lean and wiry from a distance, his beard ragged and his long black hair a receding tide which had left behind an exposed beach of tanned forehead.

He walked behind the cabin and called for me, and again, further off.

When I judged it safe, I ran across the clearing and into die Hütte. I stood at the stove and ate acorn porridge straight from the pan, scalding my mouth. The place was different after a night away, smaller, darker, but it smelled like home. I gathered a few special things together into my rucksack, but the spyglass was gone and I didn't see it again until the summer was over.

I stood on tiptoes beside my favourite wintereye, and where the three branches soared upwards from the main trunk I felt with my fingers the basin of tepid water that the tree kept in its secret heart. In this scant pool I placed a squirrel's skull. Last autumn, just to see what was inside, I had boiled the animal's head until the flesh fell away and every tooth shone white. After the skull went a magpie's feather – dark with a smear of blue, like petrol on a puddle. And lastly a dark hair, which I had unwound from the long-broken comb. It made me think of Becky's hair tied behind her unaged face. To me, Becky was forever eight.

It was right to give my treasures to the forest to thank it for keeping me safe from the boulder and to ask for some-thing, anything, different to happen. After I had given the gifts to the tree, I walked a diagonal line across the forest. The early summer sun was already warm, and the dappled shade the trees gave was a relief. Making up the rules as I went along, I ignored the deer paths and walked straight through the undergrowth, over rotten logs, scratching my legs and arms on brambles and thistles. I picked up a stick and beat them back. When the forest thinned, but before the leaf mulch had disappeared, I stopped under the gribble. It was my second-favourite tree in the forest, after the winter-eye, because it stood alone, a sad-looking tree, its trunk bowed under the weight of a bad haircut. In autumn it was covered in miniature apples, like jewelled grips coming loose from its permanent wave. Every time they appeared I couldn't resist tasting one, but the sourness always dried the roof of my mouth and snarled my lips, and I had to spit it out, disappointed.

With a flint I had taken from the shelf, I dug a neat pit under the gribble, about the size of my clenched fist. From my pocket, I took Phyllis's head. I stroked her hair, pushing it away from her face, and gave her a kiss on her forehead. I placed her head in the hole and dusted it with soil, wishing she had the kind of eyes that fell closed when her face was tipped up. Even though I no longer played with her, her head was the hardest object to sacrifice and prising it from her neck had made my eyes sting with tears. I hadn't been able to look at her headless body and so had tucked it away under the floorboards where we kept the seeds we gathered at the end of each summer. Once Phyllis was sprinkled with earth, I filled in the hole and laid two twigs on top, one over the other, in the shape of a cross.

Next, I walked a trail from the buried head, downhill to the river, to form a triangle of offerings. For most of the way I followed a deer track, until I came to the clearing. This I ran across, crouching low and scurrying more than running, in case my father was in die Hütte. The summer river disturbed me; even though it was shallower and gentler than its winter cousin, I couldn't look at the constant movement or shake off the feeling that the water was pretending to be serene with nowhere in particular to go and nothing much to do. Just under the surface it lived and breathed – malevo-lent and cunning.

In my pocket I had a leaf taken from the wintereye and another I had plucked from the gribble. Holding one in each hand, I stumbled across the muddy pebbles to the river's edge where my father fished. Tensed and holding my breath, I stretched out over the water and placed both leaves on the surface and let them go. The current took them, like it had once taken me.

'Take my love to Ute,' I called out after them, even though I knew she was dead and they would never reach her. The water danced with the leaves and spun them until they must have been dizzy and disorientated. I ran alongside calling out again, 'Take my love to Ute.' With a sudden eddy they were pulled down and out of sight, as though a hand had sucked them into a watery grave. I backed away on to the bank, frightened that the same fingers would reach out for my ankles.

As I scrambled back through the grass, I saw something lodged in the bank under the bushes – the toe of a shoe or a boot, sticking out of the mud. With a cry, I thought that all the wishing and thinking and offerings had been wasted. The river had already taken Reuben, swallowed him whole and left his bones in the earth, before I had a chance even to meet him. I tugged at the dark toe with both hands and dug around it with the flint that was still in my pocket. I im-agined Reuben's sock tucked inside the boot; his leg and the rest of his body brown and leathery, preserved by the mud, like the Tollund Man I remembered from school. I pulled again at the slippery toe, and with a sucking belch the mud let it go and I fell backwards. It was empty and it was my shoe – the one I had lost when I first crossed the river. I sat cradling it with relief and sure that magical, incredible things would happen now. I wiped the mud from the heel and saw again the leaping cat.

I held my refound shoe close to my chest and followed the flow of the river, planning to walk as far as I could until the mountain stopped me. I was dawdling, daydreaming about new green laces, when I saw the man.

20.

London, November 1985

When I reached the hall I heard the key lid open as someone clunked it against the piano frame. They scraped the stool along the parquet, and I knew it couldn't be Ute. Oskar sat at the piano, his hands poised, ready to play.

'Either come in and close the door or go away,' he said, putting on a cross face.

I went in. 'What are you doing?' I whispered. 'She'll kill you.'

He gave up the artificial frown and moved along the stool so I could slide in beside him.

'I learned this at school. If she can't be bothered to teach me, I'll have to teach myself. Do you want me to show you?' Without waiting for my answer, he continued, 'Curl up all your fingers except these two.' He pointed his index fingers side by side, like Peter and Paul in the nursery rhyme. I copied him, hiding a smile to keep my secret.

'Your job is to play these two notes.' He put my fingers on F and G. His hands felt cool and were already as big as mine. 'You have to press the notes six times. OK?'

I pressed the keys just hard enough to hear the noise of the hammer on the string. It might have been the first time I had made a piano produce a real sound.

202

'No, not yet,' he said. 'Not until I've counted to six. And do it quietly.'

Oskar spread out his fingers and started to play. Looking at him, nodding his head, biting his bottom lip, pleased me. He gave an extra-deep nod, but I was too busy watching his face.

'Where were you?' Oskar said. 'You have to be ready. After six.'

I nodded.

We were clumsy and halting, but we were making music; under my fingers' instructions, just two at a time, the piano answered. When we had played six notes he stopped.

'Why are you making that noise?' he said.

'What noise?'

'You were doing a weird kind of singing.'

'Sorry.'

'I think it might sound better if you didn't.' He took hold of my fingers again. 'Now you have to move your left finger down one, and keep your right in the same place, and play these notes six times.'

We were out of sync with each other, but it didn't seem to bother Oskar. He showed me four more notes.

'Do you think you can remember? Four lots of six.'

We started again from the beginning, with much more head nodding. Oskar stared at both his hands with intense concentration, but still his left was always a little behind his right.

'I think you might have got it,' he said.

We played the duet a few times, each round faster, until we didn't stop in between but performed the sequence again and again, until one of us went wrong and we stopped, out of breath and laughing.

'Once more!' I yelled, and we began thumping the piano as hard and as fast as we could, without thinking about the noise. After a couple of minutes Ute flung the sitting-room door open, her hands tucked inside oven gloves.

'"Chopsticks"!' she shouted. 'On the Bösendorfer!'

'Oh, Mum,' Oskar yelled back, standing up and pushing the stool with his legs, making it scrape the floor again. 'Nobody has fun in this house!' He stormed past her and out of the room, leaving me sitting alone.

Ute came to the piano. 'If you would like to learn I will arrange lessons for you.' She took the oven gloves off and started to lower the lid so I had no choice but to withdraw my fingers. 'Lunch in five minutes,' she said over her shoulder, and went back to the kitchen.

I lay my forehead on the polished wood, closed my eyes and remembered the piano my father had made, how much effort had gone into its creation, the wood turning greasy from my fingers, the pebble weights coming loose and falling between the floorboards, the song of 'La Campanella' etched into my every cell. I sat up and opened the key lid again and traced the gold lettering of the word 'Bösendorfer' with the fingers of my right hand. My left hand settled into a familiar arrangement on the keys, and when the tip of my finger reached the curlicue of the final r, my right hand joined my left.

It didn't feel as if I was doing the pressing, but more like I was sitting at a pianola, the ivory moving by itself, following the pattern of holes punched in a paper roll located somewhere deep inside the mechanism, and I was following along. My left hand played the first three notes, and my right, the high echo, then one low, two high, repeated, then the slightest of pauses.

'Lunch!' Ute called from the kitchen.

The spell was broken and the music stopped. I heard Oskar clatter down the stairs two at a time like I used to, his empty stomach overriding his brief argument with Ute.

'Peggy, lunch!' Ute called again.

I closed the piano and went into the kitchen.

21.

The man was hunkered down under the trees, his head in profile. At first I mistook him for a boulder, not one which had rolled off the mountain in the recent rainstorm, but a rock which had lain in place for years, whilst the under-growth had grown up around it and its surface had become mottled with orange and green lichen. I froze mid-step, my heart hammering. I watched him with wide eyes, waiting to see his next move before I made mine.

He had separated the wet grass and ferns like a pair of curtains and was peering intently forward through the gap. I had longed for this, offered up gifts for it, but now I wanted nothing more than to run back to die Hütte, even though my father's responses were likely to include grab-bing the axe and hunting the man down, or setting the forest alight to smoke him out. I moved one leg up and backwards. But before my foot had even touched the ground, the man took his hands out from the grass and slowly, deliberately, turned his head towards me, as if he had always known I would be there. Shaggy hair hung down to his shoulders and his beard flowed over the front of his green and orange plaid shirt like a swarm of honey-bees. His look was plaintive, as though he might be about to cry at what he had seen through the grass, but later I came to know this as his natural expression – melancholic, as if a terrible tragedy had happened that he couldn't bear to speak of. Everything about his face flowed downwards: his eyes, his mouth, even his thick, untrimmed moustache.

He lifted a finger to his lips and at the same time cocked his head, beckoning me with it. I stayed where I was, almost tempted to glance behind me to check that he wasn't nodding at someone else. He repeated the twitch of his head, and without waiting to see if I would come, he parted the grass again with his hands and stared through it. Gingerly, I went forward. If he had turned his head towards me once more, I'm sure I would have bolted, but the intensity of his stare beyond the grass drew me on. I walked towards him and crouched down beside him. He smelled different from me and my father. His scent was of the woods – bonfires, autumn berries and leather, and underneath, something sweet: soap, perhaps. Tucked under his bent legs were the boots, damp again and creased across the toes. He still didn't acknowledge that I was there; he just spread the grass wider, so I could see what he was looking at. Amongst trampled ferns, a doe licked her newborn fawn, still slippery with blood and membranes. The mother's thick tongue lapped over the baby, cleaning and checking. She raised her head and fixed her large brown eyes on us, but in the same way that the man I squatted beside had looked at me, the doe took us both in and carried on with her work. She nudged the fawn with her nose, encouraging it to stand. It staggered to its feet and the man withdrew his arms from the gap and let the grass fall back into place.

'I think that, just now, we are not wanted there,' he said, standing up and stretching as though he might have been crouching for hours. It shocked me to hear another human voice in the forest, one that wasn't mine or my father's. I wanted him to carry on talking so I would know we weren't alone. He reached his arms high over his head and cracked his elbows. He seemed to go on for ever, and I thought that when he had come into die Hütte to carve his name beside the stove, he would have had to dip his head under the door lintel to get in. I stood too and stared up at him as he yawned. His beard opened up a pink hole in the middle of his face, and I looked away, embarrassed.

'You're Punzel, aren't you?' Then he held out his hand and said, 'Reuben.'

Awkwardly, I shook it, as I had shaken the survivalists' hands when I had greeted them at our London door. He was younger than I had first thought, his face less weathered and creased than my father's, whose skin had become leathery from his time spent in the sun and the wind. Reuben smiled, and the exposed cheeks above his beard shaped themselves into pouches.

'You have the dirtiest face I've ever seen,' he said.

He reached his hand out towards my temple, and I realized I still hadn't washed off the blood from yesterday or the mud from the river. He looked down to where I clasped my shoe to my chest.

'That's an odd thing for a girl to be carrying around a forest. Do you want to clean it? And your face?'

I hesitated, and as if he understood my reluctance, he said, 'Not in the river. We can go to the gill.'

He didn't wait for an answer but walked off, away from the deer and her fawn, seeming to assume I would follow. I stood looking at his retreating back, then went after him. He seemed to know the forest as well as I did, striding along the same trails I used every day, and I wondered again how he could have been here without me seeing him. In the middle of the wintereyes he headed right and uphill, passing within a few feet of the nest.

'It looks as if there was a landslide last night after all that rain,' he said, patting the new boulder which had nearly killed me. We carried on until we stood at the lip of the steep channel. The tumble of mossy rocks had been dislodged by the rainstorm and had rolled down the gill, taking chunks of earth with them. The trunk of a tree had wedged itself crossways between the banks, and forest debris had collected behind it, water seeping through the gaps formed by a tangle of branches and logs.

Reuben picked his way down the slope with obvious practice, each foot placed with confidence, and didn't even glance at the temporary dam above us. It wasn't until he was standing on the boulders at the bottom that he looked back at me, still hesitating at the top of the bank.

'Oh,' he said, surprised I wasn't behind him, and, 'wait there.'

But before he had a chance to come back for me, I slid downwards on my bottom, the backside of my shorts gathering mud. I dug the heels of my moccasins into the bank, clung on to clumps of grass with my hands and in one blind leap I was on the rocks and beside him.

'That's one way to do it,' he said, smiling. Balancing on a green boulder, he bent down and gripped a neighbouring rock with both hands, hefting it to one side, revealing the secret, gurgling, rushing water beneath. He scraped moss from the bank and dipped it into the flow. We sat side by side so that Reuben could wipe my face with the water; I flinched at the cold shock of it.

'Sorry,' he said, still wiping. 'I've never seen so much mud and blood on one face. Hot or cold?'

I looked at him.

'Go on, hot or cold?'

'Hot,' I said, beginning to understand.

'Interesting. Town or forest?' He threw the moss away and got a new bit.

I didn't want to point out to him that his first choice wasn't available any more, so I said, 'Forest.' Up close, and whilst he was occupied with cleaning the blood and mud from my face, I noticed that every hair of his beard was a different shade – red and brown and blond, mixed on the palette of his chin until they merged to the colour of rust.

'Forest or river?'

'Forest,' I said, even though I was keyed up at the thought of the danger behind us, the sudden burst that might carry us away.

'Day or night?'

'Definitely day,' I replied, remembering the night before. I kept my eyes averted from his, but I was aware of his breathing and his concentration whilst he cleaned me. He was quiet for a while.

'Rabbit or squirrel?'

I laughed. 'Neither.' And Reuben laughed too.

'All right, apple or pear?'

'Apple,' I said, because I didn't want to tell him that I couldn't remember the taste of pear.

'That's a shame,' he said, 'there aren't any apples here.'

'There's the gribble,' I said, looking him in the eyes for the first time.

His hand, holding the moss, paused. 'Ah yes, the gribble. Sour little good-for-nothings.'

I wanted to stick up for the tree, to say something in its defence, but Reuben said, 'There, all done,' and threw the moss away. 'I think you might end up with a scar though. How did you do it?' His fingertips reached for my eyebrow again.

'It's fine,' I said, pulling back. There was a loud crack behind us. I jumped and looked towards the bulging dam and a new trickle of water which flowed between the boulders, under our feet, and continued past us, down the gill. Reuben carried on talking as if he hadn't even noticed.

'And what about that shoe you're holding? Is that fine too?'

It was still in my lap, the mud drying into flakes. He took it and plunged it into the flow that washed between us – already rushing past faster, carrying leaves and twigs with it. Reuben put his hand inside the shoe to claw out the years of compacted river mud. He rubbed at the outside, making the leaping cat on the heel clearer. A wave of homesickness came over me, but I wasn't sure if it was for London and shoe shops and pavements, or my father and die Hütte. I wanted both to stay and to run away. Reuben's face was too new; I didn't yet understand the meaning of each crease of his brow, each purse of his lips, every set of his jaw; being so close was overwhelming, like a birthday party I had been to once, where the laughing and the games and the lurid food had all been too much and I'd had to be collected by Ute and taken home. Before I could see or hear anything else, I wanted to go into a darkened room to process this new human being.

'Is it yours?' he asked about the shoe, and I could only nod. 'Aren't you going to put it on?'

I shrugged. He lifted up my right leg and rested my ankle across his knee. It was the first time his skin had touched mine. I pushed off my moccasin; there was no sock to remove – all our socks had been worn away to threadbare tubes winters before. The lace had rotted after its years in the mud and it disintegrated when Reuben opened up the shoe and tried to push it on to my foot. The inside was slimy and sodden, and I had to curl my toes up to get it on; it just fitted. My bones must have lengthened, but I hadn't got any fatter since we'd been living in the forest. Any clothes that hadn't fallen apart were still almost the right size for me. All my pants had eroded into grey shreds and my trousers had ripped so badly at the knees that we had sliced them off with the knife and sewed the bottom halves as arms on to a tunic made from rabbit and squirrel skins. For many winters I wore Ute's two dresses, but I had never grown into them and now they were ragged and worn. I cared only for my blue mittens and the balaclava – washing them regularly in a bucket of water and pinning them out over thorn bushes in the sunshine, so that the wool stretched back into shape.

But my hair had grown – bark brown in the winter, lighter in the summer; close around my face and long down my back. It stuck together in clumps so that even the few remaining teeth on the comb refused to be dragged through it. I plaited the strands that I could tease loose, and often still coiled them around my ears in the winter to keep warm.

Reuben sat back with pride, looking at my mismatched feet like the shoe fitters I remembered from Clarks on Queen's Avenue. Before he could say anything else, I blurted out, 'I have to go now,' and jumped up. As if my sudden movement had dislodged a rock or a branch, there was the creak of wood scraping against wood and a gush of water and the dam burst. I scrambled up the bank, aware that Reuben was right behind me. I could hear the water, but didn't turn to look; I just hobbled back the way we had come. Reuben called out my name, but still I didn't turn or even slow down.

'Wear both your shoes tomorrow,' he shouted after me, and I imagined his large hands cupped around his bristled mouth. I smiled as I ran, even though the tightness of my shoe made my foot hurt. I jumped over fallen trees and leaped from stump to stump where my father had felled them, full of an energy that could have kept me running for the rest of the day.

I burst into the clearing, prepared to tell my father everything, just for the excitement of having news – forgetting about our recent argument – but die Hütte's door was open, and even before I had gone inside I could hear him singing mournfully and clunking the wooden piano keys:

'And my father said to me, oh alaya bakia,

You will wed and you will see, oh alaya bakia,

All your dreams, they will come true, oh alaya bakia,

In a paradise for two, oh alaya bakia.'

I leaned, catching my breath, against the side of the cabin as his voice floated out. The summer sun dipped down behind the mountain and a fresh chill arrived, which always made me think of new beginnings. I added a harmony to my father's chorus, at first quiet and shy, then louder, with confidence:

'Oh lay oh la, oh alaya bakia.'

My father stopped playing, rushed outside and hugged me.

'Oh, Ute, I thought I had lost you. We must always be together. Promise me, we'll always be together.' He didn't stop to explain where he thought I could have gone or give me a chance to correct him. 'I have a surprise for you,' he said, releasing me and taking my hand. Inside, the walls of die Hütte had been washed clean of all his charcoal notes and writing. One of the buckets stood in the middle of the floor, and in the bottom I recognized my nightie, now a grey wet rag.

'See,' he said spreading his arms wide. I turned, taking in all four walls. 'We have lots of space for new lists, new ideas. A fresh start.' He seemed too pleased with himself.

I let him hug me and call me Ute again because I had a secret of my own. He wrapped his arms around me, and over his shoulder I read the list he had started on the wall behind the door:

Belladonna
Wolfsbane
Yew
Bracken
Corncockle
Amanita virosa

22.

I didn't tell my father about Reuben that day, or the next morning when I got up, my insides jumping with excitement. I decided to keep him for myself. In the early morning light, I worked in the garden, weeding and hoeing. I brought in wood and stacked it by the stove and turned the chicken-of-the-woods, which was laid out to dry on the shelves around the flue. I had completed all my jobs, except the checking and resetting of the traps, by the time we ate lunch. I wasn't hungry. I tried to hide my fidgeting from my father, but he raised his eyebrows when I put on a dress I had made the summer before, stitched from the remnants of Ute's camel dress, with scraps of rabbit fur for a collar. I had cut the ragged skirt, but kept it long to hide my knees, which I thought were too knobbly for a girl's. Whenever I put on the dress it made me want to stand with my shoulders back and take little steps on the tips of my toes.

'What's the special occasion?' my father asked.

'Just going out,' I said, plaiting the strands of hair hanging beside my face.

'Where to?' He leaned on the door frame, watching me, an irritating smile on his face.

'Just out,' I snapped back at him. I coiled the plaits and stuck them with feather quills. I jammed them in hard, and the thought popped into my head that if they stayed in place, Reuben would be waiting in the forest. I put my shoes on: the new one, nearly dry from where it had sat beside the stove all night, and the old one, which I had kept safe. I had sliced off the ends so I could wear them comfortably, even if my toes stuck out beyond the soles. I squeezed past my father and he gripped my upper arm, stopping me, the smile gone.

'I want you back before it gets dark.' His fingers pinched me and I pulled away, but he didn't let go. 'Punzel?' He said my name low, with an unspoken threat.

'OK!' I yanked my arm from him and walked off towards the forest. When I reached the trees, I glanced behind me. My father was still there, leaning in the doorway, watching.

I went straight to the gill and stared down into the runnel where we had sat the day before. The tree trunk still lay wedged from bank to bank, but all the forest litter which had been crammed behind it had been washed away as though it had never been there at all. The stone Reuben had lifted to reach the water to clean my face had even been put back – everything looked the same, and yet everything was different. I sat on the bank, patting my hair to check the braids were still in place. I tried out different positions and expressions, elbows on knees, looking moody; sitting up with the camel dress arranged in a circle around me; lying back in the afternoon sunshine with my eyes closed, humming. He didn't come. Our scrap of land carried on moving whilst I waited, rotating away from the sun until I was sitting in the shade. And I suddenly thought Reuben wouldn't be expecting to meet me here, by the gill; he would be watching the fawn again. I raced downhill, retracing our steps from the day before, slowing to a nonchalant walk when I got near to where I had first seen him. He wasn't there either. I crept forward and parted the grass as Reuben had done. The fawn and its mother had gone. The only evidence that the birth had even happened was a few flattened ferns.

I did my rounds, plodding from one trap to the next. Two rabbits and a squirrel went into the rucksack slung over my shoulder. Perhaps Reuben crossed the river in the mornings; maybe he had meant to collect me from die Hütte, shake my father's hand and ask if he could walk out with me. He could be there now, or maybe he was ill, dying, washed away by the river. I was a few yards from the gribble when I remembered that we had talked about its sour apples the day before, then I was upon it, and Reuben was sitting under the tree, in a patch of sunshine, his back against the trunk, writing in a book. He squinted up at me.

'Glad to see you've got both shoes on today,' he said, and I couldn't stop myself from smiling. He smiled back, and those little pouches appeared above his hairy cheeks, and I wondered how old he was and where he had been born and who his mother had been.

'What are you writing?' I could see the slope of blue words across the page, but couldn't make out what they said. I wanted to read them and take the pen from his hand and write; to remember the feeling of letters and words appearing from the ends of my fingers. He snapped the book shut.

'Oh, nothing. Just some thoughts, ideas.' He stood up and tucked the book and the pen inside a satchel he wore slung across his chest. 'Come on,' he said, then grabbed my hand

and pulled me. 'There's something I want you to see. We might already be too late.'

As I allowed him to tug me along a track towards the gill and away from the gribble, I remembered Phyllis's grave and her head buried in the earth. When I looked behind me, over my shoulder, I saw that the twig marker was no longer lying flat on the ground but had been bound with string into a cross, which now stood upright in the soil.

'Wait!' I cried out, but laughed too whilst he dragged me behind him. 'Where are we going? Why are we running?'

'Come on,' he urged. 'I promise you it'll be worth it.'

At the gill, I took a couple of steps down the steep bank.

'I've got a better idea,' he said. He still had hold of my hand, and with it he pulled me back up. 'Let's cross on the tree trunk.' It remained jammed into the bank on either side, but most of its bark had been stripped away, revealing the smooth and pale sapwood underneath. 'Hold your arms out and don't look down,' he said, stepping on to the trunk. He walked confidently along it; one, two, three long strides and he was across.

Reuben faced me. 'Easy,' he said.

I lingered on the bank, my fingertips sweating and my mouth dry. I looked up at him and down at the trunk. I stepped forward – it was barely wider than my feet. I took another step, and my centre of gravity shifted out over the gill; I compensated, moving in the opposite direction, too far. I tried another step, too fast. Reuben was bending towards me, his arms outstretched, but there was no grip on the slick surface of the trunk. And I fell. I heard myself cry out, and there was a smack of pain as my hip and chest hit the rocks a few feet below.

'Punzel!' he shouted, then he was sliding down the side of the gill and helping me to my feet. 'Christ, have you broken anything?'

My hip burned and the hand which had been under me felt crushed, but I said, 'No, no, I'm fine. Really, I'm OK.'

He held my hands in his and looked me up and down. 'Your dress is ripped,' he said. There was a tear through the beige fabric.

'It's just an old thing. It doesn't matter.'

We were balancing on the damp boulders in the bottom of the gill. I pulled my hands away from his to brush the mud and bits of moss from my dress and so I could look down whilst I worked hard at not crying. I couldn't cope with being the centre of his attention.

'What was it you wanted to show me?' I said.

'Are you sure you'd still like to go? We could see it another day.'

'Which way?' I said, starting off up the bank, trying not to limp or wince. At the top, I went left, weaving through the bushes towards the mountain, aware of Reuben following.

'Across the scree,' he said, overtaking me. 'This was why you needed your shoes.'

Behind him, I lifted up my dress to examine my hip – the skin was ragged, the area over my hip bone already reddening.

The ground underfoot shifted and moved, sliding us backwards, even as we climbed. Every year, winter frosts chipped away at the side of the mountain and the loose fragments of rock crept downhill like a grey lava flow. We scrambled up the slope for five or ten minutes until right against the escarpment the angle of the land flattened off, and we stopped to catch our breath and look back. The view carried us out over the frilly tops of the wintereyes and down to the spiked firs in the valley bottom. There was a flash of the silver river, and a green hillside rising up from the water, and, finally, the naked line of rock at the edge of the world.

'That's where you live, isn't it?'

'Come on, the sun's moving,' Reuben said, and led the way along the side of the mountain, loose stones spinning out from under our feet and clattering off the mountain-side. We came to an expanse of heather covered in a drift of purple flowers, similar to those I had found the grubs in many winters ago. In the shade of the mountain, Reuben crouched and pulled me down beside him. 'Now we have to wait.' And he sat staring straight ahead at the bushes. I thought it was a joke, but he didn't move, he didn't look at me or say anything else. So I crouched there too, until the sun crossed our backs on to the heather, which trembled in the light, lifting its flowers towards the sunshine. As we watched, the heather flexed its petals, purple and pink with black-eyed spots. Like a ripple on a still pond, the flowers fluttered in the sun's warmth and, in a chain reaction, they lifted, a flock rising and fluttering in the air around us.

'Butterflies are cold-blooded,' Reuben said. 'They can't move until the sun warms their flight muscles.' We sat until the sun had reached them all and just a few remained dancing about our heads. 'They only live for two weeks. A short but beautiful life,' he said.

When the butterflies were all gone, Reuben asked, 'Are you hungry?'

I was always hungry, but I shrugged. We continued walking along the side of the mountain, the narrow path disappearing after we left the scree, and the ground becoming grassy and uneven, lush tufts sprouting over hidden rocks and dips. I could hear water trickling beneath us, seeping out from the mountain, small rivulets which would gather themselves together in secret, amassing, joining forces until they found their way into the gill. When the incline became steeper, we headed downhill. I picked my way with care, holding my skirt and hopping from one grassy mound to the next, my hip complaining with each step. I tested the ground before I trod, wary of catching my foot in a hole and tumbling all the way down. Reuben, ahead of me, at first inched downwards in the same fashion, but then stood up and with a whoop he started to run. He leaped from one hillock to the next, his arms whirling, his body leaning out at an alarming angle as if he might spring off into the air. Well before me, he reached the grove of wintereyes and wasn't even out of breath when I caught up with him. He stood under a tree, peering up through the leaves, and then shimmied into the branches monkey-style and came back with two eggs clutched in one hand.

'Afternoon tea,' he said, offering them to me. The eggs were balaclava blue, speckled with brown.

'I can't eat them,' I said. 'I can't eat baby birds.'

He laughed. 'There aren't any embryos in these.' He held each up to the sun. 'See, no veins – infertile. Don't drop them,' he said, putting them in my hand, 'we're going to have mushroom omelette.'

We climbed the mountain and looked down on die Hütte

with its chimney smoke rising sleepily into the air and, as always, beyond it, the land across the river.

'Do you live over there alone?' I tried again, but Reuben jumped up to collect kindling for a fire and then produced the means to light it from his satchel, together with a cooking pot, knife and a pile of oyster mushrooms wrapped in leaves. We sat on the wide lip, our legs dangling over the drop, and ate with our fingers, watching my father, a pocket man, chopping wood, walking to the river with the buckets, watering the garden. We saw him lift his head and heard him call for me, and we scooted back from the edge into the shadow of the mountain, laughing.

That evening in die Hütte I hid the dress from my father, rolling it into a ball and stuffing it down the side of my bed. I knew that the rip in it and the purple bruise that had flowered across my hip would make him angry.

During that summer, Reuben and I met every afternoon. We hid from my father and walked the familiar paths, sat on the boulders in the rock forest, climbed the mountain, but we never crossed the river.

'Becky and I had a saying whenever something unexpected happened,' I told him one day when we were picking blackberries on the other side of the gill. 'It was: "We used to say it was so dull, nothing happening like in books. Now something *has* happened."'

That summer was a good one for blackberries. The bushes were taller than Reuben and covered in sweet ripe fruit, so that with one squeeze they slipped off the stalk that held them. I was meant to be taking them home, but as many were going into my mouth as into my basket.

'Unexpected like what?' he said, his lips stained dark from blackberry juice.

'Just silly things, like our teacher sneezing in the middle of a lesson, or realizing Jill Kershaw, in front of us in the dinner queue, had got the last serving of mashed potato.' Reuben had a crease between his eyebrows. 'It was a joke,' I said. 'They weren't really unexpected things, not like this.'

'Like this,' he repeated, 'picking blackberries?'

A heat rose up from my neck and I looked away, reaching further into the bush. 'It's a line from *The Railway Children*. Don't you know it? I had the record, in London. Becky and I used to listen to it all the time.'

'No, I don't think I do,' he said.

'Didn't you have a record player when you were growing up?'

'No, there was no record player.'

I wanted to ask him more questions, I wanted to know everything about him, but instead I said, 'You would have liked Becky.'

'Oh, and why's that?'

'I don't know. She was funny, interesting, clever,' I said, extricating myself from the brambles.

'Aren't you all those things?' He came towards me, a pile of ripe berries in the cup of his hand.

I could feel the blush rising again.

'Here you are.' He tipped them into my basket. 'Blackberries for supper.' He reached out and wiped the corner of my mouth with his finger. 'Wouldn't want your father knowing how few made it home,' he said, and smiled.

'What about at the cinema, maybe you saw *The Railway Children* at the cinema?'

'No, I don't think so,' he said. 'Did you know, the black-berry can be distinguished from the raspberry not simply by its colour but because the blackberry keeps its torus, the white stalk, inside it, whereas the raspberry leaves it behind when it's picked.'

'Daddy! My daddy!' It was my best impersonation of Roberta on the station platform.

Reuben shook his head.

'What did you watch, then?' I asked.

'Not much. I was never really one for watching television.'

'What about the book? You did read books, didn't you, wherever you came from?' We were walking through the forest, the basket of blackberries slung over my arm.

'Sometimes, not very often.'

I tried to remember the shelves in my bedroom in London. There had been rows of books, but only *Alice in Wonderland* came back to me.

'But you're always writing. In that little book of yours that you won't let me see.'

'You are the nosiest girl I've ever met.' He laughed, but I knew I had been warned off.

We walked in silence until we reached the trees at the edge of the clearing. I stepped out into the sunshine. When I looked behind me Reuben had already gone.

A week or so later, I showed Reuben the nest. We had been to pick blackberries again, but already they were turning – so ripe that when we touched them the soft ones fell and were lost amongst the thorns. Rain started, large droplets, sucked down by the thirsty forest floor, making the air smell of damp summer soil. When he saw the nest he was at first surprised and then seemed angry that there was a place in the forest which he knew nothing about.

The day before, I had carpeted the nest with fresh moss and woven flowers into the walls and roof, telling myself that it had needed a good tidy-up, pushing away thoughts of other reasons. With Reuben squeezed in beside me, what had seemed a large space was now cramped. He had to prop up his head at an awkward angle and bend his legs behind him; he reminded me of Alice after she had drunk the potion and grown too large for the rabbit's hall. We were inches apart, but I was conscious of every movement I made so we wouldn't touch, and yet his breath – smelling of blackberries – and his body, his presence, filled the overcrowded nest.

'How did you know my name,' I asked. 'When we first met?'

'I don't think I did,' he said. 'You introduced yourself. Thank you for asking me round, by the way.'

'You're welcome,' I said, trying to remember if he was correct or not. 'I only did it so I would get a return invitation.'

Reuben made a vague 'Hmmm' and shifted to avoid a steady drip which was coming through the fern roof.

'I'm sorry it's not very big. I was thinking of building a glasshouse, south-facing to catch the winter sunshine.'

'Then you could grow ferns all year round.'

'Orchids and grapes.'

'With birds of paradise showing off their tail feathers.'

'Pooping on the cane furniture.'

'Lovely,' he said.

We were quiet. I plucked a thistle head from the ceiling

and pulled out the strands bit by bit, letting them float between us.

'What's it like where you live?' I asked.

'Similar to this. Trees, forest, river.'

'But is it a cabin, or a tent, or what?' I tried not to let my irritation at his evasiveness show.

'It's below the ridge, amongst the trees.'

'I've never been up there. Except when we arrived, before . . .' I trailed off.

'Do you want to?'

I had imagined the Great Divide many times. It still came to me in dreams. I would stand teetering on the brink, my feet tipping pebbles into the dark, pebbles that never reached the bottom. Or I would fly above our patch of land, the mountains like cupped hands with the river running through the valley they made. But as I flew higher, I could see that we floated in an infinite black sea. I searched for other islands of life but saw nothing.

'I could take you,' he said, shifting on to his back, stretching his legs and hitting the woven sticks at the bottom end.

'Maybe.' There were strands of moss in his beard.

'Now.'

'I don't know.'

'You're always too afraid to do anything,' he snapped. 'You're going to end your days in that tumbledown hut with your weird father without having done a single thing for yourself.'

'Die Hütte is not a tumbledown hut,' I said. It was the only answer I was confident of.

'I could blow it down with one breath.' He blew through his mouth and a few white thistle tufts flew around us.

'OK, let's go now,' I said, but neither of us moved. I continued to lie on my back, watching a woodlouse crawl across the roof. I was waiting for something, without knowing what.

'Woodlice have their lungs in their hind legs,' he said, and then, 'You don't have to come back here.'

I didn't say anything, although I knew it was a question and he was waiting for an answer.

'You could stay, on my side of the river.' He didn't say 'stay with me'.

'Do you have a piano?'

'No, of course not.' With some effort he turned on to his stomach and crawled out of the nest, and I wondered if my chance for something I didn't fully understand had just been lost.

We walked in the rain, heads down, to the flat rock where every day my father lowered the bucket into the pool. It was an open and dangerous place. We stood together on the slippery green lip and looked over the edge. Drops of rain joined the river water many feet below.

'You just have to jump,' said Reuben. 'The current will take you downstream to the other side.'

The opposite bank was stepped through several layers of rock until it became level with the river. Here, thick bushes and trees crowded the water, thinning out where my father and I had crossed when I was a child.

'Can't we go in further down, past the reeds?'

'And get swept downstream, hit our heads on a rock and never come up again?' he said, and I shuddered.

I contemplated the still pool again and knew I wouldn't be able to jump. My body would resist leaving solid rock for air and water. They were the wrong elements, not meant for me.

'For God's sake, Punzel. It's only a small jump.'

'I can't do it.' I shook my head and moved backwards.

He was angry – shouting that I was a pathetic child, that he had no idea why he was bothering with me at all and it would be much better for both of us if he jumped now and never returned. I tucked my chin into my chest, letting the raindrops follow the curve of my head and run cold into the secret hollow in the nape of my neck. I wondered if he was right, whether everything would be better if I had never met this strange man and just let things play out with my father. Eventually Reuben was quiet and we left the river and went up through the trees, skirting the clearing. By the time we were sitting under my favourite wintereye, the rain had stopped, leaving beads of water clinging to the ferns. The sun came out and shone on the cabin, nestled in the crook of the mountain's elbow.

'My father told me that he and I are the only two people left in the world,' I said.

'He's lying,' Reuben said. 'I'm here too.'

He pointed to an eagle far above us, its wing tips out-stretched like fingers as it circled in an updraught. I caught the smell of blackberries again on Reuben's words and leaned closer, breathing him in.

He looked down. 'You aren't watching,' he laughed, and I thought maybe he had forgiven me for not being able to cross the river. He took my chin in his hand, tilted my head upwards and kissed me.

23.

For the remaining days of summer I stayed out of my
father's way, keeping a physical distance between us – pressing my back against the piano or the shelves when he
squeezed past. Sometimes he still caught me though, made
a grab for my dress and pinned me between his knees. I
stood rigid and kept quiet, so that later I could be sure I had
done nothing to encourage these episodes of weeping or
anger, and subsequent apologizing.

He often called me Ute, and I gave up correcting him. He
reminisced about the fuss made when they were newly married, laughing at how they had run away from a newspaper
photographer who had hounded them. He became frustrated
when I couldn't join in with the names and locations of the
hotels they had hidden away in when they were on honey-
moon. At other times, he talked about how the three of us
should be together again. This idea grew so gradually it was
impossible to remember one conversation, one defining moment, when the course of our lives changed and his decision
was made. Most nights after I was in bed, he wrote more words
on the cabin's walls, elaborate schemes and lists. He said he
had a death list and laughed at his joke. In bed I sometimes
heard him crying, muttering and burying his head under his
pillow. The nights of weeping made me feel insubstantial, as
though I existed only inside my father's head, but it was worse
when, in the dark, he tried to engage me in his plans.

'If we had dynamite – yes, dynamite would do it. Kaboom!' He gave a bitter laugh. 'We could blow up die Hütte. Bring the mountain down on our heads.' He let out a groan as if he were in pain. 'She left me – Ute. It's easy to die when you don't have to do it yourself, but you and I, Punzel, we have to work it out. We'll do it together, won't we?'

When I didn't reply, he called out my name again like a child calling for his mother in the dark. I pretended to be asleep but he got out of bed to shake me.

'Promise you'll come with me? Promise me.'

'I promise,' I whispered.

'You have to mean it. If you commit to something you have to stick with it. Not like Ute. We'll go together, won't we?'

'Yes.'

'We just have to work out how.' He sat on my bed, biting his fingernails, planning.

'Ute broke her promise,' he said, choking on the words, and he curled up on the floor, shaking and sobbing, until I put my hand out to touch him and said again, 'I promise.'

Reuben and I met after the vegetables had been watered, the traps checked and the piano played. The summer was warm, the ferns the tallest I remembered, the moss on the winter-eyes a Fuzzy Felt green, and the rain, when it fell, never fell for long. One morning there was a smell in the air, of the season turning, of leaves collecting in the crevices of the mountain, of the blackberries fermenting under a grey down of mould.

'How does the spider make his home?' I asked Reuben,

gazing at the cobwebs above our heads. We were lying on our backs under the wintereyes, the afternoon light catching on silk threads.

Reuben was silent, his eyes closed. Insects hummed about us, and I wondered whether the skin on the rest of his body was as pale as his face. I prodded him in the ribs.

'Hmm?' he said.

'The spider. How does he start? Does he spit the first thread, or jump, or what?'

'Or what,' he said dreamily, still not stirring. I ran a blade of grass down the bridge of his nose. He flapped his hands in front of his face as though a spider were crawling there. I moved the grass over his skin again, and this time he opened his eyes.

'OK,' he said, and sighed. I wasn't sure if he was irritated or tired. 'He lets the wind take it,' Reuben said, 'and wherever it lands, that's where he builds his home.'

'Like you. You live wherever the fancy takes you, don't you?' I asked.

Reuben had already closed his eyes.

I shut mine too and let the warm afternoon carry me. In my dream I lay on my bed in die Hütte. Reuben was curled behind me, his arm over my waist, his fingers moving rhythmically between my legs. His beard and warm breath tickled the back of my neck, and more than anything I wanted the bite of his teeth against my skin. I lay quiet, listening to the curious creaking noise the circular motion of his hand made, as if something inside me needed oiling. Still dreaming, I rolled over on to my back and saw the soles of my father's boots just above my head, slowly swinging, and realized that his body was hanging from one of the rafters. I woke with a cry, the sun in my eyes. Reuben had gone from beside me, leaving behind the shape of a body in the flattened grass. I looked up and saw him sitting on a branch, his feet dangling high above me. Behind him, the shadow of the mountain crept forward.

'What can you see?' I said, standing up.

'Your father. He's looking for something under the beech trees.' My stomach lurched. Reuben was holding his book, but he wasn't writing.

'My father's searching for destroying angels,' I said, trying to sound nonchalant.

'*Amanita virosa*: the deadliest of the poisonous mushrooms. Eat any part of its pure white body and its toxins will bind to your insides, your liver, kidneys and even your brain. No known cure.' With one vicious motion he ripped a page from his book. 'Wrong trees. Tell him to look under the pines. It's still too early for destroying angels anyway. Come up and see.'

It took me several attempts to scramble on to the lowest branch of the tree; once there, I edged towards the trunk and levered myself up until I was at Reuben's level. He didn't look at me or shift from his position. I scraped my knee on the rough surface, and when I lifted up my skirt, beads of blood rose through the ripped skin and tears came to my eyes. I gripped the wood and, with sweating fingers, shuffled sideways towards him. On the ground, a branch lay in the long grass. Its bark had fallen away, leaving a bleached bone underneath us.

Reuben had rolled the paper from his notebook into a cigarette and stuffed it with dried grass; I could make out a few words: 'all no good', spiralling around in blue ink. With matches he lit the brown filaments which stuck out of the end; they flared and the paper caught. He held the cigarette out towards me, holding his breath. 'Want some?'

I shook my head, overwhelmed with loss, watching the words he had never allowed me to read glow and change to ash as he blew the smoke out through his nostrils.

'Everything looks perfect from far away, doesn't it?' Reuben said.

My father, bending down every now again, could have been picking meadowsweet for the table.

'He's kept me safe for a long time. He's very good at chopping wood and skinning rabbits.'

'What does he want destroying angels for?'

'And squirrels. He can skin a squirrel in two seconds flat.'

'Wants to end it all, does he?' Reuben sucked on his cigarette and it burned fiercely.

His beard and moustache had become yellow on one side. He flicked the stub off his thumbnail and we both watched it land in the grass. A minute later, a thin column of smoke rose into the still air and I prayed my father would look up from his work and come running. But he was examining something; he held it close to his eyes and placed it into the reed basket strapped to his waist.

'He's looked after me for a long time,' I said.

'I'd be careful about eating what he gives you for dinner,' Reuben said, and laughed. I swung my legs, but the sensation of not having anything solid under my feet made me feel sick and I stopped after a couple of kicks.

'He's a good cook.'

'*Amanita virosa* stew, with corncockle salad. A deadly combination. Is he going to eat it too?'

'He says he's seen them there before.'

Reuben raised an eyebrow and stroked his beard. It made the sound of dry leaves.

'Is that so?'

'He says we have to go together.'

'Go where? What does that mean?'

'He says I couldn't survive here without him.'

'You seem to manage pretty well – for a girl.' Reuben winked at me.

'He says it's not right for the last person in the world to be on their own.'

'Tell him there are three people left.'

'I can't do that,' I said quietly.

'But you're not going to go through with it, are you?' he said, surprised.

I shut my eyes, but I felt I was falling backwards, so opened them again. A trickle of sweat or an insect crawled across the small of my back, but I couldn't let go of the branch to scratch.

'I promised him.'

'What? You promised him you would die with him?'

'Yes.'

'Promises can be broken. Punzel?' Reuben's face was even paler than normal, his eyebrows raised, as though he had only now realized I wasn't joking. 'Just because some old man wants to top himself, it doesn't mean you have to join him in his crazy suicide pact.' Reuben sounded out-raged.

'We've agreed; as soon as he finds the mushrooms.' I said it matter-of-factly, but whilst I watched my father walking up the hill towards die Hütte, my body trembled at the thought of what lay in his basket and a chill spread across my back as the shadow of the mountain reached us.

'He says we've survived a lot longer than most of the world, but now it's time to go.'

'Tell the fucker he can go if he wants, but you're staying.'

'I promised,' I said again.

'This is ridiculous.'

Reuben grabbed hold of my wrist; the grass and rocks below me shifted in response and I thought I might throw up.

'I have to go home now,' I said, although it wasn't clear to me how I would get back down the tree. I made a movement along the branch and the forest spun around me.

'Punzel, promise me you won't eat those mushrooms.' He paused, and we both stared at his fingers around my wrist. They reminded me of my father's. 'I don't . . .' he paused again and didn't finish; instead he let go of me and I continued my shuffle back towards the trunk. Reuben stayed where he was, looking out over the landscape.

I had wanted us to say goodbye properly. I had wanted him to kiss me again. It was even harder climbing back down than going up; I couldn't look below me, so I pressed my cheek into the bark and prodded for where to put my feet. I jumped the last part, landing on the side of my ankle.

When I was under the branch, Reuben called, 'Promises can be broken.'

From my position on the ground I saw his incisors, large and pointed like a cat's, and I wondered how I hadn't noticed them before. I walked from the shade into the sun, imagining Reuben's eyes on me. I kept my back straight and my head up, but when I reached die Hütte I couldn't resist turning for one last look. I half raised my arm to wave, but the branch was already empty.

In die Hütte, my father was chopping the carrots I had picked and washed that morning. On the floor beside the table was his basket.

'Did you find any?' I asked.

'A few; enough,' he said, still chopping.

'Are you sure that's what they are?'

'As sure as I can be. I thought we would have them for breakfast. One final dinner tonight,' my father said, smiling. 'Stew and acorn dumplings, baked potatoes and honey cake. Nice?' He sounded so sane.

'Will it hurt?'

'Oh, Punzel. I wouldn't ever let anything hurt you. No, I think we'll just fall asleep and not wake up.' He put the knife down and stroked my hair. He tilted my chin. 'You know this is right.' It wasn't a question, but I nodded.

After dinner we went straight to bed. For once, my father didn't talk; I supposed there was nothing left to say. I heard him crying though, but I didn't have the energy for reassurance. A while later he got out of his bed and padded across to mine.

'Ute, let me in,' he whispered, and tugged at the fur cover.

I pretended to be asleep.

'Ute, please,' he whined.

I pinned the cover down with my knees and gripped it with my hands.

'It's our last night,' he said, and yanked on the covers so that they came free from under my body and he was able to climb in beside me.

I lay still with my arms straight down and my eyes shut, and thought about the view I had seen from the tree, how the land curved gracefully down to the river and up the other side. How the wintereyes and beech across the water did look perfect from far away, like the dark green heads of curly kale that I grew in the garden, complex and convoluted. And I thought about how all the bad things – the snake that ate the bird's egg, the eagle that ripped the mouse into bloody shreds, the ants in the honey – were the necessary details in a world that would still be here after we were gone. After a time my father went back to his own bed and I heard his breathing change as he fell asleep. I lay awake in the dark for a long while, climbing the tree again, but without difficulty this time, and standing on the branch with my arms out. I dived off and a warm breeze caught me, and like the eagle I flew over the mountain ledges, the gribble, the butterfly heather and the wintereyes.

'Punzel,' Reuben hissed my name in the dark. 'Punzel!' his voice came again beside my ear.

I opened my eyes; I was still in my bed, there was the first dull light of dawn and Reuben was bending over me. He had on a blue woollen hat I hadn't seen before, his hair tucked up inside it so that in the half-light he might have been bald.

'Come on.' He pushed the covers off me and pulled me upright. He took my hand in his and together we crept out of the cabin. The first mist of late summer washed across the bottom of the valley.

'My shoes! I have to get my shoes,' I said, as soon as we were outside and I could feel stones digging into the soles of my feet.

'There's no time,' he said, and he ran uphill across the clearing, drawing me along behind him.

'Wait, slow down. It hurts.' I said.

'Quick!' Reuben's eyes were shining, excited. Drops of water hung in his beard as if the dew had caught there.

'Where are we going?'

But he was already pulling me off into the forest. We ran to the nest, me on tiptoes, trying to keep my feet in the centre of the worn paths to avoid the worst of the twigs and stones. In the grey light, I saw that the outside of the nest had been newly woven with ferns and, once we were inside, I realized the ground had been laid with fresh moss.

'What now?' I asked when I'd got my breath back.

Reuben and I crouched side by side like two seeds in a green pod.

'Your father can eat his own stupid mushrooms,' he said, pressing his palms against the roof a few inches above his head.

'Take his own medicine,' I said, and we laughed. 'No, really, what now?' I asked, worried, but Reuben leaned forward to kiss me. His beard and moustache prickled my cheeks and chin and made me laugh again. 'It tickles.'

Reuben pulled away. 'I've been thinking about cutting it off,' he said, stroking his beard.

'No, don't do that. I like it.'

I pushed my fingers into it, making hollows, and pulled his face towards me and kissed him back. He opened his mouth and I put my tongue inside. He tasted salty and I wondered what he had been eating. He reached out his fingers and touched my breast through my nightshirt. It had been my father's shirt, a faded green that came halfway down my thighs. It was ripped and stained in places, and I worried that I should have put a dress on. I tugged at the bottom of the shirt, trying to cover my legs. It flattened over my breasts and Reuben moved his fingers over one of my nipples, which rose under his touch. The shirt was missing all but two buttons and Reuben slipped his hand inside and cupped my breast in his palm; cold against my skin. He undid one button and bent to take my nipple in his mouth, and between my legs I had the sensation of the seconds before a thunderstorm begins. His hair tickled me again, and made me want to scratch and giggle, but I stayed silent. He kissed my other nipple and then my mouth. The full length of our bodies came together and I tried to undo his shirt, but his had all its buttons and the nest was too small; our legs tangled together and by accident I kicked his ankle so that he yelped. Eventually I lay still whilst Reuben contorted himself to undress, taking off his hat, pushing his boots and clothes to the end of the nest with his feet. His pale body was almost luminous in the restricted space, like an exotic deep-sea creature. I tried to focus on the moss and twigs caught in the hair on his chest, so that I only saw his upright thing, which stuck up from its own nest, out of the corner of my eye. Reuben helped me take off the shirt and I covered myself with my hands.

'I don't have any pants,' I said.

'You're beautiful,' he said, and pulled my hands away and, taking one of them, wrapped it around him.

I felt his hardness and his heat and wondered if that was why his hands were so cold. After I had held him for a while, Reuben began to move his body, so that he slid backwards and forwards inside my hand, until I learned to copy the movement. He breathed into me and pressed his face down on to mine so that our teeth clashed and his tongue was in my mouth. The sharp edges of stones in the dirt floor under the moss pressed into my back, as he traced the shape of my waist and bony hip with his hand, the undulation of my thigh, and down to the graze on my knee, then up again between my legs. His fingers explored me and circled around the bit of me that I didn't have a name for. He made me forget to kiss him, forget to keep my hand moving. He shifted his body over mine and opened my thighs with his. His thing nudged me, and for a second I felt his full weight. Leaning on one elbow, he used his other hand to push inside my body. A cry, almost of pain, escaped from me and there was a low answering echo from him. He propped himself up on his elbows and we looked at each other. Daylight was coming in through the opening of the nest, and I watched a smile grow on his face.

'I've been thinking about this for a long time,' he said.

He took my hand, guiding it between our bodies, and moved his hips up and forwards. Slow at first, then faster, and all the time my fingers kept rhythm with him. He buried his face into my hair and moaned. His nose to mine, he pushed into me harder, his face changing, his eyes losing focus, and I went with him, breathing heavier and faster, until that moment when a kind of fire spread up from between my legs and I convulsed and I heard Reuben's deep, animal noise. And from a long way off, perhaps down by the river, I heard my name being called.

'Punzel!'

Reuben's body tensed again and he rolled off me, on to all

fours, and stuck his head out into the day. I wriggled to the bottom of the space, found my nightshirt and put it on.

'Punzel!' my father's voice came again. Urgent, closer.

'I have to go,' I said, pulling on Reuben's arm so I could get past him to the opening.

'What?' he said, turning his head to stare at me, incredulous. 'No. This isn't going to happen. Not now.'

'I don't have a choice.'

'We'll hide,' Reuben said. His thing hung between his legs, still wet, but soft now. He dragged his clothes up towards him with his feet and put them on.

'He'll find me.'

'We'll cross the river,' he said, feeding buttons into the wrong holes on his shirt.

I stared at my hands, calloused, already old.

'OK, not the river. We'll climb the mountain.'

'I didn't bring my shoes.'

'Christ! You want to die with him, don't you?' He was almost shouting. 'Fight back, damn it.' He held me by the shoulders and shook me, and I just wobbled with him, feeling the tears welling. He gave me a despairing push.

'Punzel,' came the call, once more from the forest. Drawn out; a howl.

Reuben and I sat in the nest, our knees touching, not talking, until at last he said, 'I don't want you to die,' and I let him take me by the hand to lead me out into the morning.

We went left towards the gill, but slowly; I couldn't run, I had to pick my way along the paths, but still my legs and feet were stabbed and scratched by stones and brambles. The liquid that Reuben had put inside me trickled down my thigh, congealing on my skin whilst I walked.

'We'll work our way round, back to die Hütte, and get your shoes.'

'Your hat,' I said, pulling back on his hand. 'You left your hat.'

'It doesn't matter.'

When we reached the gill, I glanced behind me and was sure something moved between the trees, following us through the forest. The gill was damp and mossy as always, but easier to navigate than the forest floor. All thoughts of the water which tumbled beneath us disappeared as I followed Reuben down, hopping barefoot from one slippery boulder to the next, catching my balance at the last minute with clawing fingers. I slid on my bottom, grazing my skin, jarring my elbows, the nightshirt becoming a darker shade of green. The scab on my knee reopened and blood trickled down my shin.

Reuben was always a few steps ahead, looking around to say, 'Hurry, hurry up.'

When we had ducked under the log bridge, he scrambled up the bank and I turned to look back the way we had come. My father stood at the top of the green tunnel, his feet planted on adjacent boulders. He stared down at me, then Reuben was grabbing my hand and pulling me up into the trees.

We traversed a wide loop through the forest, almost down to the river, and without me saying that I had seen my father following us, we crouched low under the ferns, crawling on hands and knees over rotten logs and through bushes which pulled at our hair and tore at our cheeks as if the forest, too, wanted me to stay. When we reached the trees, at the edge of the clearing, we paused to catch our breath. I couldn't see anyone behind us, but I was sure my father was there. Die Hütte stood in a pool of sunshine. It was perfect: logs stacked in rows against an end wall, the purple stems of chard standing to attention in the vegetable garden, but the door was ajar and the interior dark.

'Perhaps I should go in alone,' I said.

'No, I'm coming with you.'

The grass was high around die Hütte, waiting for my father to come with the scythe and slice it to stubble. We strolled through it, although my heart was hammering. When Reuben reached the doorway, we looked behind us, as if checking that the owner of the little house was not somewhere close by. With one hand he pushed at the door. It resisted. He put his shoulder to it and something heavy on the other side scraped along the floor, and then he ducked his head under the lintel. Inside, it took a moment for my eyes to adjust to the gloom – nothing was where it should be, everything had been turned over, smashed and scattered. The stove tilted on two legs, its door open, spilling cinders. The shelves were empty, my bedcover had been thrown off, as if my father had thought I might have been hiding underneath it, and the base of my beautiful bed was cracked in two. My father's bed had been ripped off the wall, and the contents of the chest – the food, the clothes, the tools, nails and seeds – had been flung around the room. I picked up my balaclava, sticky with honey. And when I turned to the window, I cried out at the sight of the piano. The keys were in disarray, like broken teeth, the pebble weights strewn across the floor, catching under my bare feet. The table was cleaved almost in half, and the axe was wedged in the gap.

Reuben took the handle and tried to lever it free, but it

wouldn't shift. I nudged a couple of the broken things with my toes and righted a stool. I had my hand on one of my shoes when the door was pushed wide. My father stood there, a black shape against the white morning.

'You promised,' he said coldly.

I glanced at Reuben behind the open door. My father stepped inside and I saw he held the spyglass in his left hand. The sunlight caught something in the other, and I realized, without surprise, that he also carried the knife.

'I'm sorry, Papa,' I said. 'I can't do it.'

From the corner of my eye I could see Reuben pulling at the axe handle. My father moved closer, holding both his hands out as if asking me to choose between the two objects he gripped. I still clutched the balaclava, but I lurched forward without any clear intention. At the same time, my father's right hand sliced upwards. The knife slashed across the side of my head, and although I didn't feel any pain, when I looked down, the petals of a dark bud were growing and flowering with immense speed across the shoulder of my nightshirt. I put my hand up to the side of my face and it came back slippery with blood. I swayed, closed my eyes, heard a dull thump and thought I must have fallen, but when I opened them again, I was standing over my father, who lay on the floor, his body turned sideways and his head resting on the rug.

'Papa?' I said, and kneeled beside him. Blood dripped from my face on to his. I pulled at his shoulder and he fell on to his back and I saw that the other half of his head was wrong, missing. I rolled him on to his side again and was pleased at how peaceful he looked. I put one of our straw pillows under his head to make him more comfortable and tucked my bedcovers over him up to his neck.

'He's dead,' said Reuben, stepping forward from behind the door. The axe hung in his hand. He laid it down beside my father. There were smears of blood across the handle and Reuben's face and shirt were splattered with it. 'Let me look at you,' he said. He leaned forward over my father and tilted my chin.

I could feel fresh blood flowing when my head moved.

Reuben picked up a piece of clothing and pressed it to my temple. 'I think he got some of your ear.'

'What now?' I asked for the third time that day.

I knew the words he would say before they came out of his mouth: 'You have to come with me. You have to cross the river.'

24.

After lunch, on my way upstairs, I stood and read Ute's framed newspaper review, still hanging in the hallway – 'Despite her young age, one can tell that Bischoff has lived with the music and its world for a long time; her passion flows from every note she plays' – and I noticed for the first time that the review was of her performance of 'La Campanella', when she had met my father.

The review hung next to the central heating thermostat. I turned it down, again. Ute had sent me up to my bedroom to get changed before Becky and Michael arrived. Instead, I spread my father's lists across the bed, picking odd ones up which caught my eye, and rereading them. I got a notebook and a pen from my desk, and at the top of a blank page I wrote, 'Things I have missed'. I followed the title with:

Butter and cheddar cheese
Salt
Apfelkuchen
Toothpaste
Socks
Getting to know my brother
Baths

Mirrors?
Becky
Nine Christmas dinners
Trifle
Boyfriends (and I crossed this out)
Omi

In my bedroom, the radiator gurgled as the central heating was turned up.

'Peggy?' Ute called from the bottom of the stairs. 'Are you getting changed?' I sat amongst the pieces of paper and waited. I heard her climb the stairs, out of breath by the time she came into my room.

'Oh, Peggy, you haven't even started,' she said, looking at what I was wearing. 'Come on, they will be here soon, and you want to look nice. Don't you?' She sat down heavily on the edge of the bed and I started to gather up the lists scattered across the blanket.

'What are all these?' she said, picking up a list describing and calculating lengths and quantities of four-by-fours to build the bunk beds. A line formed between her eyes as she grasped what it was. 'Oh my goodness, where did you find these? I thought that everything was gone out of the house.' She picked up another piece of paper with a list of underwear and other items of clothing.

I watched her reading them. I wanted her to know that it wasn't going to be possible to just throw away all evidence that my father had existed, that it was never going to be that simple. Before I had time to stop her, Ute picked up the piece of paper which lay on my lap: my own list. We were both silent whilst she read it.

'Oh, Peggy,' she said, 'I am pleased, at least, that you don't feel you missed out on boyfriends. There is plenty of time for that.'

She really didn't have a clue, I thought, as I took the list from her and collected all of the others together.

'Where are all the pictures of Papa?' I asked her. She looked taken aback and composed her answer before she spoke it.

'I threw them all away. Angela and I – Mrs Cass and I – decided it would be for the best when I found out what had happened.'

I thought about the photograph she had missed, the one I had cut my father's head from.

'Isn't it odd for Oskar that he has no photographs of his father?'

She shrugged. 'I think he understands.'

'What about the note? I know you didn't get rid of that.' It came out sharper than I had intended.

'What note?'

'Oskar says that Papa left a note. Please don't lie.'

'Peggy,' she said. 'There's something –'

'Where is it?' I cut in. 'I want to read it.'

She sighed. Her hands were in her lap, clasped together. As she spoke she released them, and I could see red crescents where her nails had dug into her skin.

'You can read it,' she said with forced patience. 'I will get it for you.'

She went to her bedroom and came back with a piece of paper which she handed to me. 'Ute' was written in green biro on a folded square, which had been scored flat many times. My father had used graph paper torn from my maths exercise book. The staples had caught and ragged the sheet. I opened it and scanned it.

> I think it's better for everyone if I go now. I'm taking Peggy with me – you can keep the other one. That's fair, don't you think?

And my father's signature, scrawled, as though he was in a hurry.

'This isn't what you told Oskar. He thinks his father loved him. He's been living with a fantasy that Papa would come back for him. Why did you lie?' I shook the paper in Ute's face.

She gave the slightest movement of her head away from me. I read the note again, slower this time.

'The other one,' I said. 'What did he mean, the other one?'

Ute opened her mouth to speak, but I carried on talking.

'Oskar! He meant Oskar, didn't he? He knew you were pregnant and he didn't want it. Is that why he left?' I could hear my voice rising as if I had stepped outside it. 'But why did I have to go with him?' The voice was a shriek. I stood up and ripped the note in half again and again. 'You know he went mad in the forest? He tried to kill us both and there was nothing I could do. He said everyone was dead and I believed him.' My cheeks were burning and my head jutted forward. 'He told me the world had gone, disappeared in a puff of smoke.' I threw the note into the air and pieces of graph paper flew about us.

Ute flapped her arms trying to catch me, to quieten me. 'Peggy,' she kept saying, 'Peggy.'

'Oskar's right. It's all lies. You should have stopped him. You should have been here!' I shouted at her like a devil.

She slapped me, hard, against one cheek. Instantly we were still; only the bits of paper fluttered. Bile rose in my throat.

'I'm going to be sick,' I said, clamping a hand over my mouth.

'The bathroom, quick.' Ute pulled me off the bed and out of the door. We ran past Oskar, standing flat against the wall on the landing, listening. I saw his red cheeks and his hands held in fists as we rushed past him.

I no longer had a fringe for Ute to stroke out of my eyes. A nurse had shaved off my hair in the hospital. I hadn't understood what he had said, although his tone had been reassuring, but as he forced the electric trimmers between my scalp and my hair, tears had formed in his eyes and rolled down his cheeks. My hair had come off in a single matted ball. The nurse had carried it like a dead cat, his hands in see-through gloves, and he had put it in the yellow bin which stood in the corner of my room. Since then my hair had begun to grow back, and it now lay short and flat across my scalp. Ute said I reminded her of Mia Farrow in *Rosemary's Baby*.

In the bathroom I hung my head over the toilet whilst she stroked my forehead.

'There, there,' she cooed until we heard the doorbell ring.

25.

In die Hütte, Reuben wrapped the wound on my head with my dungarees, tying them on with cloth torn from Ute's camel dress. He washed his face with the water from the one bucket which hadn't been overturned and helped me search for my missing shoe. We looked everywhere: upending the broken beds, emptying the chest, shifting the stove, even hunting around outside, but we couldn't find it. I sat in the doorway and cried – my shoe was lost again.

'You need shoes. You'll have to take your father's,' said Reuben. He leaned against the shingles outside, puffing on a cigarette made from another page of his book. I saw the words 'all my born days' go up in smoke. He seemed a different man from the one I had done such private things with earlier.

'But he needs them,' I said, shading my eyes and squinting up at Reuben.

'He doesn't. He's dead.'

I went back inside. It was already warm in the cabin, stuffy. My father was still resting, although he looked paler. I stroked his cheek and pushed back his hair. His head had a halo of blood spread out over his pillow.

'I'm sorry, Papa,' I said, lifting the cover from his feet. His boots were laced with home-made twine. I undid them and prised them off. His feet were bony and white, with black hairs sprouting from the toes; a dirty crust had collected between them and the nails were thick and yellow. His feet made me want to weep. I put on his boots.

'Get some stuff together,' Reuben called from outside. 'Clothes, food, the knife, whatever you think you'll need.'

I got down my rucksack from the back of the door, much repaired but still usable, and kicked through the debris that was scattered across the floor, trying to sort the useful objects from the broken ones. I was light-headed, watching a girl inside a cabin pick up one blood-splattered item after another and decide without any logic what to take and what to leave behind. I found one of the hairless toothbrushes and put it in my bag; the broken comb went in too. I remembered the headless body of Phyllis under the loose board, but the stove now lay across it and I couldn't shove the metal box aside on my own; the effort made my head swim. My anorak was on the floor behind the door; I went to put it on but dropped it when I saw it was speckled with bloody lumps and unidentifiable scraps. The knife, the axe and the spyglass lay on the floor, close to my father, as though they had been arranged to make packing easier. I touched the axe with the tip of my father's boot but couldn't bring myself to pick it up. I looked at the knife too, but I thought my father might need it, so I chose the spyglass, put it in my bag and walked out into the sunshine.

Reuben and I sat on the rock above the river. I couldn't look over the edge, even though I knew the water below us would be calm. My head throbbed, the day was too hot, the sun too bright. I didn't need to tell him I couldn't do it.

'Shall I go first or second?' he said, standing up, stretching and yawning. 'First!' he shouted, and before I knew what he was doing, he had leaped off, one minute his legs pedalling in mid-air in front of me, and the next, all of him gone.

There was a splash, and I scrambled back from the drop as if his sudden fall might pull me with him. I lay on my stomach and peered down into the water. Reuben's head, his hair flat and dark, was already bobbing downstream, as he was swept towards the opposite bank. I got the spyglass out of the rucksack, and after a bit of searching and focusing on rocks, I watched his shoulders rise up out of the water. He waded through it, churning the muddy bottom, and when he reached the bank he shook his head like a dog, his hair spraying drops of water as it spun outwards. He was framed in the spyglass's circular window; I saw him smile at me, raise one hand, perhaps in a wave, perhaps beckoning, and then he stepped amongst the trees.

I looked over the top of the spyglass to see if I could follow his progress through the bushes, but there was no movement on the opposite bank. 'Reuben!' I called; no reply came. I couldn't believe he hadn't waited. Panic rose in my chest; I needed him here to tell me that I must go after him. I sat up, hugging my knees and rocking, with my eyes squeezed shut. If I rocked for long enough, when I opened them I would be able to stand and walk back through the trees into the clearing and hear the regular beat of the axe as my father chopped the wood, and I would call out to him, 'Squirrel for dinner!' And tomorrow afternoon, I would meet Reuben in the rock forest. He would be lounging against a boulder, smoking a cigarette, and he would tell me that the cuckoo lays its eggs in the afternoon.

When I stopped rocking and opened my eyes, nothing had changed. Still holding the balaclava and spyglass, I stood up and stepped off the rock, into the void. I hit the water sideways, with a vicious slap and a stinging pain that shocked me as much as the cold. The fall took me to the bottom of the river, and the momentum spun me so I wasn't sure which way was up. I would have been happy to stay down there, washing back and forth with the pebbles and the fish, but the current snagged me, popped my head out like a cork, coughing and choking, and deposited me on the opposite bank where Reuben had climbed out. It wasn't until I had wrung out the balaclava that I realized I had jumped without the rucksack. And the river had taken the spyglass from my hand. I imagined it spinning downstream and dropping into the Great Divide. The wound on my ear had opened again, and a trickle of watery blood flowed down my neck, but the river had washed the red flowers from my nightshirt. I turned and pushed my way into the trees.

All the rest of that day I traipsed through the forest on the other side of the river. Once or twice, I thought I saw a tree or a path I recognized from when I had been there years before, until I saw the same tree again and understood I had gone in a circle. The land on Reuben's side of the river was steeper, and more crowded with trees and tangled bushes than mine. I walked through it, calling out for him and searching for signs that he had gone before me, but there were no broken branches, no footprints, nothing. In the late afternoon, I was even brave enough to climb a tree to try to spy the smoke from his campfire, but the branches became too thin to bear my weight and I had to return to the ground. My head throbbed with every step, and my skin was scratched and sore from the thickets that tried to trap me. I lumbered uphill through a copse of wintereyes, all the time thinking that beyond the next tree Reuben would be sitting on a log, his kettle whistling and his boots steaming in front of the fire. He would kiss me, laugh and say, 'What took you so long?'

I walked until the light left the sky and it became too dark to see my feet. A hook of tree root sent me sprawling; I put my hands out just in time to prevent my head hitting the ground. As soon as I sat down, my body began to shiver and the thought of the bedcovers and anorak discarded on the floor of the cabin tormented me. I tried to pull the balaclava over my head, but the dungarees still tied there made it too difficult and stabs of pain shot down the side of my face, so instead I rubbed my legs with the damp wool. I eased off my father's boots, my toenails tender to touch, and tucked my feet inside the balaclava and tried to curl up on the lumpy earth. I couldn't stop my teeth from chattering, so I sat up again and rested my forehead on my knees. It was impossible to sleep. I hummed a few phrases from 'La Campanella', but they didn't distract me. I was alert to every noise the trees and hidden animals made; jumping when an owl hooted, wondering what was roaming in the midnight forest, but ever hopeful it was Reuben coming to find me. After a few hours I must have dropped off, because I saw my father emerging from the river with the sodden bedcovers draped around his shoulders. He was talking to me but his language was unrecognizable, garbled, his mouth distorted as if it moved underwater. He turned and I saw that the corner of his head was still missing. I woke with a start, in the middle of the forest.

It was the longest night, but when dawn broke, it was with a slow lightening of the sky; there was no sun. When the plants around me grew more distinct, I put my father's boots back on and climbed higher, calling again for Reuben. I climbed with the idea that, near the top, I would have a view over the trees to see the column of smoke from his fire. I didn't think about what was on the other side; I was scared of the swirling blackness of the Great Divide. Near the top, just as on my side of the river, the trees thinned and the ground became stonier, but here there was no towering cliff. I kept going, until I came to bare rock, carried on up it and looked backwards over the valley. An autumn mist hung along the river and its banks. There was a gap amongst the trees which must have been our clearing, but the roof of die Hütte was hidden from me and there was no smoke. I turned away, and on my hands and knees crawled forward with my eyes closed, terrified of being sucked over. The boots sent showers of stones skittering down the hillside as I scrabbled for purchase. My heart hammering, I opened my eyes, my head already spinning with anticipated vertigo. In front of me, I saw another valley falling away. Wintereyes and beech and more mist stretched down to a distant hill, and beyond that, another. What I saw was beautiful.

For a long time I didn't understand. I pivoted around to check I hadn't become disorientated and was looking back at the way I had come, but even after I had turned several times the land beyond the ridge was still there. I threw a stone into it, expecting ripples, as though it were a pool reflecting my world back to me, but the stone bounced down the rocks and into the undergrowth. My father had been mistaken. The Great Divide wasn't an infinite blackness but a mirror image of our world. I put down one foot, the way I used to test the ice on the boggy shore near the river in winter. The ground held under my weight. One final time, I looked over my shoulder for smoke, a sign of Reuben, but there was nothing, so, clutching the balaclava to my chest, I went forward into the new land.

I trudged downhill, using a stick to fight my way through tangled bushes and past spiny trees. I could manage only a short distance at a time before I had to stop and rest. Inside my father's boots my bare feet slid about, my ankles banging into the tops, and the leather rubbing my heels into gory blisters with each step. I discovered that if I found a mossy spot I could put the balaclava under my head and lie down with my eyes closed for a few moments, to stop the banging pulse in my temple, but something always made me get up again and continue walking. When the midday sun passed overhead, the land turned upwards again, and I staggered to the crest of a small rise. More wooded hills and another valley sloped away before me. I slid over the top, navigating the way down on my bottom. At the base was a gill, similar to ours – a long green tunnel with a tumble of mossy rocks – and for just a second I thought somehow I must have walked in a circle and crossed the river without noticing. After climbing down, I shifted a stone in the way Reuben had, and cupped my hands to drink from the icy flow. I followed the gill downhill, clambering from rock to rock until the hidden stream burst out from underneath the boulders and the gill became a proper force. Scrambling up the bank, I pushed my way through bramble and holly to walk beside the water. Every time, when I reached the top of each small rib of land, or negotiated a thicket, with nervous anticipation, I expected to see the edge of the world.

All afternoon I walked, concentrating on putting one foot in front of the other, until the gill widened and became a river and when I next looked up there was open land falling away into the distance and rising again. I stood at the edge of the forest, watching the wind race across the meadow and the shadows of clouds wander over the grass. It was the darkening forest at my back that forced me onwards and out into the open. I cut a path downwards, over a long sloping hill, until in the distance I could see dotted across it, at intervals, towers of straw. I had seen them before, but the name of them wouldn't come back to me. Before the daylight had gone, I reached the first one – twice my height and smelling of new-cut hay. I tucked myself inside it and slept.

In the morning, as the sun was rising, I hobbled across the meadow. In the night, my raw heels had dried and stuck themselves to the back of my father's boots, and walking reopened the wounds, so that with each step pain shot up my legs. The dungarees around my head had shifted and fresh blood dripped down my cheek, which I caught with the palm of my hand and smeared upwards, out of my eyes. I walked past more towers of straw and the sun got higher and hotter, so that I regretted leaving the river and forgot the pain in my head and my feet, and thought only of how thirsty I was. At the end of the meadow, over the brow of another small hill, I looked up and saw the red pitched roofs of houses. They clustered around a church, its white spire reaching above a line of trees. A thin grey road uncurled from the houses, running alongside the meadow. How many people would be in that village? I wondered. Fifty? Twice that? And I knew my father must have underestimated the number of survivors. There weren't two people left in our world, or even three, counting Reuben; there were more than a hundred. Without any clear plan, except the idea that perhaps the reason Reuben had always been so reticent to tell me where he lived was because he lived in this village, I walked down the hill and the road became closer and wider and greyer. The meadow went right up to it, with a shallow ditch dividing them. I stepped over and stood on the tarmac, dusty, man-made. Its hardness resonated through my knees and hip bones whilst I walked, and the loose chippings with their regular sides caught under my father's boots.

At the start of the village, I passed a large house with many windows and doors. The ground floor was painted white, and its top storey, shaded by a steep roof, was wooden. I thought about knocking on the front door to ask the owner for a glass of water, but the shutters were closed. A dog barked twice and whimpered from an inside room. Beyond the house were a field and another house, smaller than the first, but the same shape and style, after these there were no more gaps, only buildings. I carried on walking until a man with a moustache and a child came towards me.

I glanced right and left to see how I might escape, but they walked quickly, and when I looked back they were a few feet away. The man stopped and pushed the child behind him, as though afraid I might leap forward. The child, with blond curls and a face that could have been a boy's or a girl's, peeped out, wide-eyed, from behind the man's jeans.

'Please, do you have any water?' I said to the man with curly hair, similar to the child's but darker and thinner. The dungarees tied around my face, crusty with blood, pulled against my skin as I spoke. The man said something I couldn't understand, touched the side of his face with his hand and moved towards me, the child still clinging to his leg.

26.

I awoke in a room where everything was white – bed, floor, walls. Uniformed people came in and pressed needles into my arms, shone lights in my eyes and peered into my mouth. I lay still and let them examine me. They spoke in gentle, questioning voices, but I couldn't understand what they were saying and I didn't know what to tell them anyway.

Sometimes I whispered, 'Is this the Great Divide?' but they didn't answer. I was amazed at the different faces human beings can have, at the noises they made – from the squeak of their shoes on the white floor, to the clink of a wedding ring against a metal dish. I remembered the toy doctor's set that Becky owned, with its medical instruments strapped into a carry-case. She would make me lie on her bed so she could listen to the beat of my heart through the plastic stethoscope. We never worked out what we were supposed to do with the hammer which was also included, so I used it to beat out a rhythm on her headboard and in a deep voice she would say, 'AI, that's an AI heart you have there, Miss.'

In the white room I drifted in and out of sleep. Reuben came to check up on me, sitting on the end of the bed with a leaf stuck in his hair. I asked him whether it was autumn yet, but he wouldn't say.

One day I woke properly. I was aware of the shape my

body made in the bed, knees curled to my chest, hands clasped under my chin. I stretched out my feet towards the cool end, lifted up the white sheets and the white gown which covered me, and stared at my naked body; it had never been so clean. I got out of bed and put my feet on the cold, hard floor and stood at the window. Curving away to my left was a white building, three storeys high. The sky beyond its flat roof was still dark and all the windows were illuminated. Shapes and shadows of people walked past them, all busy going somewhere, doing something. The building formed a semicircle around a dull patch of green, not a quarter the size of the clearing. In the middle was a bench under a solitary tree – a spindly thing with leaves that were already turning brown. More than anything I wanted to breathe the same fresh and cool air the tree was breathing. I couldn't find a catch to open the window; I tried to slide it, pushing one way, then the other, but it wouldn't move. I pressed my cheek up against the glass, leaving behind a smudge, and then walked around the bed to a white sink and turned a tap. Water gushed out. I turned it again and the water stopped. On, off, on, off, on. It amazed me. I thought I would tell Reuben about it, and the idea that I might never find him in this huge white building made me sick with worry. Still standing at the sink, I looked up and was shocked to see a girl right in front of me, nose to nose. Her eyes were deep-set and her cheeks hollow, her head was shaved and bandaged, her face a more adult version of mine.

There was a sharp knock, and behind her a door opened and a group of people came in: men and women in white coats and an older lady in a blue uniform. I spun around, clutching at the gaping gown behind my back, and the group all started talking at once. I recognized the sound of their words; how odd that they speak German in the Great Divide, I thought. The blue lady came forward and gently but firmly ushered me back into bed, whilst someone else turned off the tap.

'I can do it,' I said, as she pulled back the sheets.

The oldest man in the group came towards me and all the others fell into place behind him.

'You are English,' he said, with some hesitation over the words. He started to say more, but gave up and spoke to the white-coated people, until a man at the back raised his hand and stepped forward.

'Dr Biermann would like to know your name,' said the young man. His thin hair was combed flat to one side, but a cow's lick leaped out from his parting.

'Punzel,' I said, more into the bed sheets than as a reply.

'Rapunzel?' he asked, and his hand flew to his hair to flatten it.

'Just Punzel,' I said.

The man spoke to the others and said the name 'Rapunzel' in the middle of his German.

'Do you know where you are?'

Everyone was silent, waiting, looking at me. I stroked my own head, feeling the soft bristles growing straight out from my scalp, whilst the overhead lights reflected in Dr Biermann's glasses winked out a warning. The glare from his glasses grew, spreading like drips of bleach on sugar paper, until his eyes were white, his face was white and finally everything was white and I had the same sensation of falling that I had felt on the road in the little town.

*

The man with the cow's lick was sitting on my bed when I woke up. He bounced a couple of times, as if he was testing its springiness, and smiled at me. On the chair in the corner of the room, an older, fatter man took a pen and notebook from his jacket pocket. I tried to read his writing upside down and thought I could make out the words 'keep off the line', but then realized he would be writing in German.

'So, you are English?' the man next to me said. I nodded.

'I'm Wilhelm, medical student, final year,' he said, and laughed even though he hadn't said anything funny. 'And this is Herr Lang. He is a policeman . . .' He indicated the man in the corner. '. . . a detective. Dr Biermann asked me to come to speak to you. Rapunzel, do you know where you are?'

'In the Great Divide, or I may be dead, or both,' I said.

Wilhelm laughed again, a girlish giggle, and I thought it must be true. He talked to the detective in German, and the man gave a snort.

'You're certainly not dead,' said Wilhelm, turning back to me and smiling. 'You're in a hospital.' And his hand flew upwards towards his hair. 'You hurt your ear and you lost a lot of blood and you were very . . .' He paused, searching for a word. '. . . thirsty, when you were found. I think you are perhaps a little confused. We would like to find out more about you. Would that be all right?'

I nodded.

'For instance,' he said, 'where do you live?'

'In die Hütte,' I said.

The man behind us shuffled around in his seat, and Wilhelm made a surprised sound in the back of his throat. He asked me a question in German.

'I only speak English,' I said.

After a pause, he tried again. 'Where is die Hütte?'

His tone was gentle, but the action of his flying hand made me suspicious, and I wondered whether he was trying to catch me out. Perhaps he knew where die Hütte was, had already been there and discovered my father on the floor.

'Out there.' I waved towards the window, and Wilhelm looked behind him, as though he might see die Hütte on the other side of the patch of grass.

'Who do you live there with?' he asked.

'My father,' I said.

'Is he still in die Hütte?'

'And Reuben,' thinking whilst I said it that it was almost true.

'Reuben,' said Wilhelm. 'Is he your brother?'

'No.' But I didn't know what to say he was.

'Your grandfather?'

'No.'

Wilhelm's hand rose halfway then dropped. He kicked his heels against the floor so they squeaked, and he smiled again, and I wondered if he found the noise funny instead of irritating, like I did.

The man in the corner spoke sharply, and Wilhelm said, 'How old are you, Rapunzel?'

'I'm not sure,' I said. 'I haven't had a birthday in a long time.'

'And what is the name of your father?' I knew that Papa wasn't the answer he was looking for.

'James,' I said.

'Does he have a surname?'

I thought for a few moments. 'I can't remember,' I said

honestly, but Wilhelm raised his eyebrows and translated without turning around. The man in the chair scribbled.

'Would it be OK to speak to your father? Perhaps on the telephone? He must be worried about you.'

'He's resting,' I said, and then, 'Reuben said he's dead.'

The man in the corner coughed and I thought he must have understood me. My answer seemed to surprise Wilhelm; his hand moved even faster than before, patting down his wayward hair.

'Oh, I'm very sorry. How did he die?'

'Reuben hit him with the axe,' I said.

The detective asked a question, but Wilhelm ignored him, instead leaning forward with a look of concern.

'Did Reuben hit you too?' He raised his hand towards the bandage on the side of my head.

'No, of course not.' I flinched, alarmed that he was getting the wrong idea.

The man in the corner started to talk with more force, and Wilhelm translated as I spoke.

'Papa did that with the knife.'

'And what about your mother? Does she live in die Hütte?'

'She's dead,' I said, and a wave of panic washed over me at the thought that they were both gone, and Reuben too, and that I was here in this white land alone.

Wilhelm frowned. 'It's OK, Rapunzel.'

'Punzel,' I said again.

He laid a hand on my arm. 'Did Reuben hit her? You're safe; you can tell me what happened.'

'No,' I said. 'She died a long time ago. I lived with my father in die Hütte. I was going to live with Reuben in the forest on the other side of the Fluss, but I couldn't find him.'

'Where is this forest man; where is Reuben now?' Wilhelm asked, his face level with mine.

'He crossed the Fluss before me, he went into the trees and then he was gone.' I put my face in my hands, my body doubling over. 'He left me.' Dry heaves were coming up from my stomach. 'I didn't know what to do. I thought he might come for me in the night, I was so scared, but he was gone. And then I saw the Great Divide . . .'

Wilhelm moved closer and put his white arm over my shoulder and pulled me in towards his chest. I heard my gasping noises, but no tears came. Up close, underneath a smell of medicine, I sniffed something floral. He held me until the dry sobs had subsided, and I pulled away from him.

'What is the Great Divide? I don't know the German for this,' he said, and spoke to the detective.

I shrugged. It was too much to explain. The three of us sat silent.

'Do you know what the date is?' Wilhelm asked after a minute or two.

I shook my head.

'It's the twenty-first of September 1985,' he said. 'We think you walked to Lügnerberg. Do you remember if it was far? How long it took you?'

'Nine years,' I said.

Wilhelm shook his head. 'My English is not so good. You were walking for nine years?'

'What's Lügnerberg?'

'The village where you were found. You were worn out, Rapunzel, your feet are damaged. You must have walked a long time.'

I shrugged.

'Do you think you could draw a map of where you came from? The policeman,' he indicated the man with a twitch of his head, 'will need to help your father and to find Reuben.'

He spoke to the detective again, who tore a page from his notebook and handed it over. Wilhelm took a pen from the top pocket of his white coat and, resting the piece of paper on the clipboard that had been hanging on the bottom of my bed, handed them to me. It was the first paper I had touched since I had held the sheet music for 'La Campanella' before the forest fire. But this was blank, apart from faint blue lines on both sides. Wilhelm gave me the pen. I looked at him and at the paper. He took the pen back and clicked the end of it so the nib poked out from the bottom. He nodded at me – go on, he seemed to be saying. I pressed the end too and the nib disappeared; again, and out it came. The detective had moved forward to stand beside the bed, watching me. His gaze made my hand shake. I was worried he would tell me off for wasting his piece of paper, that he would laugh at my drawing. I hadn't drawn a picture since I had been at school, but I put the pen on the paper.

In the middle of the sheet I drew a little house with one window and a door and a metal chimney poking through the pitched roof. Woodsmoke puffed into the summer sky.

27.

The following morning, a woman with translucent skin came into my hospital room lugging a plastic bag. She tipped a pile of clothes out over my bed, a kaleidoscope of unnatural colours; they smelled of unwashed necks and damp blankets, they smelled of die Hütte. I drew my knees up to my chest.

'This is very nice,' she said in English, picking up a long checked skirt, similar to the one she was wearing.

With my eyes, I traced the pale blue journey of a vein from the bottom of her cheek up to her temple.

'And about your size, if we can find you a safety pin.' She smiled and she held it out, trying to measure it against me. 'I hear you were found in the woods,' she said, examining my face. 'You had a lucky escape by the look of it.' She burrowed into the heap of clothes. 'Here's a blouse that will do.' The collar, a nylon ruff, had a rind of grey around the inside. The woman excavated a jumper, red, green and purple stripes zigzagging across the front.

'Do you have any underwear?' I asked.

'Bras? Pants, do you mean? I'll have a word with the nurses on my way out. They should be able to find you some paper knickers at least.' The woman's eyes had become watery, but she carried on. 'Now, how about shoes?'

'I have my own.' I leaned over the side of the bed for my

father's boots and remembered that I hadn't seen them since I'd worn them when walking through the village.

'I was told you needed shoes, so you'd better have some. What about these?' She held out a pair of patent T-bars.

The shine had been scuffed from the toes, but I liked them. I pushed the bedcover off my legs and stuck out my feet. A little cry came from the woman, but she covered her mouth to hide it. My feet were swollen and purple bruises had blossomed, mutating into green algae where they reached my toes. A nurse had wrapped my ankles with bandages where the skin had been rubbed off. I eased my feet into the shoes, pressed the tongues on to a corresponding patch of bristles and then ripped them off, with a sound like tearing paper. I did it again.

'Velcro,' the woman told me before she left.

I put on my new clothes. They were an improvement on the hospital gown, but their smell made me worry about the health of their previous owners. I played with the Velcro and wondered whether the detective had found my father yet. I thought about Reuben and tried to imagine him in this new white world, but his hair was too long, his beard too tangled, his smile too natural. He didn't fit. For the rest of the morning I stood at the window and watched the wind in the leaves. I breathed on the glass and, with a fingertip, traced the outline of the tree on the misty pane. Only the visits from the nurses coming in to perform their regular checks and the arrival of food broke the monotony of the little white room. Thin soup, watery porridge, rubbery egg, rice pudding – all of it wonderful.

In the afternoon, when Wilhelm poked his head around the door, I was pleased to see him.

'Rapunzel, Rapunzel, let down your . . .' he started to say as he came in, but he blushed, and his hand rushed to his own hair.

He seemed even younger than he had the day before. He was walking awkwardly, with one arm hiding something under his white coat. I hoped it was food, but instead he whipped out a newspaper and slapped it down on the bed.

'You're famous,' he said.

On the front page was a line drawing of a girl with sharp cheekbones and a small, downturned mouth. The artist had drawn her crudely, her eyes too big for her face, and part of her ear was missing. The writing underneath wasn't in English, but above the drawing was a headline starting with a word I knew.

'Rapunzel, the forest girl,' Wilhelm said. He picked up the paper and translated: 'Police are trying to trace the family of an English-speaking teenager who was discovered wandering in Lügnerberg, a Bavarian village about twenty miles north of Freyung. The girl, who says her name is Rapunzel, claims she has been brought up by her father in a remote forest cabin. After a . . . after a . . .' Wilhelm struggled to find the words. '. . . deadly fight between her father and a wild man of the forest, the girl, who is about fourteen, walked . . .'

'I'm seventeen,' I said.

Wilhelm stopped reading and his eyes widened.

'I worked it out.'

'Seventeen,' he repeated.

'If it's 1985.'

Wilhelm gave a whistle and a roll of his head. 'What else?

Have you remembered anything else?' He sat down on the bed and smoothed his hair. 'Were you born in die Hütte? What about the rest of your family?'

'They're all dead,' I said. 'But I remember London. We had a big house, with a grand piano.'

Wilhelm bounced. 'Did you play it?'

'There was a cemetery at the end of the garden.' Wilhelm was getting more excited, but when I thought of the garden, my bedroom and the glasshouse, I remembered they had all been sucked into the Great Divide years ago.

'What else?' said Wilhelm, but I slipped back under the sheets, fully clothed, and turned my head towards the window.

After a while Wilhelm left. I stared at the white bedside table until it came into focus. A nurse had put a plastic jug of water there, with a pink beaker, a box of tissues and a soft toy which had a squirrel's tail, a mouse's snout and the paws of a bear. It was a ridiculous animal. I gazed at it for a long time until the room grew cloudy, and it was then it came to me that the old world had carried on rotating without me. That Becky had grown up and started secondary school, that double-decker buses still drove past the fish and chip shop on Archway Road, that my bedroom continued to overlook a north London garden and cemetery, that Omi still visited from Germany, that Ute still ate Apfelkuchen on Sundays and that my father had lied.

I got off the bed and, holding my skirt tight to my waist, I hobbled around the room, searching the cupboard beside the bed, the yellow bin, the shelf above the sink, and behind the machines that I was occasionally plugged into. I had no plan. At the back of the drawer in the bedside table I found a metal hair grip. With my teeth, I pulled off the plastic ends and gave it a flick with my fingers. I went into my private bathroom: toilet, bath, towel, rubber mat, another sink. I sat on the loo with the lid down and examined the toilet-roll holder. With the hair grip I worked at one of the screws which held it to the wall – poking the metal end into the screw-head, working it loose until it turned and with my fingers I was able to withdraw the screw. It was long and thin. Plaster dust lay in its threads. I ran the pointed end down my middle finger, across my palm and over the pale blue veins in my wrist. I thought about the woman with thin skin who had brought me the clothes, and whether her husband, or whoever she lay next to at night, would be able to see her pupils and irises when she closed her eyes and slept. There was something loose inside me, rolling around in my head or my stomach.

My shoes sounded like the nurses' and doctors' as I squeaked painfully back into the white room. I didn't think it was going to be possible to fit into this new world. I crouched in the gap between the bedside table and the wall, and with the point of the screw I gouged an 'R' into the wall's white plaster. The R's tail curled; an 'e' followed it, and after a 'u', 'b', 'e' and 'n'. I sat back to admire my work, joined up, cursive. From an oblique angle the writing was clear, highlighted by the evening sun. Then I scratched the name 'Punzel' next to his. When I stood up at the window the light was all but gone from the garden. A bearded man with long hair was sitting on the bench under the tree, looking up at my window. He raised a hand in a half-greeting, then dropped it.

For a minute we stared at each other. He picked up a bag beside him on the bench, slung it over his shoulder and hurried across the grass towards the building.

'Reuben!' I said, and my breath steamed the window. I ran, limping, to the door of my room, opened it and stepped out into a long white corridor. To my right were several closed doors, leading to a high desk with a nurse behind it, her stiff hat just visible as she bent down over an unseen chart or paper. I turned the other way, and the swing doors in front of me opened to let in a man pushing a mop handle that stuck out of a bucket on wheels. Fighting the urge to run, I hobbled around him with my head lowered and my bandaged ear towards the wall. He let me pass without a second glance. Through the doors I was in another long corridor, wide and empty except for a queue of wheelchairs waiting for their next passengers. I went left and broke into a loping run – pain in my ankles, new shoes already rubbing my heels, skirt loose around my waist. Up the slope, past tall windows providing glimpses of the tree and the bench. I couldn't see Reuben. I ran past more swing doors and a white-coated man who turned to stare. He called out, but I kept going. At the top, there were lifts, their doors pressed together. I pushed the down arrow and waited. Pushed it again. The doctor shouted, and I looked back to see him hurrying towards me. I slammed through the doors beside the lifts – 'Notausgang', the sign said. Stairs. I ran crookedly down them, the smell of fresh air drawing me on. Another door – Notausgang again. I shoved its horizontal bar. The door opened into space and green and sky. Behind me a siren wail rose, insistent. I looked for Reuben. The man with the beard was running towards me. He lifted a camera to his face.

'Rapunzel!' he shouted, as his flash went off.

I stayed in my room after that, with the curtains closed. The detective came back with another man, who spoke English. This one sat beside my bed, and I watched his grey moustache move in a circular motion whilst he asked lots more questions about die Hütte and Reuben and the forest. I told him about the journey there with my father, and what happened the day before my father died – sitting in the tree, collecting the mushrooms – and the day after, but from embarrassment I left out what Reuben and I had done together in the nest. They took my fingerprints, rolling each finger against a pad of ink and pressing them on to a card which the fat man had in his jacket pocket. Nobody thought to wash my hands, least of all me, so that when the nurse came in, she tutted and huffed at the black smudges on my pillowcase and sheets and made me get out of bed so she could change them.

Wilhelm came to visit, telling me hospital stories to try to make me laugh or at least smile. A day later he brought an English newspaper with him. So many words – news, ideas, thoughts, events – more words than I knew what to do with. The front page showed a woman with candyfloss hair, and a young boy. 'Pupil Prince's Debut', the headline read. Wilhelm flicked forward a couple of pages to my photograph – crew cut, emaciated and wide-eyed, with the emergency door open behind me. I kept the paper under my pillow with my balaclava and read it when he had left. The print was small and I had to follow the lines with a finger, but even then the words jumped about the page, especially those I didn't understand. The piece repeated much of the story Wilhelm had translated from the German newspaper, playing up the theory of the wild man and saying that inhabitants of Lügnerberg and the surrounding area had been asked to stay vigilant and make sure their doors were locked at night.

The next morning the detectives came back, this time looking serious. The fat one settled himself in his usual corner, whilst the other remained standing, his hands clasped behind his back.

'Are you Margaret Elizabeth Hillcoat?' he said, his accent heavy but his English perfect.

I was shocked to hear that name again, to recall my surname. But before I had time to answer, there were shouts from the other side of the door, raised German voices, and Ute burst into the room, followed by a nurse who had hold of her coat sleeve. Ute had widened, but it was her. Her eyebrows were still plucked into perfect semicircles, her dark hair still swept back from her face, her lipstick still neat. When she saw me she stopped shouting and the nurse let her go. Her eyes looked me over, compared me with an image I supposed she kept inside her head. I put my hand up to my shaven hair and bandaged ear. I wasn't sure I would match up.

'Peggy? Mein Gott, Peggy?'

The police officer stood back to let her pass.

'Is it really her?' she asked him in English, as though I weren't there.

'We have more questions,' he said.

Ute came to me and took my face in her hands, moving it this way and that – examining me like a mother might check her newborn baby. She touched the scar that ran through my eyebrow where the hairs hadn't grown back. She held my hands in hers, turning them over, tutting at my calluses; at my fingernails, short and cracked; at my red skin – the hands of an old lady. She spread my fingers out against her own and looked up at the detective.

'Peggy always had good strong fingers and a wide span,' she said to him. 'I used to think she would make a fine pianist one day.'

It was funny, I thought, that I had never heard her say that about me before. When she turned back to me there were tears in her eyes, but mine remained dry. I was one step away from the action, watching it unfold in front of me, curious to find out what would happen next.

'Are you Margaret Elizabeth Hillcoat?' the detective asked again.

'Of course she is,' Ute snapped. 'Do you think I would not know my own daughter?'

'In which case,' he said to me, 'I have to inform you that we have recovered the body of your father in the location you described to my colleague.' He nodded towards the fat man. 'Frau Hillcoat,' he used her married name, 'has already provided positive identification.'

'Oh, Peggy,' said Ute, sitting beside me on the bed, shuffling me along to make room. 'What has happened to you?'

'And Reuben?' I asked the police officer. 'Did you find Reuben?'

'We would like you to explain again what happened on the day your father died.'

'Did you find his camp?'

'Ja,' said Ute, 'did you find this wild man?'

'It wasn't like that,' I said. 'He isn't a wild man.'

'We are doing everything we can, Frau Hillcoat, but for the time being we need your daughter to tell us again what happened.'

'Meine Tochter,' Ute said in awe, and stroked my cheek.

'But I've told all of it already,' I said.

'Again, please,' said the policeman.

I sighed. 'Reuben woke me up, early in the morning.'

'Why was that?' said the policeman, his moustache moving.

'I told you, that was the day my father was going to kill us both.'

Ute put her head in her hands. 'Nein, nein,' she said.

'And what happened when Reuben woke you up?'

'We ran away, into the forest, to my nest, my den, and then down the gill and across the forest back to die Hütte. My father was crazy, he was hunting us like we were animals. I didn't have my shoes, we had to go back to get them. He came in with the knife, he was angry with me for running away. He wanted me to choose – the knife or the spyglass – then he lashed out at me so Reuben hit him, with the axe.'

'Are you certain?' he pressed me.

'I'm certain.' I raised my hand to my ear.

'What happened after that?'

'My father fell down, of course!' I shouted.

Ute put her arm around me and gave my hand a squeeze.

'What happened to the axe and the knife?' The detective's tone didn't change: level, calm, infuriating.

'What do you think happened? Do you think Reuben ran around chopping at everything?' I spat out, and looked away towards the window, shaking.

'The cabin had been ransacked by someone.'

I turned back to him, pushing my anger down into my stomach. 'That was my father,' I said. 'He destroyed everything before Reuben and I returned.'

'Peggy,' he said, pulling up the chair next to my bed and sitting down. 'May I call you Peggy?'

I nodded.

'This is very important. Did you touch the axe or the knife after Reuben hit your father?'

'Reuben told me to go back in, to get things to take with me. I left them on the floor; I only took my father's boots, the spyglass and my balaclava.'

'So you didn't touch the knife or the axe?'

'No,' I said.

'We found a bag near the river with some items in it.'

'My rucksack, with my toothbrush and the comb.'

'So you did take something other than the boots and balaclava?'

'Yes. No. I left them by the river.'

'Does she have to answer all these questions right now?' asked Ute. 'Surely you can do this another time.'

'It is important.' The detective spoke in German to his colleague. 'You said Reuben lived with you and your father in the cabin.'

'No,' I said. 'Not in the cabin, in the forest.'

'I thought Reuben's camp was the other side of the river – the river you crossed.'

'It was. It is.'

Ute held me tighter and gave the man a hard stare.

'But you lived together in your den?'

'I only meant . . . we spent some time there,' I said, my

voice rising again. 'We ran there from my father. You can see it for yourselves. I'll draw you another map.' I turned to the fat man in the corner. 'I need more paper and your pen,' I said, making drawing motions with my hand.

The man stood, but he didn't give me the paper.

'Reuben left his hat there. Reuben left his hat behind.' I knew I was gabbling. 'We were running away from my father, for God's sake. Reuben saved my life!'

'That's enough!' said Ute. 'She needs to rest.'

Both detectives were standing now, and the one who had asked the questions inclined his head towards Ute in agreement.

'I would like to take my daughter home,' said Ute, 'to London.' The two men talked together in German, and Ute interrupted them. They appeared to have forgotten that she understood them. They spoke for a few minutes, back and forth, arguing until an agreement seemed to be reached.

'What about Reuben?' I said.

Ute's arm tightened around me again. 'The police will carry on looking. They have agreed you can come home, Peggy, to London.' There was a catch in her voice. 'They will telephone us when they know something more.'

The big man coughed, a clearing of his throat behind his fist, and we all looked at him. His large face was flushed. He held out his hand to Ute across the bed. Ute's face took on a practised smile. I had forgotten it, but as soon as her lips closed and curled I knew it was the one she saved for her audience or photographers, the one on her albums in London. She released me, placed her hand into his and he bent down to kiss it.

'Ute Bischoff,' he said. 'Enchanté.'

She bowed her head.

As the men were leaving, I said, 'Reuben carved his name in the cabin – under the shelves, beside the stove.'

They looked at me but didn't reply.

When the door had closed behind them, Ute sat on the chair beside the bed, seeming to take strength from the detective who had just left it.

'Omi died whilst you were gone,' she said, and her face crumpled and folded in on itself like a glove puppet squeezed by an invisible fist.

I looked for the tissues on the bedside table but they had been removed, along with the peculiar animal. I reached for the blue balaclava under my pillow and held it out to her. She took it, burying her face into it and inhaling. I thought she might be checking if it still held Omi's perfume, but I could have told her that it smelled of blood, dirt and honey.

28.

In my bedroom I picked up the purple skirt from the floor where it lay crumpled and forgotten. I took off my dress, and the bra I had cut in half, stuffing it back into my under-wear drawer but not bothering to get out another. I put the skirt on. I couldn't do the zip up to the top, and when I sat down it gaped open. What would Becky be wearing? I tried to imagine her grown, but she stubbornly remained a smiling eight-year-old in flared jeans and a yellow T-shirt. In my memory her face seemed pink and white, lips stretching wide over teeth and gums. I could remember a turned-up nose, a thick fringe which stopped short of her eyebrows, so fair they were almost invisible; but none of these features would be still for long enough to form a face. I took off the skirt and put the dress I had been wearing back on.

Downstairs, in the sitting room, Ute stood with her back to the windows, talking about me.

'. . . a very difficult time,' she said before she trailed off, and all heads turned at once.

A man, tall and good-looking, stood up.

'Oh, Peggy, you didn't get changed,' said Ute.

'The skirt doesn't fit me. Nothing fits me any more,' I

said, looking at the girl on the sofa. Her hair was unexpectedly brown and curly; I wondered if she'd had a permanent wave. Her legs, in tan tights, were pressed together, knees pointing the other way to her body, which she held upright on the edge of the seat. She smiled at me, her mouth splitting her face in two, revealing the pink of top and bottom gums, and then her lips closed as if she were trying to restrain her escaping teeth. Smoothing her skirt over her bottom, Becky half rose but thought better of it and sat back down.

'It's nice to see you again, Peggy,' said the man.

He seemed about to step forward and shake my hand. I pulled at the hair over my ear and stayed near the door.

'Peggy, this is Michael,' said Ute. 'Do you remember Michael? One of your father's . . .' I knew that Ute was about to say 'friends', but she tailed off with a weak 'group'.

'A survivalist?' I said, and shook my head. I couldn't place him; I tried to imagine him in black and white, with a beard, but I was sure he wasn't in the photograph I had found that morning.

'A Retreater,' he said, and gave an embarrassed laugh. 'But that was a long time ago.'

'Please, sit down, Michael,' Ute said. 'Oskar, perhaps you would put the kettle on and make us tea.'

He was standing by the bureau, but she didn't look at him when she spoke. He walked stiffly from the room. Michael sat on a chair in front of the windows and Ute sat opposite Becky. I remained standing, ready to bolt.

'Your mother is looking very happy,' said Michael. 'She was telling us she's started playing the piano again.'

Ute dipped her head.

'I was just asking her if you or Oskar played.'

'Not really,' I said. We were all quiet, listening to the rumble of the kettle coming from the kitchen. I decided it was safe to sit at the other end of the sofa from Becky. I wanted to stare at her, soak up the image of her face and replace the outdated one I had stored inside for nine years.

At last Michael spoke. 'It must have been very odd to come back and find you have a brother you knew nothing about.'

'Everything's odd about being home,' I said. 'I thought you were all dead.'

'Oh,' said Becky. 'We all thought *you* were dead.'

And we were silent again, whilst Becky's mouth flashed white and pink with embarrassment.

'We visited the cemetery,' I said to fill the gap.

'You're going to have a funeral?' Michael said to Ute. The words seemed to come out much faster and louder than he expected.

Ute looked at me, as surprised as Michael.

He hesitated, started and stopped twice before he said, 'There's something I've been wanting to say. I'm ashamed I once counted James as one of my friends. That we all did. As far as I was concerned, all that survivalist stuff was only talk, bravado, boys playing games . . .'

Michael trailed off as Oskar came in with the tray laden with the best teapot, the bone china cups and saucers from Germany with the ivy pattern, and the Apfelkuchen that Ute had set out earlier. He slammed the tray down, so the china tinkled and tea slopped out of the pot, and then he sat on the floor with his back to the bureau. Michael reached forward and grabbed at a camera that was on the corner of the coffee table, wiping off a few drops of spilled tea on to his trousers. The camera reminded me of the man in the grounds of the hospital.

'Speaking for myself, I don't know if I could go to James's funeral,' continued Michael.

Perhaps I should have stopped him and told him that I hadn't meant we would be having a funeral, but I didn't.

'The others of course might feel differently, not that I'm in touch with many of them.' He looked down at the camera and twisted the lens so that it moved in and out.

'Oliver Hannington,' said Ute. The words came out of the blue; they weren't even a question.

Michael looked up sharply.

'I mean, do you still know Oliver?' she said more lightly.

'I haven't heard from him for years,' Michael said. 'I'm pretty sure he went back to the States after James disappeared. He didn't join in the search in France; I have a vague recollection of him tying one of those yellow ribbons on the trees at the front. He's probably hiding in a bunker with a stash of guns, although I always thought Oliver was only in it for the attention.' Michael lifted the camera up to his face, focusing on the piano at the other end of the room. 'Playing games with us all,' he said, and in a smooth, practised motion he turned his body and the camera towards me and clicked.

I flinched as if he had slapped me.

'Sorry,' said Michael, dropping the camera back into his lap. I understood then why he wasn't in the photograph of the survivalists.

'Tea,' said Ute. 'Becky, would you like some tea?' She leaned forward and poured out five cups.

'Any news from the police on that wild man? Have they caught him yet?' said Michael.

Watching him take a sip of milky tea made my stomach flip.

'They are meant to be telephoning today,' said Ute.

'He wasn't a wild man,' I said at the same time.

'Let's hope they have good news, so we can all sleep a little sounder,' said Michael.

'Is he here then, in Highgate?' said Becky, sitting up straighter.

'No, no, of course not,' said Ute.

'He wasn't a wild man,' I repeated. 'He was my lover.'

All movement in the room stopped: Becky with a lump of cake in her cheek, Michael with his teacup halfway to his mouth, and Ute. Ute was looking straight at me and I saw her eyebrows lower, her open mouth close and her eyes move down over my chest and come to rest on my stomach. Something changed in her face – understanding, realization – as I knew something was changing in mine.

It seemed that everyone was still for minutes, but eventually Becky said, 'You should have some cake, Peggy. It's lovely.'

'Peggy has got a bit of an upset stomach today,' said Ute.

Becky looked at me whilst she took another bite of Apfel-kuchen. 'I sold another story, the one about the King of the Mussels, so there'll be buns for tea,' she said with her mouth full, and we both laughed. There were crumbs of cake in her teeth, but I didn't mind; instead I felt a burst of hopefulness, as if perhaps sometime in the future we might be friends again.

★

When Michael and Becky had left, the three of us sat down in a row on the sofa with Ute in the middle.

'When your brother was born,' Ute said, 'I was on my own. I telephoned the hospital and called for a taxi. I was very frightened, I did not know what to do – the baby was coming at any moment.'

'Mum,' complained Oskar, and rolled his eyes.

'I open the bedroom window and call to an old man walking down the street. He takes a long time to look around him and find who is shouting. "Ich habe ein Baby!" I yell, and only when another contraction has passed do I realize I have been calling to him in German. Finally he understands, but he takes a long time to get into the house because all the doors are locked for reason of security, and he has to break a window. So much glass smashed in this house.' Ute leaned back on the sofa, remembering. 'By the time the man came to the bedroom, my little Oskar had arrived already. Do you know why I name him that?'

'It was the old man's name,' Oskar said, as if he had heard this story a million times before. He had taken my father's leaving note out of his pocket – the pieces taped back together – and was holding it in his hands.

'No, that is not correct,' said Ute. 'There have been too many lies. It was Oliver Hannington's middle name.'

My brother and I stared at her, confused.

'I was angry with James for leaving, for taking Peggy, for not coming back, for me having the baby all by myself. So I call the baby Oskar.'

'After Oliver Hannington?' I said, trying to make things clearer in my head.

'Yes, Oliver Oscar Hannington,' she said. And then to my

brother, 'He was your father's friend . . .' She paused, choosing her words with precision. '. . . and mine. When I became pregnant, I did not know if the father was Oliver or James. I told your father that, on the telephone from Germany. This is why he left.'

I remembered how I had often thought Oliver Hannington was a dangerous influence on my father, but now it seemed I had been worrying about the wrong parent.

'I should have kept quiet,' continued Ute. 'Of course, as soon as you were born I could tell James was your father. But by then it was too late, he was gone. And Peggy with him.'

Oskar stared down at the note.

'It is all my fault,' Ute said, and was about to say more, but the telephone rang. She and I looked at each other, then she hefted herself off the sofa and left the room. I heard her pick up the phone in the hall.

'Hello?'

'What? What is it?' said Oskar, looking at my face.

'Shh,' I said, standing up and walking to the doorway. 'It must be the police.'

Ute wasn't talking. When I peeped into the hall, she'd sat down on the telephone seat, the same one that had been there when I was a child. She looked at me and her face drained of colour whilst she listened to the voice on the other end.

'Have they found Reuben?' I said to her. But she put her hand up to silence me, still listening.

'No, I think you must be not correct,' she said into the receiver. 'This is not possible.'

'Have they found him?' I hissed at her again, but she turned her back on me.

'What about the name carved into the cabin?' she said down the phone.

'Why are the police calling?' said Oskar, tugging on my sleeve.

I yanked myself loose. 'They went back to die Hütte, to the cabin, to look for Reuben. They said they would phone today.'

'Yes, that is correct, but she is receiving treatment for the past two months,' Ute was saying. 'Yes, OK. Tomorrow.' She replaced the receiver with care and stood up.

'Have they found him?' asked Oskar. Ute came back into the sitting room, went to the piano and held on to it. Without turning around, she said, 'I would like you to go to your bedroom, Oskar. I need to talk to Peggy alone.'

'Why?' he complained. 'What did they say?'

'Please now, Oskar.'

Her voice frightened me, and it must have scared my brother too because with a pout he left. I heard his feet on the stairs, although I suspected he may have been marching on the bottom step and was still listening outside the door. I needed to see Ute's face, but she didn't seem about to turn around, so I went to the piano and sat on the stool in front of the closed key lid.

'He's dead, isn't he?' I said, already worried for the creature inside me.

'No, Peggy, he is not dead.' She turned to look at me and I held her gaze. 'They said he never existed.'

Her eyes slid away from mine and I opened the key lid and saw again the row of polished teeth.

'They only found your fingerprints . . .' She paused. '. . . on the axe.'

With quiet deliberation I laid my fingers out across the keys in the position for the start of 'La Campanella'.

'They searched the other side of the river, but there was no camp. Do you understand, Peggy?'

Softly, I pressed my fingers down, but the piano didn't make a sound. I thought again about the beautiful silent piano in die Hütte cleaved in two with the axe that Reuben had used to kill my father.

'They found your den, but they didn't find Reuben's hat. There was no hat, Peggy!'

I lifted my fingers off the keys and heard the muffled click of the hammers moving.

'They only found blue mittens, that is all there was.' Ute leaned forward and the concave scoop of the piano held her. 'They found two names cut in the wood. But they told me that when they cleaned your room in the hospital, they see that you cut the same names into the wall. Peggy?' She looked at me, wanting answers, but I had none to give her. 'They said you have invented Reuben, but if that is so, then it wasn't Reuben who killed James. And if Reuben isn't real, it means the baby . . .' She looked at my stomach again and didn't finish her sentence.

I pressed the keys once more, harder this time, and let my fingers follow the flow and pattern they knew by heart. I was aware of Ute turning towards me, of a sharp intake of breath which she held whilst I played, but I closed my eyes and went with the music. And when Ute propped open the piano lid, the room was filled with a magical sound and I knew the music came from somewhere real and true.

★

My mother stood at the kitchen sink, peeling potatoes. I put on my duffle coat and lifted the torch from a hook behind the cellar door.

'I won't be long,' I said to her, and stepped outside the back door before she could stop me. Even though it was night, the frost was gone and the air warmer. I let my eyes get used to the dark, following the same route down to the bottom of the garden that Oskar and I had taken earlier that day, to the chain-link fence. I lifted it up and slipped underneath. The smell of ivy and undergrowth in the cemetery was stronger than before. I still didn't put the torch on, but let my memory guide me through the trees until I came out beside Rosa Carlos. I switched the light on and shone it up into the angel's face, illuminating the underside of her chin, the concern in her brows and the narrow slit of her eyes as she looked sorrowfully down at me. I bent and scrabbled in the same dirt I had dug in only hours earlier, and with the help of the torch I found James's face, undamaged despite his time in the ground. I put him in my pocket and switched off the light, letting the night settle around me, and went home.

'Let's have some hot water, Mrs Viney,' I said to my mother as I went past her in the kitchen.

She gave a half-hearted laugh and carried on preparing dinner. I went into the sitting room, and from the bureau drawer I got the photograph with the hole where James's face should have been. On my way upstairs to Oskar's room I turned the thermostat down and heard the heating click off.

'Have you got any Sellotape?' I asked him.

He was lying on his bed, reading a book about knots.

'Desk,' he said, without taking his eyes off the page. 'Did you know, the only animals that are able to tie knots are the gorilla and the weaver bird?'

I fished the dot of James's face from the corner of my coat pocket and placed it on a piece of tape. I put the photograph over the top so that James's face slotted back into the space he had left earlier that day. I left the picture on Oskar's desk; he didn't look up from his book when I went from his room.

In the bathroom, I ran a shallow bath and took off my clothes, letting them drop on the floor. I slid into the tepid water, watching the very top of my belly rise above it like a tiny island. I closed my eyes and remembered the warm summer sun turning the tips of Reuben's hair orange.

Acknowledgements

Many thanks and much love to Tim, who not only tolerated me spending so much time writing, but encouraged it, and without whom our family would be hungry and without clean clothes. Thank you also to India for her critical eye, and to Henry for the fishing advice.

I'm incredibly grateful to Jane Finigan for her enthusiasm and guidance, as well as the rest of the team at Lutyens & Rubinstein; to Juliet Annan for making every page stronger and to everyone else at Fig Tree and Penguin who has had a hand in publishing this book; and to Masie Cochran and Janie Yoon for their invaluable suggestions.

For reading and giving feedback, thank you to Louise Taylor, Jo Barker Scott, the rest of the Taverners, Heidi Fuller and Steve Fuller. Special thanks to Ursula Pitcher for the German. I'm also hugely indebted to Judy Heneghan for her unfailing support and advice. Finally, thanks to Sam Beam for providing my writing soundtrack.